SUNSHINE CHIEF

Also by Eric Peterson

Life as a Sandwich

The Dining Car

SUNSHINE CHIEF

ERIC PETERSON

Escondido, CA

Published by Huckleberry House
P.O. Box 460928, Escondido, CA 92046
www.huckleberryhousebooks.com

This is a work of fiction. Where certain long-standing institutions, entities, and government agencies are named, the characters connected with these organizations are wholly products of the author's imagination. Any resemblance to actual persons, living or dead, is entirely coincidental.

Book design and jacket design by Kathleen Wise
Story and line editing by Jennifer Silva Redmond
Copyediting by Laurie Gibson
Cover photograph © setthawuth/Adobe Stock
Additional photography © Sean Lorentzen
Amtrak photograph courtesy of Michael Minn
Location photography by Cannon Daughtrey

Sunshine Chief
First edition
Library of Congress Control Number: 2021907720

ISBN 978-0-9824860-8-5 (hardcover)
ISBN 978-1-7369834-0-9 (paperback)
ISBN 978-0-9824860-9-2 (ebook)
10 9 8 7 6 5 4 3 2 1
Printed in the United States of America

For Teresa,

with gratitude for this wonderful life.

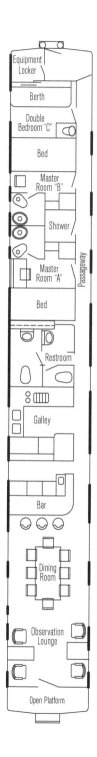

Pioneer Mother

Business Car

Features: Open-platform car with comfortable observation lounge. Two master staterooms, each with a queen bed and private lavatory. One double bedroom with day sofa-seating, upper and lower berths, and lav. Guest restroom and separate shower. Dining room seats 8. Spacious walk-behind bar seats 3. Interior paneled in teak and mahogany throughout.

History: Pullman-built in 1932 as AT&SF business car 21. Acquired by Horace Button and Lincoln Whitehead in 1973 for *Sunshine Trails* magazine. Renamed *Pioneer Mother*. Extensively upgraded in 1988 and again in 2014. Richard Nixon used the car one year to travel to the Army-Navy football game.

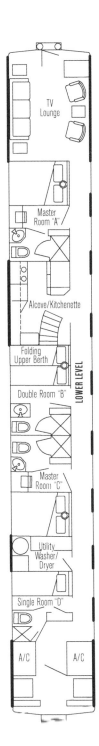

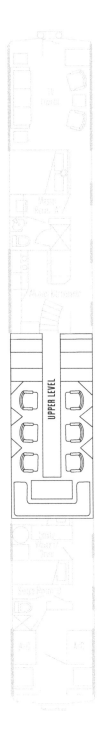

Alaska

Dome Lounge—Sleeper

Features: Half-domed car with upper and lower lounges, two master staterooms; each with a queen bed and private lavatory. One double bedroom with day sofa-seating, upper and lower berths, and private lavatory. One single bedroom. Guest restroom and shower. Kitchenette. Utility room with washer and dryer. Lounges and bedrooms are adorned with handcrafted Honduran mahogany paneling throughout.

History: Built in 1957 for the Great Northern Railway by the Budd Company, the *Alaska* served on the Empire Route between Chicago, Seattle, and Portland. In 2005 the car was fully restored and modernized as a dome-coach by the BNSF Railway, with seating for 45. Recently the car was acquired by Horace Button, editor in chief and publisher of *Sunshine Trails* magazine, who reconfigured the car as a vista dome-sleeper.

ONE

WE CAME TO A STOP IN THE SLASHING RAIN, our headlights illuminating the barn doors of the motor house on the other side of the circular driveway. The delicate wipers flailed across the windshield of our right-hand-drive, 1962 Rolls-Royce Silver Cloud III.

I shut off the engine and killed the lights, steeping us in darkness.

"You're a straight-A student, Jane. You can't keep doing these stupid things."

Jane Pepper slumped in the passenger seat beside me. She wore the skirted blue uniform of Creighton School, but her lanky frame and short bob haircut made her look like a tomboy. Arms crossed and a scowl on her pretty face, she stared defiantly at a spot on the floorboard, a pose of aggrieved indignation every thirteen-year-old girl has mastered.

"A month ago it was single malt scotch in a flask," I continued. "Last week it was cigarettes. I don't know what to say. You've never been in trouble like this before."

Jane glanced at me.

"Florabelle's my best friend."

"Maybe it's time for a new best friend. When they let you back in school, that is."

Jane glowered at the dash. "This is so unfair."

Her anger charged the air, mixing with the smell of wet wool and the stink of gasoline from the old car's finicky carburetor.

"What will your uncle have to say about this?"

"*He* smokes cigars," Jane said. "He'll probably laugh."

"Well, Wanda and I aren't laughing."

Jane jerked furiously at the door handle. "You're not my parents." She pushed open the door. "My life is over. I'll probably flunk all my classes."

"Jane, wait," I said as she bolted from the car, leaving the door open to the rain.

Marching across the lawn and past the reflecting pool full of leaves, Jane stomped up the wide granite steps of the well-lit porte cochere. "I'll never make it into St. Ignatius!" she called back to me. "I'll never go to college!"

Inside, I found Wanda in the professional-grade kitchen of the Italian Mediterranean Revival mansion we all shared. This strong, beautiful woman who wore chef's togs and worked seven days a week was stirring a simmering Madeira sauce. A rich bouquet of butter, onions, and wine rose from the pan, drawn upward by one of the exhaust fans inside the massive range hood.

"What was that all about?" she asked.

"One of us got suspended from school today."

Wanda looked at me with alarm. "Suspended, why?"

"I'll fill you in later." My hand went instinctively to the small of her back and I gave my wife a quick peck on the cheek. "Don't go leaving any torch lighters around."

By the time I entered the library, my employer had made a shambles of the daily mail. Envelopes torn open, sheets of paper shredded into bits or wadded into balls and tossed here and there; consequently, gathering up the pieces and making sense of it would fall to me. Engrossed in reading a letter, Horace Button sipped the last of a martini. He was a big man—well over 250 pounds, tall and portly with a Roman nose and sagging jowls. In the year and a half I'd known him he was always clean-shaven and impeccably dressed, as he was now. He looked up at me from behind his desk.

"Ah, Jack, there you are!"

I took my customary seat in the wingback chair across from him.

"Anything interesting?" I asked.

"A shocking note from an old friend," Horace said. "You think you know what's enduring in life, and then lightning strikes. I've lost my faith in God." He studied the letter again.

"Bad news?" I asked.

"Have I ever told you about my friend Bunny Lorillard?"

"Doesn't ring a bell."

"The kindest, most generous person you'd ever want to know. I'll tell you a story about Bunny. Some orphans once wanted to see a Chinese dance show, and she heard about it. She bought out the entire theater, a matinee performance. The dancers played exclusively to the orphans. And every child went home with a truck, doll, or game."

"A saint, in other words."

"Indeed. It's made her the toast of Tucson society. She's the only reason I say yes to this charity stunt every year. Fortunately for us freeloaders, she keeps her place stocked with an ample supply of Dom Pérignon."

"Another Tanqueray martini, Mr. Button?" Pierre stepped from the library's shadows. Small in stature with a swarthy complexion, he wore white gloves with his black tie and tails.

"Thought you'd never ask." Horace looked at me and winked.

Pierre collected Horace's empty glass and turned to me. "What about the trusty sidekick? Are we drinking tonight?"

"Thank you, Pierre," I said. "I'll wait and have wine with dinner."

"Very good." Pierre left the library.

"You say you do this every year?" I asked Horace. "And you call it a charity stunt?"

"A tried-and-true fundraising scheme. They call it Best Chef Tucson. It's a jail-and-bail. As honorary chief of police, I issue an arrest warrant for Tucson's best chef, and we take him into custody until his friends and patrons raise enough money to bail him out. In the meantime, he cooks for us—seats at the intimate Friday dinner party routinely go for thousands of dollars apiece. And Saturday night's the big gala fundraiser. The ladies will be in formal gowns and the men in black tie."

"And it's all for charity."

"Well, in my case it's all for Bunny."

Something behind me caught Horace's eye. He lifted his broad face and beamed.

"Speaking of prisoners," he said, "there's our little convict right now."

Jane was entering the library, taking tentative steps on her coltish legs. She had a heavy woolen blanket wrapped around her shoulders. The rest of the blanket trailed behind her like a queenly robe.

"Please, Uncle. Don't tease me about this. It isn't funny."

"Word has it the headmaster gave you the heave-ho."

"Ten days without school."

Horace turned to me with a smile. "Don't throw me in that briar patch!"

Jane slipped into the chair next to mine. She curled up her legs and adjusted the blanket. "Maybe I'll go to Egypt and be a travel writer. I could live on a river barge."

Pierre approached the desk. He carried a fresh martini glass and a silver shaker on a serving tray. Setting the glass down on Horace's desk, he poured the icy gin. He turned to Jane. "May I get you something to drink?"

Jane looked up. "No, thank you. Wanda's making me hot tea."

"Will there be anything else?"

"No, thank you, Pierre," I said. "We have some family business to discuss."

"Of course." On his way out, Pierre quietly closed the double doors.

I looked at Jane. "So, tell us. What the heck happened today?"

"It wasn't my fault. See, there's this boy named Aiden O'Brien, and he's really mean to Florabelle. She wrote a secret poem about being in love with…" She regarded me with discriminating eyes and sighed. "You wouldn't know him. He's a totally famous movie star. Anyway, Aiden stole her poem and was going to read it out loud in the gym, where the whole middle school was taking rainy-day lunch. I told him to give it back or I'd set his backpack on fire."

"Sounds reasonable to me," Horace said.

I shot him a baleful look, but his eyes were on his glass as he took a long pull of gin.

Jane turned to me. "Aiden says Florabelle's mother is crazy as a cuckoo bird, did I tell you that?"

"We're talking about you. Headmaster Kruttschnitt said you were smoking a cigar. What's that all about?"

"Florabelle and I had a contest to see who could smoke one for the longest. I won the cigarette contest last week when she threw up on Matilda Muslusky after five puffs. Matilda's still in seventh grade because she's dyslexic. She has a horse named Rembrandt. He's a hunter-jumper."

"Where are we going with this?" I said. "You're starting to lose me."

"The cigars, remember?" Jane said. "Florabelle wanted to go double or nothing, so I said okay."

"In other words, in order to carry out this dim-witted idea of a smoking contest with Florabelle, you risked your entire career as a student at Creighton School? I can only guess where you got the torch lighter and the cigars."

I glanced across the room at the massive built-in bookcase, the centerpiece of which was Horace's humidor.

Jane turned to her uncle. "Did you miss them?"

"Not in the least," Horace said.

Jane gave me an I-told-you-so look.

My face grew hot. "Jesus, Jane, it's not about whether your uncle missed the cigars. It's that you took them in the first place. There's so much bad judgment here on so many levels, I don't know where to start. And we haven't even gotten to the fire trucks."

"Fire trucks?" Horace asked.

"The city of Palo Alto dispatched three engines," I said.

"Ha!" Horace lifted the martini to his mouth, licked his lips, and took another sip.

"Like I said, it wasn't my fault," Jane said. "Aiden's backpack was really hard to light, even with the torch lighter. It just sort of melted and got gooey. A teacher was coming, so I threw my cigar over the fence into the parking lot, but Florabelle panicked. She ditched hers in a trash can that turned out to be a recycling bin. It was insane. Paper burns really fast."

"But according to Mr. Kruttschnitt, *you* started the fire," I pointed out.

"Mr. Crunch-Nuts is a moron. He doesn't know anything."

"He did you a big favor today, not expelling you from school."

"I don't care. I hate him and I hate that stupid paper he's making me write."

Horace perked up. "Paper?"

"She has to write a six-page paper profiling a good citizen who's contributing to the betterment of the community," I said. "Smoking cigars and setting fire to recycling bins is counter to the school's motto."

"'High moral character and service to community.'" Horace shook his head. "Where do these delusional hacks come up with this poppycock?"

"Poppycock or not, it's what she has to do to get back in school," I said.

"Uncle, maybe I should write about you," Jane said.

Horace blinked at her. "Me? God forbid, child, I'm no good citizen. I inherited my father's cold-blooded banker's heart. If you want to write about a good person, you should meet my friend Bunny, in Tucson. I was just telling Jack about her. In fact, since you're out of school for ten days, you should come with me to Arizona and meet her."

"Really? Can Florabelle come? She got suspended, too."

"No!" I said quickly.

"I don't see why not," Horace said.

I looked at him gravely. "I think we should talk about this first."

"What is there to talk about? We've plenty of room. Florabelle can have the upper berth in Jane's bedroom on the *Alaska*. We'll treat it like a family vacation."

The *Alaska* was Horace's latest purchase, a 1957 blunt-end half-dome observation car. He already owned a vintage Pullman-built business car, the *Pioneer Mother*. He traveled everywhere by train.

"But suspension from school is supposed to be punishment," I argued.

Horace's frown chided me. "Being loyal to a friend—what in that deserves punishment? Besides, it'll be a valuable lesson for our two mischief-makers—seeing firsthand how a person of means makes a difference in the lives of the less fortunate."

"I can't wait," Jane said, her eyes sparkling. "This is going to be so much fun!"

"All right, Jack. Here are your marching orders: Clear it with Florabelle's parents. And notify our friends at Amtrak. Have them add the *Alaska* to the train, but make it clear in the train orders I want the *Pioneer Mother* on the rear. We leave from San Jose on the Coast Starlight first thing Tuesday morning."

That night I lay in bed reading the chronicle of a doomed voyage, *Dead Wake: The Last Crossing of the Lusitania*, by Erik Larson. Out the black window, the storm raged. Wanda, fresh from the shower and wearing a gray sleep shirt, crossed to her side of the bed and sat, the scent of her vanilla body lotion trailing behind her. She took a small tube of hand cream and squirted a dab onto one palm.

"Here's what I'm wondering," she said, rubbing the lotion into her hands. "To name your daughter Florabelle, wouldn't you have to be at least a little bit crazy?"

"I don't even want to think about it," I said.

"This thing with Jane and Florabelle's really eating at you, isn't it?" Wanda opened the drawer of her nightstand and took out her wedding rings. The diamonds weren't large, but they were high grade—Horace had spearheaded the shopping. Wanda slipped them onto her ring finger.

I marked my place, closed the book, and set it on my nightstand.

"Mr. Button's got this completely wrong," I said. "Loyalty to a friend can never override the need for law and order. That's gang mentality, and it can't be condoned—not in a school, not in society, not anywhere."

Wanda gave me an amused smile. "You should've stayed at Stanford and been a philosophy professor."

"Yeah," I said. "Now I get to spend ten days on a train with Florabelle Sackett. When do I get my life back?"

Wanda's sleep shirt rode up her legs as she climbed under the covers. She looked at me. "Maybe this trip can be your next book."

"What makes you say that?"

"Ten days on a train with Florabelle, and Mr. Button acting as chief of police and arresting Tucson's best chef. What could possibly go wrong?"

I stared at my wife.

"It screams material," she continued. "Your writer's block won't stand a chance."

"It isn't writer's block. I've been busy with this trustee business, is all. They're rebalancing the portfolio and I have to approve every stupid little trade." I switched off my reading light. "Besides, I write biographies, not horror novels."

Wanda hesitated before turning out her light. "You never told me. What was the distressing news about Bunny Lorillard?"

I fluffed my pillow. "Her billionaire husband is divorcing her. He's moved into a hotel in Beverly Hills."

"Is that such a big deal?"

"Mr. Button seems to think it is."

THE SUN STREAMED THROUGH the foyer's pedimented windows, bathing the gallery in the golden light of morning. Wearing her backpack and carrying her pillow, Florabelle tiptoed down the curved marble staircase, casing the joint like a cat burglar. She was small for her age and slight of build. Her stringy hair was ash blond. Having met her father for the kid handoff the previous day, I saw where she got her prominent nose. She paused at Horace's pride and joy, an oil-on-canvas original by Frederic Church, and ran a finger along the sunset's roiling pink clouds. She crossed the tiled foyer and carefully examined a Remington bronze, a cowboy on a rearing horse. I half expected her to try to put the statue in her backpack.

"You can set your things by the door," I said, surprising her.

She smiled gamely as I continued past her and up the stairs.

The enormous master bedroom suite was in a state of chaos. Closet doors stood agape. Silk pajamas spilled from a drawer of the Louis XVI armoire. Suits, shirts, and ties were strewn across the rumpled bed. Horace mulled over a favorite cashmere overcoat. I stepped around a steamer trunk and pointed urgently to my watch.

"Mr. Button, it's time to go. We'll miss the train."

"Tucson in February, Jack. The warm days and frigid nights have me in a quandary."

"What about the things Pierre laid out for you?"

"The gray plaid suit was too informal. I woke up with the night sweats, practically screaming. Chef Jean-Claude cooks classic French.

I decided to go with my striped navy, and it's triggered a slew of fashion adjustments I wouldn't wish on my worst enemy."

"I don't get the connection," I said. "French cuisine requires more formal attire?"

The question was horrifying in its ignorance, apparently. Horace's popping eyes and slack mouth declared me a country bumpkin.

I took a breath.

Expect nothing. See the good. Accept what is.

"What can I do to help?" I asked.

"Pack that police badge into my valise."

On the desk, beside stacks of papers and manuscripts, was a silver badge that said *Chief* and *Tucson Police*. I reached for it. Four blue stars floated in a gold ribbon.

"And inside the top drawer... double-check that that gun isn't loaded," Horace added.

I opened the drawer. A holstered Smith & Wesson .38 snub-nosed revolver lay among scissors, rolls of stamps, and personal checkbooks.

"You're not really taking this thing to Arizona—"

"What thing?" Horace glanced around the room.

"This pistol."

"Don't be naïve, Jack. A chief of police without a gun would be laughed out of town." He was picking through neckties. "In my other closet you'll find a brown leather duster and my white Stetson. Pack those into the trunk with my red anteater boots, will you?"

*   *   *

Horace marched us through the brick building's cathedral-like waiting room—why do all train stations smell like a dusty post office?—and out to Track 1, where the southbound Coast Starlight sat idling. It was a long train: nine silver double-deck Superliner cars, a baggage car, and, leading the charge, two postal-blue locomotives, their blunt noses and narrow slits for windshields making them look wicked as pit vipers. Hitched to the last Superliner car was our silver-fluted vista dome *Alaska*. Bringing up the rear was Horace's forest-green business car, the

Pioneer Mother. Pierre stood on the *Pioneer Mother*'s back platform in his white waiter's jacket, taking aboard the pieces of luggage as they were passed up to him.

*   *   *

"Cutting it a little close, aren't we?" Wanda said, her back to me, whisking hollandaise in a stainless-steel mixing bowl. I lingered in the galley doorway. Eleven hours on the train today, a twenty-five-hour stopover parked in the Los Angeles Amtrak yard, a fast overnight run to Tucson, where Horace would be eating two dinners away from the train—this would be an easy trip for my wife. She turned to me. "How was your night with the girls?"

"Pizza and Netflix and a lot of laughing up in Jane's room. I doubt they slept more than a few hours."

"What did the grown-ups do for dinner?"

"Chow-Bella."

"The food delivery service?"

"Lobster pot pie from the Kennebunk Inn, prime New York strips from Snake River Farms. How bad could it be?"

"Steak and lobster without the chef. Should I be worried?"

"I still had to tip the delivery guy." I couldn't help myself—I stepped forward and kissed Wanda's nose, that narrow Swiss milkmaid's nose with the cute little crook. "Trust me, you're irreplaceable."

With a sudden jolt, our train began to move.

I noted the time: 10:14. We were departing San Jose seven minutes late.

*   *   *

"Can't we eat up here?" Florabelle said. She lolled in the big barrel chair, her high-top Vans pressed firmly against the mahogany paneling.

I stood at the top of the stairs, gripping the handrail. The Coast Starlight was highballing on a long, straight stretch of track through the rolling green hills south of San Jose. The vista dome's curved panes of glass afforded a 360-degree view. Trucks and trailers were moving on Highway 101.

"That's one of the rules," I said. "Jane eats with her uncle."

"He must eat a *lot*," Florabelle said. "He's one of the fattest men I've ever seen."

"He eats for a living," Jane said. "He's a food and wine writer."

"Another rule," I said to Florabelle. "No feet on the furniture."

Florabelle quickly retracted her Vans from the wall.

"And when the train is in motion, always wear shoes. The steel plates in the vestibule move around, and they've been known to eat toes. When you're passing through the cars, be sure to hold on to something—a handrail, the back of a chair. These things can pitch and roll when you least expect it."

Jane burst out laughing. Florabelle had lodged two short wooden coffee stirrers between her upper lip and gum to make beaver teeth. She wagged her head derisively as I spoke.

My temper rose, and I eyed her harshly.

"If there's a whiff of trouble, I'll take you both back to Hillsborough on the next flight out. This isn't a vacation. Schoolwork comes first, and I expect you to be on your best behavior. Are we clear?"

Florabelle, still with the teeth, stared at three red roses in a crystal vase, which sat on a brass table at the front of the dome lounge.

I turned to Jane.

"Are we clear?"

"Yes," she said, looking down.

Behind me, Pierre entered the lower lounge, striking a succession of quick notes on a dinner chime.

"Good." I gave both girls an encouraging smile. "That means breakfast is ready. Let's not keep your uncle waiting."

*   *   *

I pressed the control panel on the electro-pneumatic power door. It slid open with a hiss. I followed the girls into the shadowy vestibule, the clickety-clack of steel wheels mere feet away, the brisk air a shock. The next power door opened with a similar hiss. We made our way down the *Pioneer Mother*'s narrow hallway, Jane and I following Florabelle, who pawed at the handrails and bounced off walls like she was drunk. Jane guffawed at her friend's helplessness.

Two thirteen-year-olds, setting off on an adventure.

THREE

SUNSHINE FILLED THE *PIONEER MOTHER'S* observation lounge, and the smell of fresh coffee was in the air. Franz Schubert's Symphony in B minor played over the satellite radio. The Coast Starlight had slowed suddenly, and it now rolled along at a leisurely pace through the oak-covered hills and wilderness canyons of San Benito County. At the dining table, the china plates and crystal stemware gleamed.

"A good appetite, ma chérie?" Horace laid down his newspaper and smiled at Jane.

"Starving!" Jane took her customary seat beside Horace.

"Mademoiselle?" Pierre stood behind the next open chair and nodded at Florabelle.

Florabelle glanced around. She brought an uncertain hand to her willowy chest.

"Am I supposed to sit there?"

Pierre gave his best butler's smile. "As you wish."

Florabelle let out a nervous chuckle. "Okay, I wish."

When Pierre had pushed in her chair and was hovering solicitously behind her, Florabelle dropped her chin and spoke to Jane in a small voice.

"Um, what's this guy doing?"

"That's Pierre. He's going to serve us breakfast."

"May I?" Pierre plucked the napkin from the center of Florabelle's plate, unfurled it flamboyantly, and situated it in her lap. "Fresh squeezed orange juice for you?"

"Uh, okay, I guess." Florabelle's eyes bugged.

"First time on a train, kiddo?" Horace asked.

The tips of Florabelle's ears reddened, her head drooped, and her shoulders slumped. She pressed her hands together, glanced at Jane, and looked at Horace.

"My dad took me once on Caltrain. To a Giants game."

"Caltrain," Horace said, frowning. "Like a chicken bus. No comfort to speak of. The hicks are always getting off at the wrong stop, and the bums use it to commit suicide." He raised his newspaper and resumed reading.

Pierre poured coffee.

Our train had passed into Monterey County and was crossing the shallow waters of Elkhorn Slough when Florabelle shrieked suddenly and pointed out the window.

"Oh my gosh, look at all those animals!"

Startled, Horace lowered his newspaper.

Florabelle sprang from her chair and went to a window. "They're everywhere! Over there... and there... and there's some more!"

Jane craned her neck for a better look at the gray mounds that littered the mudflats of the tidal creeks and marshes. Some small, some larger, many basking in groups, each mottled mound of blubber with dark round eyes and catlike whiskers—they were harbor seals, hundreds of them.

Florabelle pressed her hands and face to the glass. "One, two, three, four, five, six, seven, eight, nine..."

Horace made strong eye contact with me.

"Eleven, twelve, thirteen, fourteen—"

"Florabelle, that's enough. We see the seals," I said. "Sit down."

She looked at me. For a moment she appeared to bare her teeth and snarl.

Pierre served the meal: eggs Benedict, mixed organic greens, and oven-baked fingerling potatoes.

Holding her fork like a ball-peen hammer, Florabelle waved it over her plate.

"What's this weird jelly thing on top?" she asked. "Are we supposed to eat it?"

"That's a poached egg," Jane said.

"It looks like seal poop."

Jane began to laugh but caught herself when she saw me glaring.

Florabelle shredded the Canadian bacon with her hands, she licked butter from her fingers, she chewed with her mouth open. Horace Button, the incomparable raconteur, was struck dumb by her lack of manners.

"Remember the frog's eyes Crunch-Nuts made when he saw that thing on fire?" Florabelle asked Jane, dipping chunks of English muffin into the egg splatter and stuffing them into her crowded mouth. "How 'bout the look on Matilda's face when I barfed on her shoes?" Florabelle's rasping laugh shot specks of egg and bread across the table.

I looked at Horace. He gripped his chair and gaped incredulously.

I pictured myself throwing the little shit off the train.

At the next scheduled stop, Jane and Florabelle went out to the open platform to wave goodbye to the disembarking passengers.

"Auf Wiedersehen, sayonara, adios!"

Horace turned to me. "Quick, let Jane in and lock the door. We'll leave the horrid little monster in Salinas."

"We can't do that," I said.

"All right, Paso Robles. That'll give you time to pack up her things."

"We can't do that, either."

"Of course you can. Why not?"

"Because her father's on a plane to Europe and her mother's in a mental institution."

"Which is where I'll be if I have to suffer another meal with that… Oh, lordy. I feel sick. We can't expose her to Bunny like this. She's expecting us for brunch." Horace turned to Pierre. "You're the etiquette expert. You'll have to work with her. Give her a crash course in table manners."

"What makes you assume she's salvageable?" Pierre asked.

"Be a miracle worker, Pierre. You've got two days."

Pierre gazed out the window to the back platform, where Florabelle was swinging from one overhead handgrip to the next, like they were monkey bars. "It's as though I'm Henry Higgins and she's Eliza Doolittle. And a time bomb's ticking under her chair."

Horace looked at me and rolled his eyes.

Pierre finally said, "Okay, I'll do it if Jack can cover for me as bartender."

"Fine," I said. "It's not like I haven't done it before."

*　*　*

We were approaching King City, traversing a mesa that ran parallel to the Salinas River, which meandered through a wide green valley. Pierre stood in the sunken aisle of the *Alaska*'s vista dome lounge, facing Jane and Florabelle, who sat in matching booths on either side of the aisle. In front of each girl was a full place setting: soup bowls, china plates, crystal stemware, and cutlery.

"Back straight, elbows off the table, hands relaxed and resting comfortably in your lap," Pierre was saying. He saw me standing on the staircase but didn't acknowledge me. "The soup course has been served. Your eyes are on your hostess as she takes up her spoon. This is your cue to follow suit. Soup spoons up…"

*　*　*

Five minutes later I was back in the *Pioneer Mother*, hovering in the galley doorway. "I love watching you do dishes."

Wanda handed me a dish towel. "Here, dry."

As we worked, I could tell she had something on her mind so I asked.

"I do, as a matter of fact. What would you say to giving Pierre the day off tomorrow?"

I glanced around and then eyed my wife quizzically.

"Why do you look so shocked?" she asked.

"Because leniency with the hired help isn't generally in your nature."

She scoffed. "The Sunset Limited doesn't leave Los Angeles until ten o'clock tomorrow night. He wants the day off to go to Disneyland."

"Disneyland? A grown man?"

"He has a friend who works there. And he's offering to take the girls."

"Absolutely not."

"Jane's never been to Disneyland."

"She's never been in this much trouble, either."

Wanda slipped past me, stowing a sealed container of greens in the refrigerator. "So two friends got in a little trouble at school. You're acting like they should get the electric chair."

"Not the electric chair. But not a day at Disneyland, either."

"Don't be a grump. It would probably do us all a world of good to let the girls off the train for a day."

"You mean before I strangle Florabelle?"

"I mean before we all strangle her."

"The answer is no, Wanda. I'm trying to make a point. This isn't a vacation."

The service chime rang. Wanda looked at me peevishly, not for the interruption but for my stubbornness. In the galley doorway, I stopped and turned.

"Thirteen is a formative age," I said. "We need to be careful here."

"Maybe you're expecting too much."

"Meaning what?"

"Meaning none of us are perfect. And that goes for the friends we pick."

In the observation lounge, Horace sat in his favorite parlor chair, puffing a torpedo cigar. A cloud of sweet, nutmeg-scented smoke drifted up to the ornate ceiling. The old railcar rocked gently from side to side. Afternoon shadows, set in motion by the train's subtle turns, floated through the old Pullman's interior, dipping toward the floor, rising over the walls.

"You rang?" I asked.

Horace pulled the cigar from his mouth.

"I'm no eavesdropper, Jack, but I'm siding with Wanda on this one."

"Excuse me?"

"Pierre and Disneyland. Give him the day off. And by all means, encourage him to take Jane and that feral wolf child with him."

I stared at him. "I don't think it's right."

"No?"

"It's antithetical to being suspended from school. Three days in and we send them to Disneyland? That hardly constitutes punishment."

"Punishment for what?" Horace said. "Smoking and playing with matches? It's what bright children do when they grow tired of adding sums. May I tell you a story? This is from Mark Twain's autobiography."

Somewhat incredulous, I lowered myself into the adjacent parlor chair. Twain's autobiography was a big, difficult book.

"You've read it?" I asked.

Horace gave me a smile. "Twain had a favorite daughter, Suzy. She was a bright child, full of life. It was hay-cutting season. At eight years old, Suzy and her sister were looking forward to a promised ride on the family hay wagon, a great privilege that had never before been bestowed on these young children. Suzy was counting the hours to the big event. And then calamity struck. The two sisters fought. As punishment, Twain denied them the hayride. Poor Suzy died of meningitis at an early age. But Twain was the one who paid the price, the lasting penalty, for the punishment. The recollection of Suzy's lost hayride caused him pangs of remorse for the rest of his life."

"You're equating Suzy's hayride to Disneyland?"

"I may have told you this before. At the National Cathedral, in Washington, DC, during the service for Ruth and her husband, I saw a light. Whether it was a dream, I can't say. But we had a little conversation, Ruth and I, in which I promised to care for Jane. And now, whenever I'm faced with a difficult decision, I treat it as though her mother were in the room. We've only got five more years with her, Jack, and then she'll belong to the world. No, a dosage of devilry in the schoolyard can be forgiven, but to miss a day at Disneyland for strictly punitive purposes—I'm afraid Ruth would never forgive me that, and I might never forgive myself. You'll understand when you get to be my age. Time is fleeting. There's little virtue in being iron-fisted with the innocent."

"So that's your answer—yes to Disneyland?"

"You don't agree."

"You're her legal guardian. Whether I agree is irrelevant."

Horace turned and looked out the window. We were passing through working oil fields—rows and rows of oil derricks nodding like gangly birds pecking at the ground. "It means you'll have to work tomorrow. I hope you didn't make plans. I have an important friend joining me for lunch."

"A friend?"

"A gifted and savvy businessman, but his mindset has turned depraved. I have no choice but to intervene. He'll be at the rail yard at noon."

FOUR

AN ALARM CLOCK SOUNDED, and in my exhausted state I thought, *You've got to be kidding*, and turned over in our warm bed. I'd been up most of the night. By the time our two railroad cars had been uncoupled from the Coast Starlight and parked on a track in the Amtrak yard, the eastern sky was turning blue. The alarm was Wanda's, but with so much going on—getting our three travelers fed and on the road to Disneyland, and after that, assuming my old role of train steward for Horace's important lunch—staying in bed contravened my self-image. Full nights of sleep were for the indolent.

I was honored and, frankly, caught off guard when Horace appointed me trustee of the David and Ruth Pepper Family Trust, the multimillion dollar trust to which Jane was sole beneficiary, but Horace's reasons for doing so had more to do with protecting his ownership interest in *Sunshine Trails* magazine than in any altruism or belief in my extraordinary capabilities—after all, at that point I was merely his bartender. There were times I missed the plain, straightforward duties of being Horace's factotum and steward aboard the *Pioneer Mother*, which is one reason I offered to monitor the overnight moves of our railroad cars in Los Angeles. The other reason was this: In retrospect, that I'd been so determined to deny Florabelle a day of fun at Disneyland, punishing Jane and Pierre in the process, seemed monstrous behavior on my part, and letting Pierre have a full night of sleep before his day visiting the happiest place on earth was my way of saying I was sorry for opposing the plan.

I had poured my first cup of coffee and was making my way through the *Pioneer Mother*'s observation lounge, switching on table lamps and raising window shades, when Wanda called me into the galley. She was scrambling eggs.

"I forgot to take these off," she said, pressing her two wedding rings into the palm of my hand. "Would you mind running them back to the stateroom?"

I closed my hand over the rings and smiled. "If I didn't know better, I'd swear you were ashamed to be married to me."

Wanda turned back to the eggs. "Don't rule it out, Majordomo. The priests tell me there's still time for an annulment."

It was Wanda's running joke, but I knew better. Chefs don't wear jewelry—it's an inviolate rule of cooking, one of the first lessons learned in culinary school. Can you imagine a patron breaking a tooth on a loose diamond? My wife found solace in wearing her wedding rings at night.

I took the rings back to our dimly lit stateroom—the shades still drawn, the lights off—and tucked them safely in the top drawer of Wanda's nightstand. As I turned to leave, a wave of drowsiness hit, I yawned, and the bed beckoned me, but then my gaze settled on the throw pillows and bedspread Wanda had so carefully fashioned back to perfection, and I left the bedroom and returned to the *Pioneer Mother*.

In a few minutes, with bacon sizzling in the galley and a trace of husky smoke making its way around the crystal prisms of the cut-glass chandelier, the dining table was bustling with activity. Jane and Florabelle were crouched over a curious assortment of clutter: denim shirts, black baseball caps, and dime-store sunglasses. In the center of the table was an open fishing tackle box filled with middle-school art supplies.

"This is supposed to be a breakfast table, not a quilting bee," I said to the girls, somewhat peeved that their clutter encroached on the formal place settings I'd laid out. "What are you up to, anyway?"

"Making disguises," Jane said, studying the heated tip of a glue gun.

"And why do you need disguises?"

"Because we're famous actresses."

"I don't follow."

"It's a story we made up last night. We're in Hollywood to shoot a Ram Urban movie."

"And who's Ram Urban?"

Florabelle dropped her head and looked sideways at Jane. "Is he serious?"

"Ram Urban is a famous writer," Jane said, her tone betraying a hint of impatience as she hot-glued rhinestones to one of the shirts. "He writes about two girl detectives who solve crimes. *Old Man Goss and the Ornery Ape* is probably the best book ever written."

"I thought you were reading *To Kill a Mockingbird.*"

"That was three whole books ago, before Florabelle introduced me to Ram Urban. Now we're hooked on solving mysteries."

"Well, don't get so busy solving mysteries that you forget your homework."

Florabelle was hunched over the hats. She used a silver marker to draw stars on their bills.

"So what exactly are these disguises supposed to be?" I asked.

"We're going as ridiculous tourists," Jane said. "We can't afford to be recognized or we'll be mobbed by our fans."

"You ridiculous tourists need to wear a lot of sunscreen today," Pierre said, emerging from the hallway. "It's supposed to hit eighty." He wore tight white shorts and a green tank top that said *Cape Cod*. Nestled in his dark hair was a pair of black sunglasses. His white Adidas looked fresh out of the box. He sat at the table and pored over a map of Disneyland while I ferried out platters of eggs, bacon, and fruit.

"You girls need to set that stuff aside and eat," I said.

About halfway through breakfast, Wanda called me into the galley. "Did Jane talk to you about money?" She spoke in a hushed tone.

"No, why?"

"Don't go crazy—"

"What about money?"

"Florabelle doesn't have any."

I searched my wife's eyes. "I told Pierre to use the credit card."

"But the girls want spending money. For souvenirs and stuff."

I looked in the direction of the dining table, dismayed by the request, flustered by my lack of sleep. I took Wanda by the hand, led her from the galley, and showed her into the privacy of the nearby powder room.

"I'll be damned if this day is gonna be all fun and games."

Wanda shot me a look. "You're still mad about the cigars—"

"Maybe."

"Let it go, Jack. Give these kids their fun."

"And dole out cash as a reward? So they can blow it on crap from a gift shop?"

"Not crap. Mouse ears and maybe a picture frame—"

I cut her short. "You know, if you ask me, it's the height of irresponsibility to pack your kid off for almost two weeks without money. Her father's using us, Wanda, while he gallivants the world for his computer business. If he and his crazy wife weren't intending to care for the pain in the ass, they shouldn't have given birth to her in the first place."

From behind me came a whimper. For a split second Florabelle remained in the doorway, an expression of horror on her face, and then she was gone.

I stared at Wanda. Both our mouths fell open.

"Oh, Florabelle, I am so sorry," I said, squatting beside her chair at the dining table. She sat glassy-eyed, her knees drawn tightly to her chest. She breathed into her cupped hands. "There's no excuse for what I said. It's not what I meant to say. I'm tired. The wrong words came out. The truth is—listen to me—we're glad you're here. We appreciate that you're such a good friend to Jane, and we want you to have a nice time at Disneyland, okay?"

"Sweetheart, are you all right?" Wanda leaned in close and studied Florabelle's eyes. Florabelle appeared to be in a trance. She puffed into her clenched fists.

I looked at Jane.

"What's wrong with her?" I asked. "What's she doing?"

"She did this before at school," Jane said. "She needs to breathe into a paper bag."

"Is that right, sweetie?" Wanda asked. "You need to breathe into a paper bag?"

Florabelle fluttered her eyelashes.

"Hang on." Wanda hurried into the galley and came out with a brown paper lunch sack.

Pierre, Jane, Wanda, and I looked on anxiously as Florabelle breathed into the bag, which popped in and out like an accordion.

"That's it, Florabelle," Wanda said. "You're going to be all right." She looked at me and mouthed the words *panic attack*.

Soon the color returned to Florabelle's face. She managed to sit up and drink the cup of water that Pierre had brought. Eventually she stood.

"I need to use the bathroom," she said.

"I'll go with you," Jane said.

"No, I'd rather go alone."

Florabelle made her way unsteadily up the *Pioneer Mother*'s darkened corridor, past Horace's locked stateroom door—he had yet to appear for breakfast.

Jane stared at me with contempt.

"Truce, okay?" I said. "From now on we just enjoy the trip. I promise you. We'll treat this like a vacation."

FIVE

I VENTURED TO THE THRESHOLD of the observation lounge and sounded the chime. Lunch was served.

When Horace and his guest finally stood, I collected their crystal flutes of Veuve Clicquot on my silver serving tray and showed the men to the dining table. Charles Lorillard was well into his eighties. Short and fat with a comically round head, he walked with a stoop, pushing forward with determined effort. He was telling Horace of his ordeal moving into a penthouse apartment in his Beverly Hills hotel.

"Suffice it to say this girl at the reception desk is intent on stone-walling me. She says there's an Arab sheikh in my apartment, and he hasn't checked out yet. She bats her fake eyelashes and says, 'Won't you have a seat in the lobby, Mr. Lorillard, and I'll let you know when your suite is ready?' And I says, 'Hold on a minute, honey. Do you know who the hell you're talking to?' 'Of course I do,' she says. 'You're Mr. Charles Lorillard, and you're the owner of this hotel.' 'In that case, sugar lips,' I says, 'you tell that Arab sheikh to haul his ass outta my apartment, the sooner the better. And when that room is ready, it'll be the goddamned general manager of this hotel who informs me so, not you. And he better have his assistant general manager standing at attention at his side, just to show a little goddamned respect around here.'"

Horace chuckled. He clapped his guest on the back.

"Charlie, you're the last of the truly classy rich. You still know how to kick the galley rowers in the teeth, and you aren't afraid to do it."

I held the chair at the head of the table for Horace, then helped Charles into the seat immediately to Horace's right. I presented a chilled bottle of Château d'Yquem, the French Sauternes that Wanda had selected for the first course. Horace gave an approving nod. Pulling a corkscrew from the pocket of my white waiter's jacket, I removed the cork with a soft pop, and poured the wine. The two gourmands tucked their neckties inside their shirts and draped starched napkins across their ample midsections. They took up their forks. Their ravenous eyes followed the food as I brought out two plates of a classic terrine of *foie gras*.

Horace studied fat people when they ate. He noted the measure of their bites, the way the food went into their mouths, the way their tongues extended, how they chewed and swallowed. He watched Charles intently.

"So tell me, Charlie," Horace said, "is this thing going to blow over?"

Charles looked darkly at Horace. "The divorce?"

Horace gave a quick nod.

Charles turned his gaze downward and toyed with his knife. "Not a chance, Horace. It's beyond hope."

"Nothing's beyond hope."

"This marriage is," Charles said. "It's over." He stared at Horace. "When did she talk to you?"

"She wrote me a letter. Asking my help. In convincing you to reconsider."

"Listen, Horace, I got a great deal of respect for you. That's why I came today. But this thing can't be saved."

"She says you're throwing her out in the street."

Charles tightened his grip on the knife. "She threw herself out in the street. What else did she say?"

"She fears for her future."

Charles's face reddened. "I been a good husband, Horace. I always gave her anything she asked for —"

"I know you did —"

"—houses, cars, furniture, trips around the world. Hell, I just bought her a goddamned wing at the big cancer hospital. The ink on the check is barely dry."

"I have a proposition for you." Horace leaned in. "We arrive in

Tucson at 7:30 tomorrow morning. Ride with us. I'll broker a truce."

Charles waved a hand dismissively. "No, I'm finished with that town. And I'm finished with her."

"You're no spring chicken, Charlie. Are you prepared to die alone in a hotel room in Beverly Hills?"

Charles locked eyes with Horace. "What's wrong with that? Look at you. You'll die alone, too."

Horace appeared stung.

The table fell silent.

Charles avoided making eye contact with his host. He pushed the *foie gras* around on his plate. "I'm sorry, Horace. This has been a very painful experience. Let's talk about something else." The fight had gone out of his voice.

I poured the last of the Yquem and cleared the first course. When I carried the dirty dishes into the galley, Wanda turned to me expectantly. I shrugged.

She raised an eyebrow.

After the incident with Florabelle, I didn't dare utter my opinion out loud, not even as a whisper in my wife's ear: *Charles Lorillard is a horse's ass.*

At the sink, running hot water over the plates, I studied Wanda's profile — her imperfect nose, her downcast eyes. Standing round-shouldered in the galley, her long, ringless fingers working their magic, arranging slices of black truffle just so, she was wholly absorbed in her art form. A wisp of hair fell across her forehead. In that moment I ached for her.

"Stop looking at me like that, Majordomo. I'm not going anywhere."

I shut off the water and dried my hands with a chef's towel.

Wanda pressed two shallow bowls of braised sweetbreads into my hands. "Second course. Serve it with the Château La Louvière Blanc."

By the time I cleared the second course and served the third, a ragout of lamb shoulder with sautéed potatoes, the conversation at the dining table had come full circle back to Charles's divorce. Standing over the two men, I opened a bottle of 1990 Château Latour, a celebrated Bordeaux that Horace had painstakingly selected hours earlier. Neither man paid any attention to me or to the wine.

Charles raised his voice to interrupt Horace's defense of Bunny. "That goddamned ungrateful bitch—"

"Now, Charlie—"

"—she says it's all my fault, on account I've become unsocial. I take naps. I have zero desire to travel. The thought of eating in a noisy restaurant sickens me."

"It's the age difference, Charlie. What is she, twenty years your junior? Twenty-five? You made a deal with the devil."

"She complains I never take her dancing. Dancing! Look at me. I can barely walk."

"Now, these aren't irreconcilable differences. What about seeing a counselor?"

"Not a chance, Horace. This ship has sailed." Charles raised his eyes and his gaze turned distant. Suddenly he balled a fist and pounded the table. "I brought her up from dirt! She was nothing when I met her—a goddamned gypsy! I gave her everything in the world—everything!"

Horace observed his friend coolly. From my post behind the bar, I, too, studied the apoplectic octogenarian.

Will I have to usher him out?

His hand quivered as he reached for his wine glass and took a slug of Bordeaux.

"Help me understand, Charlie," Horace said. "You say Bunny threw herself out in the street. Do you mean she left you?"

Charles sneered. "No, I left her."

"After all you've built together? After all these years? It makes no sense."

"I hate that bitch. More than anyone I hated all my life."

"Hatred is a flame. It burns hot, but a flame can be extinguished."

Charles tapped his temple with a blunt fingertip. "But contempt, contempt lives up here, and it lives forever."

"Do you have someone else?"

"No."

"Then tell me, Charlie. What happened?"

"Nothing happened. I just woke up one day and decided I don't want to be married to her anymore."

"I have a friend," Horace said, "who was acting irrationally. They sent him for a brain scan. And, well, they found a tumor."

Charles's face went crimson. "You think I got a brain tumor?"

"You're angry, Charlie, as angry as I've ever seen you. You've left Bunny for no apparent reason. I'm thinking maybe you should get a brain scan."

"You think I'm sick in the head?"

"I'm simply looking for answers."

"She's having an affair, Horace. There's your *answer*. She's in love with someone else!" Charles stared at Horace with bulging eyes. The veins in his neck pulsed.

Horace stiffened in his chair.

"I intend to kill the bastard," Charles said. "I got the means to do it, too." His voice was low and resolute.

"You're talking nonsense. You can't be serious."

"No? Ever heard of a sparrow?"

"A sparrow?"

"You fly him in from the Philippines. In and out in a day. One simple shot in the head and the assassin disappears."

"You're talking murder."

"Damn right I am."

"It's crazy, Charlie. You can't go around talking about knocking people off. They'll put you away for that."

"They can have me. At least that playboy freeloader will be six feet under."

"You know who he is?"

"I know exactly who he is."

Horace lifted an eyebrow. "Tell me."

"I won't dignify his existence by speaking his name."

"Where is he? Is he in Tucson?"

Charles raised his face and blinked at the ceiling.

"I'll warn him his life is in danger," Horace said. "It could spare you the death penalty. Please, Charlie, you must tell me who he is."

"Check the obituaries. You'll know soon enough."

Horace sat back in his chair and regarded his guest. "If you weren't like a brother to me, Charlie, I'd guess you were serious. But you're no more a killer than I'm Jesus Christ Glorified. Now let's drop this mindless blather and enjoy our lamb before it gets cold."

SIX

AT 9:35 P.M. WE WERE COUPLED to the back of the Sunset Limited and parked on Track 12 at Los Angeles Union Station. The Limited was taking on passengers. Horace sat alone in the *Pioneer Mother*'s observation lounge, sipping cognac and smoking an after-dinner cigar. I stood at my post behind the bar, keeping an eye on the station platform. Jane, Pierre, and Florabelle had yet to return from Disneyland.

Horace caught me checking my watch.

"Don't worry about them missing the train, Jack. For the young there's always a Plan B."

"But the next train is two days away. Maybe they're having trouble getting an Uber."

"Pierre could always get a hotel for the night, rent a car, and drive out in the morning." Horace took a drag on his cigar and exhaled quickly. "No, the ones we need to worry about are those on the verge of losing everything, and who, due to their age, have little hope of ever earning it back."

"A thinly veiled reference to your friend Mrs. Lorillard…"

"Lunch today was wasted. The food was all but ignored, and he talked murder the whole time. I can get that eating with a German."

"When we see Mrs. Lorillard, are you going to mention your conversation?"

Horace sat forward and frowned. With the tap of a finger he sent a nugget of cigar ash tumbling into a crystal ashtray. "In front of the children? No, I don't believe that's a good idea."

"But when you have a moment alone, don't you think you owe it to her to warn her?"

"Charlie's no killer, Jack."

"But you said so yourself—what if he's mentally unbalanced or has a medical condition that's altered his personality?"

"Has he misplaced his crackers? The question deserves thought. I keep turning it over in my mind. If not for the double Jack Daniel's, I can't imagine how I would've slept this afternoon. What's your opinion? Does he strike you as a man capable of contracting out a hit?"

"I wouldn't know. But this is an instance where you should err on the side of caution. You have no choice. You have to say something to Mrs. Lorillard."

Horace sat back in his chair. He brought the snifter of cognac to his mouth and took a thoughtful sip.

"He has the motive to do it if she's really having an affair," he said. "And he certainly has the means to hire an assassin. But then again, what divorcing spouse hasn't fantasized about strangling the other? You must consider the whole, Jack. Charlie Lorillard owns hotels all over the world. A man of big accomplishments is necessarily a man of risky visions and outlandish dreams. Giving voice to your fantasies doesn't make you a murderer." Horace rubbed his brow with a meaty hand. The diamonds in his pinky ring caught the overhead light and sparkled. "You have to ask what's best for Bunny. This fundraiser is two nights of spectacular parties. The last thing I want is to ruin her big weekend."

The heavy door to the back platform flew open. With a ballyhoo of animated voices and laughter, Jane, Florabelle, and Pierre paraded through the observation lounge. They sported Mickey Mouse ears and carried oversize Disneyland shopping bags. A knot of purple and pink helium balloons, tethered to Florabelle's wrist, nearly cuffed Horace on the side of his head.

Pierre deposited his shopping bags on the dining table.

"Nice of you to join us," I said, shooting him a nasty look. "The train's about to leave."

"Lost track of time," Pierre said buoyantly. "What a day! You should've come with us."

"Someone had to work lunch." I forced a smile.

Jane came behind the bar, opened the refrigerator, and took out two bottles of water. I surveyed her painted face: feline eyes, a blackened nose, long whiskers. Florabelle's face was painted like a rat. The embroidered names on their Mickey Mouse ears said *Sky* and *Cassidy*, respectively. Pierre's said *Ram*.

"You girls have a nice time?"

"It was amazing," Jane said. "We got caught up in a case!"

"I saw him first," Florabelle said. "His cape looked like a dress—"

"—he wore a black hat and sunglasses—" Jane said.

"—and gloves to hide his fingerprints—" Florabelle added.

"But we saw through the disguise," Jane said.

"Girls," I said, "what are you talking about?"

"A real-life blackmailer," Jane said. "Our client pointed him out, and we followed him!"

"Your client?"

"…even cut the line when we had to, so we wouldn't lose him—"

Florabelle clutched Jane's arm. "Oh my gosh, the Matterhorn!"

Jane turned to me breathlessly. "We had to abandon our bobsled and climb the catwalks and ladders inside the mountain. We chased him all the way to the top!"

"And I'm afraid of heights," Florabelle said.

"But she couldn't leave me alone with a possible killer," Jane added.

I looked at Pierre, searching his face for a clue.

He smiled apologetically and shrugged.

I transferred my puzzled gaze to Horace. He looked straight ahead and sipped his cognac. I turned back to Jane.

"This is starting to sound like a fish story," I said.

Jane's spirit visibly sagged. She opened her mouth to protest, then stopped.

Florabelle turned away.

"Tell me about your blackmailer," Horace said suddenly. "Describe his crime."

Jane turned to her uncle and brightened. "He's a school principal who preys on his best students. They have to pay him two hundred dollars or he'll ruin their lives."

"And how might he do that?" Horace took a puff of his cigar.

"He has the passwords to the grading system," Jane explained. "He can log in and give them all Cs and Ds."

Horace exhaled slowly. The smoke rose to the ceiling. "And your client is one of these students? A he or she?"

"She. Emma."

"Emma was at Disneyland today to make the payoff, and that's when you two gumshoes got involved? You happened onto her... where? On a ride?"

"We found her crying on a bench on Main Street."

"Crying because she couldn't afford to lose the two hundred dollars, which she might've earned babysitting. You finally unmasked this miscreant and brought him to justice."

I felt stupid. That I had failed to play along with Jane's and Florabelle's active imaginations revealed something lacking: the nuances of parenting were foreign to me.

Jane smiled. "Do you like our story, Uncle? Do you think it would make a good book?"

"I think it would make an excellent book. You must write it at once. But before you start, I have one correction. The crime you've described is extortion, not blackmail. Sit down and I'll explain why."

The girls quickly sat.

Horace studied his cigar. He took a moment to peel away the paper band, which he set in the ashtray. "There's a basic difference in the two crimes, you see. With blackmail, the criminal demands a sum of money for not disclosing some spurious or damning information that would ruin the victim's reputation. The victim pays the blackmailer for his silence. The extortionist, on the other hand, demands money under threat of violence or harm. In the case of your school principal, he's asking his students for money in exchange for not lowering their grades. That's extortion through abuse of authority."

Florabelle leaned into Jane. "How does he know all this stuff? I thought he was a food writer."

"He's an honorary police chief, too," Jane said.

Florabelle blinked at Horace. "Wow. Have you ever shot anyone?"

Horace narrowed his eyes at Florabelle and tapped away his cigar ash. "Only once. A brash Newport sommelier served a Chablis grand cru warm enough to crack a wine glass. I only winged him, but he got the message."

Florabelle looked wide-eyed at Jane.

"Speaking of messages, girls," I said, "your school emailed a batch of homework. I printed it and left it for you in the TV lounge on the *Alaska*."

"It's all busywork," Jane complained. "Do we really have to do it? I could tell Crunch-Nuts we never got it."

"Tell him anything you want, Jane," I said. "Your grades are up to you. You know that."

She made a sad face. "Sometimes I get so bored with schoolwork I want to cry. I'd much rather write our mystery novel."

Horace checked his wristwatch. "You girls should go out to the back platform. We're about to leave."

"And when you finish there," I said, "Wanda has a surprise. She made you a special dessert."

"What did she make?" Jane asked.

"Bananas Foster."

Jane let out a whoop. "My favorite!" She turned and grabbed Florabelle by the arm. "Have you ever had it?"

"Bananas what?" Florabelle asked.

"Bananas Foster." Jane turned to me. "Can we have it up in the vista dome while we start our homework?"

"Starting homework?" I asked. "This late?"

"I've got it all planned out. We'll do school stuff until we reach Ontario at 10:54, work on our book until Palm Springs at 12:36, and then we'll go to bed."

Horace smiled indulgently. "She knows the Limited's schedule better than I—and I've been riding this route for forty-five years."

"It's your call, Jane," I said. "Like always, you're responsible for your own sleep."

Florabelle looked at Jane with awe. "We can stay up as late as we want?"

"Why not?" Jane said. "We're practically in high school."

"Keep in mind," I said, "you've got a big day tomorrow. Brunch with your uncle and Mrs. Lorillard, and then at three o'clock she's taking you to tea."

For the Sunset Limited's departure, I joined Jane and Florabelle on the *Pioneer Mother*'s open platform. There was no train horn. With a gentle bump, precisely at ten o'clock, we began rolling. Few people remained on the station platform to see us off. We crossed the tracks at Mission Junction—our railcar rocked hard from side to side and there was a series of sharp clacks—and we passed over the Los Angeles River. The lights of the city were all around us. The cold air and whirling dust stung our faces and soon forced us inside. Back in the observation lounge, the girls said their goodnights to Horace.

"You smell like a cigar," Jane said, kissing her uncle's ruddy cheek.

Smiling, Horace watched the girls make their way up the hallway toward the *Alaska*.

By the time our train cleared the expansive, bustling freight yard east of Ontario, Pierre was dressed in his black slacks and white waiter's jacket and back on duty. Wanda and I were both exhausted and ready for bed. I was shutting our stateroom door for the night when Pierre passed by in the corridor, headed for the dimly lit vista dome lounge. On his tray were two servings of bananas Foster.

"Our mystery authors are calling for seconds," he said, flashing his snaggletooth smile. At the staircase, he stopped and turned. "Thanks for covering. We had a nice day."

"You saw your friend?"

"Yes, and he loved meeting the girls. He envied their energy. It really was a wonderful day."

I was in bed reading when Wanda came out of the bathroom in her robe, freshly showered. She sat on the edge of the bed and brushed out her wet hair.

"Your bananas Foster was a big hit," I said, looking up from my book.

"Was it?"

"I just talked to Pierre in the hallway. He was taking the girls seconds."

"Good. Glad to hear it." Wanda switched on her lamp. She pulled open the top drawer of her nightstand.

"Okay, Majordomo, what gives?"

"What is it?" I asked.

"My rings."

"What about them?"

"They're not here."

"Yes, they are."

"No, look—" She felt around in the drawer. "They aren't… Are you sure you put them back?"

"Wanda, I'm positive. Look again."

"I'm looking. They're not here. Anywhere."

"That's impossible. They have to be there."

We finally pulled out the drawer and emptied it. We pulled out the nightstand's second drawer, too, and we combed the carpeting around the bed. Wanda was right. Her rings were gone.

THE ROAD UP THE MOUNTAIN grew narrow. Sand blew across the asphalt. Natural stands of giant saguaro cactus, with arms like gunfighters, populated the steep rock-covered hillside. The views were sweeping, a verdant basin rimmed by a crown of purple mountains. At this elevation where the stately, gated homes were widely separated, the city of Tucson felt clean, crime-free, and full of money.

The global car rental company, a longtime *Sunshine Trails* advertising client, had done it again. No matter how remote the railroad yard, the corporate executive staff always managed to outfit Horace with the newest, most luxurious SUV in their fleet. Our black Cadillac Escalade handled the climb in stride.

"You girls ready for this?" I asked, glancing at Jane and Florabelle in the rearview mirror. They sat two rows back. Horace was seated in the row behind me, reading, catching up on work, jotting notes on a yellow legal pad.

"I don't know why, but I'm nervous," Jane said.

"No need to be nervous," Horace said. "Just imagine you're breakfasting with the Pope."

*   *   *

"Staghorn Drive. Follow the main road past the hotel lobby," said the guard, highlighting our route with a yellow marker. "Take the first right after the tennis courts. The golf course residences will be on your right."

His uniform matched mine: charcoal slacks, blue blazer, conservative rep tie. An earpiece wriggled up behind his ear. The dry, temperate air that drifted in through my open window was tinged with the minty scent of sage and carried sweet hints of the desert ironwood that was about to bloom.

The long steel gate opened, and we entered the five-star resort that was the Saguaro Mesa Resort & Spa. In the distance, framed by towering palms, a copper-colored concrete-and-smoked-glass hotel blended into the rocky hillside behind it.

Bunny Lorillard lived in the sort of cookie-cutter home that is ubiquitous to upscale Sonoran golf resorts—a single-story duplex unit with thick walls, heavy exposed beams, and a rustic front door. In the red-tiled courtyard, tiny birds flitted among the stripped vines of a dormant bougainvillea that cascaded down a wall. Beneath the laced branches of a desert willow, a small corner fountain burbled, giving the enclosed courtyard an air of tranquility.

A striking brunette with sapphire eyes answered the door. She wore a peasant dress.

"Horace, my love, you've arrived!" She wrapped her suntanned arms around Horace's neck. She had well-toned, muscular calves. I saw how she might drive a scorned husband mad.

"The unsinkable Bunny Lorillard," Horace said. "Still sailing upright, I see."

"And alone as a shepherd's crook," Bunny said. "You're the first decent person I've seen in ages. How was your trip?"

"A wonderful trip," Horace said. "The girls saw Disneyland."

Bunny turned to Jane and smiled warmly. She put out a hand, which looked bony and frail. A diamond bangle bracelet hung loosely from her wrist. "Jane. I'm Bunny. I'm so glad you came."

"Thank you." Jane did a sort of curtsy, flexing her knees and bowing her head.

Bunny said to Florabelle, "And you're the special friend I've heard so much about. Please, tell me your name again."

Florabelle shifted and drew back, as if Bunny's piercing gaze were a heat lamp.

"Um, Florabelle," she said.

Bunny smiled. "Florabelle. Our beautiful flower. Are your parents French?"

"I don't know. Maybe. They speak English at home." Florabelle's nervous chuckle came out sounding more like a grunt.

"And you must be Jack," Bunny said, offering her hand. "Welcome to Tucson."

Given the firmness of her grip and the scale of her diamond rings, I feared breaking her fingers.

Bunny brought us inside.

"Excuse my little cracker box," she said. "Charles left me poor as a church mouse."

Vaulted windows looked out onto the golf course. The sunken living room, two steps down, had an improvised seating area—a floral uphol-stered sofa, matching love seat, and a Queen Anne wing chair. Stashed haphazardly around the edges of the room were antique dressers, gilded mirrors, and statuettes in bronze.

"Forgive the chaos," Bunny said. "The downsizing was a bit sudden." She led us to a small dining room with a round table. "We'll eat here."

While Horace and the girls got situated, I followed Bunny into the kitchen.

"It's a nice surprise that you came," she said. "I read your book. We all did. The ladies of my book club loved it. I don't imagine you'll be running out of material anytime soon, being Horace's biographer."

I laughed. "That's an understatement."

She opened the refrigerator, took out a platter of smoked salmon, and began stripping off the plastic wrap. "What are you working on now?"

"Nothing at the moment. Although my wife keeps pushing."

"Wanda? I'd love to meet her one of these days." She took out another platter, this one with egg salad sandwiches with their crusts cut off. "How's Jane?"

"Doing surprisingly well, considering."

"My heart goes out to her." She turned back to the refrigerator and took out a bag of bagels and a tub of cream cheese. "I'd like to do some-thing for her. Would you mind if I took them shopping after we eat?

Maybe choose some new outfits."

"I'm sure the girls would love that."

Bunny arranged the bagels and cream cheese on a serving plate. Adjoining the kitchen was a laundry room with stark white walls.

I turned to Bunny. "Is there something I can help you with?"

She gave a sidelong glance to the laundry room. A stepladder stood near the washing machine. A tool belt lay atop the dryer.

"No. Just fiddling with some lights before you came."

"I'm pretty good with lights."

"Changing out some bulbs is all. Here's one thing you can do." She pulled a bottle of Dom Pérignon from the refrigerator and handed it to me. "There's a bucket of ice on the sideboard."

*   *   *

Florabelle shrieked.

The weighty silver platter of smoked salmon, too much for her slight arms, went sideways, knocking over a pitcher of ice water, sending water, salmon, bagels, cream cheese, capers, and lemon wedges spilling onto the floor. The falling platter left a gouge in the edge of the highly polished dining table.

Bunny was gracious. She brought a stack of paper napkins from the kitchen and we all pitched in to clean up the mess—all except Horace, who topped off his champagne and continued to drink.

"Send me the bill for getting that nick rubbed out," I said to Bunny.

She wouldn't hear of it.

*   *   *

"Pass these around the table, would you, Jack?" Bunny said.

The small cellophane gift box was black and decorated with gold fleurs-de-lis. It opened like a book. Arranged fussily inside were two rows of white-and-bronze, rough-textured cookies.

"Do you need this?" I asked Bunny. A printed notecard was tucked inside the box.

"What is it?"

"'Enjoy these sweet treats. We're a local company. We provide catering services for corporate and private events. We'd love to consult with you on your catering needs for your next Los Picadores event—'" I looked at Bunny.

"Forget it," she said. "Trying to gain a foothold in our special events— people send me these things all the time. Last week it was maple-glazed donut cookies. This week it's coconut macaroons, which I thought the girls might enjoy."

I slid the card into a side pocket of my jacket. We passed the cookies around as Bunny donned a pair of reading glasses and walked us through the timeline for the next day's events.

"We start with an eleven o'clock presser in the chief's conference room," she said to Horace. "You'll announce Jean-Claude as the winner. After the press conference we have a catered lunch in the visitor's parking lot: Texas barbecue on a trailer rig, big tent, open bar. Our squad-car caravan departs promptly at 12:45. You and I are in the old parade car. Jack can be our driver if he doesn't mind." She peered at me over her reading glasses.

"Love to," I said.

"We arrive at Saguaro Mesa by 1:15. Horace, you'll slap the cuffs on Jean-Claude. Ten minutes of photo ops and general tomfoolery before we hit the road. That puts us back at police headquarters by two o'clock for Jean-Claude's public appeal for bail, in time to make the evening news. By three he's cooking at the convention center. The show kitchen's in the Apache Ballroom this year, sponsored by Wolf. Dinner's in the Cochise Ballroom, starting at eight. We go till whenever. Seem doable?" Again, Bunny peered over her glasses and glanced around the table.

Munching on macaroons, Jane and Florabelle followed the timeline with great interest. With their college-ruled notebooks open in front of them, poised with their pens, hanging onto Bunny's every word, they suddenly seemed quite grown up. They were certainly on their best behavior.

"Saturday night's the big formal gala," Horace said, "and then we catch the train Tuesday night for Los Angeles."

"And we all get our lives back," Bunny said. "Until next year, that is."

Slightly confused, I scanned the schedule again.

"It says here the caravan arrives at the Saguaro Mesa Hotel at 1:15," I said to Bunny. "Isn't that where we are now?"

Horace looked at me and raised an eyebrow.

"Jean-Claude's restaurant is here at the resort," Bunny said. "Papillon. It's off the hotel lobby."

"Got it," I said.

Horace gave the timeline one last look and transferred his gaze to Bunny. "These other chefs—they know they're finalists and not the winner?"

"They all know."

Horace made a note on his copy of the timeline. "Who are they again? I'd like to acknowledge them as finalists."

"First runner-up is Tatiana Wong and Sebastian Root at Family Bone. Honorable mention is Miguel Ramirez at El Whisky."

"Family Bone," Horace said. "That's the one my editors fawned over."

"They liked El Whisky, too. We all do. It was close tallying, the tightest we've ever had, but in the end the steering committee chose to go with Jean-Claude. I hope your editors will forgive us."

Horace shook his head. "I had a long talk with them about that. It's your charity and your event. You have the right to go with whomever you choose."

"Still, they made it known Jean-Claude wasn't their first choice."

Horace frowned. "In that case, I'm the one who should be apologizing. You can't have the soup bossing the kettle." He quaffed what remained of his champagne and pushed back from the table. "Bunny, may I use your washroom?"

"Go right ahead," Bunny said. "And then you boys need to scram. The girls and I are going to do a little shopping. It's in our DNA, right, girls?"

EIGHT

I ALWAYS ENJOY THE RELAXED PACE of cocktail hour on the road. It's diametrically distinct from passing the same hour at the mansion in Hillsborough. Sitting in a remote railroad yard—in this case the Union Pacific yard off 22nd Street in the Pueblo Gardens neighborhood of Tucson—we were free to contemplate matters without the distraction of going through Horace's mail, which often included unsolicited manuscripts and letters from murky charities cadging money.

Horace signaled Pierre for another martini.

"You're moving at a good clip tonight," I said. "Is something troubling you?"

Horace looked over at me with his weepy hound's eyes. "Is it that obvious?"

"Mr. Lorillard?"

"No, not specifically Charlie."

We sat a moment without speaking. Behind the bar, a martini shaker rattled. Outside our windows there was the blast of an air horn and a low, steady rumble. A long train of red and orange double-stacked containers was making its way eastward in the twilight, bound for darkness.

"Do you believe in skeletons, Jack?"

"Skeletons?"

"I'm guessing you've never found one dwelling in the closet of a close friend. But then again, you have no close friends."

I smiled, flattered to be the object of Horace's humor—it was his way of saying I mattered.

"I have my Stanford teammates," I pointed out.

"Your Stanford teammates have all been rendered brain-dead—"

"And I have you, Mr. Button."

"Dependability and loyalty are the two breasts that feed a friendship. It's why you find my companionship so reassuring. Ah, thank you, Pierre." Horace grasped the new martini glass by its stem. "Today at Bunny's house, when I went to the washroom, it had nothing to do with the call of nature. I was acting a sleuth, in search of clues."

"And you found a skeleton?"

"A leather dopp kit. In a cabinet beneath the sink."

"Not exactly incriminating."

"But inside the kit—"

"You opened it?"

"—a prescription bottle. With a man's name on it... a familiar name."

"Who was it?"

"I'd rather not say."

"No?"

"To unmask him would be unfair to Bunny. It calls for further investigation."

"But you're certain the prescription was in this man's name?"

"Certain."

I leaned forward. "Here's something to go with your dopp kit. This morning at Mrs. Lorillard's, when I was helping in the kitchen, I saw a stepladder and a tool belt in the laundry room."

Confused, Horace stared at me.

"Think about it," I said. "What elegant society lady straps on a tool belt and climbs a stepladder to change a light bulb?"

"So you agree that a gentleman may be residing on the premises? A paramour?"

"I believe it's possible, based on what I saw. I think you need to warn Mrs. Lorillard."

Horace cocked his eye at me.

"There's probably a simple explanation for the stepladder and tools. A helpful neighbor, perhaps, or an absentminded handyman."

We sat in silence as the freight train passed.

*   *   *

"Take these," Wanda said.

The two wire baskets were lined with wax paper. Each contained a ramekin of fresh-made guacamole and several handfuls of tortilla chips. I delivered the snacks to Jane and Florabelle, who were encamped in the *Alaska*'s vista dome lounge. They sat with crossed arms, sagging posture, and glazed eyes. Wadded balls of notebook paper littered the floor. Our happy solarium had turned into a gloomy detention hall.

"What's the matter, girls?" I asked.

Without looking at me, Jane fisted a clump of hair and pushed it off her forehead. "It's this moronic paper Crunch-Nuts is making us write. Everything sounds so stupid."

"I thought you enjoyed your time today with Mrs. Lorillard?"

"We did, but we forgot to take notes. We'll never be allowed back in school."

"It can't be that bad."

"It is."

I swiveled the nearest barrel chair to face Jane and Florabelle.

"Approach it like you're working journalists," I said, sitting. "If you do that, there's no such thing as writer's block."

Jane eyed me with disbelief. "Wanda says you have writer's block."

"I don't have writer's block. I just have nothing to write about. But I still write in my journal every day."

"You write stories?" Florabelle asked.

"Not stories. The *who, what, when, where*, and *why* of my day. It's a surefire method. Here, let's try it. Jane, you be team leader. Take notes."

She shot me a black look.

"I'm serious," I said. "We're going to write it down—everything you remember about the afternoon."

Jane begrudgingly picked up a pen and flipped to the first blank page in her notebook.

"You went shopping. Where did you go?"

"A big mall," Jane said. "They had an Anthropologie. Like at the Stanford Shopping Center."

"She bought you each a dress?"

Jane looked at her friend and laughed. "Florabelle tried on like a million dresses."

"Not a million," Florabelle said quickly.

"At least a hundred." Jane turned to me. "And then Mrs. Lorillard took us to Ann Taylor for shoes and purses."

"So she's patient and generous. Write that down, Jane. After shopping you went to the hotel for tea. Who else was there?"

"Lots of people," Florabelle said. "It was crowded."

"Mostly ladies?"

"All ladies."

"And how were they dressed? Casual or formal?"

"Formal," Jane said. "Dresses and high heels."

"Lots of red lipstick and turquoise jewelry," Florabelle said. "We had pearl necklaces."

Pearl necklaces? I looked from Florabelle to Jane.

"Mrs. Lorillard let us borrow them," Jane said.

"And these ladies at the tea," I said. "Were they sociable or did they keep to themselves?"

"Sociable," Jane said.

"Everyone came up to talk to Mrs. Lorillard," Florabelle said. "She was like a celebrity."

"So she's popular and well-liked. Make a note of that, Jane."

Florabelle reached for a chip. "What's Los Picadores?"

"Did she tell you about that?"

"It seems like some sort of club," Jane said.

"—that you have to be superrich to join," Florabelle said. She munched the chip.

"It's a service club," I said. "They do a lot of good for the community."

Jane drummed her pen against the page of her notebook. "We should probably know more about that."

"Good," I said. "Make a separate list for follow-up items."

"What does a picador do?" she asked.

"Picadors help the matador in a bullfight. They prepare the bull for the next stage of the fight by stabbing it in the back. They cut the bull's shoulder muscles so he can't raise his head."

Jane crinkled her nose. "I think bullfighting should be illegal."

"It is, in this country. At least you're not allowed to kill the bull." I looked around the dome. Under the indirect lighting, the mahogany paneling glowed the color of honey. Jane and Florabelle had grown quiet again. They were staring at their feet. "Let's get back to the tea. Was the service attentive or lax?"

Jane looked at Florabelle.

"Attentive," they both said.

"And what happens at a ladies' tea?"

"You drink tea," Florabelle said.

I looked at Jane.

"We had our own teapots and picked out our own tea," she said. "I had chamomile. Florabelle had lavender. The waiter brought finger sandwiches and scones."

Florabelle jumped in. "He had red hair and stuttered—f-f-finger sandwiches and s-s-scones." She turned to Jane. "And remember, the chef-guy came out, too?"

"Came out to do what?" I asked.

"To see Mrs. Lorillard."

"So this is good," I said. "How did Mrs. Lorillard react to the stuttering waiter and the chef-guy coming out?"

Florabelle glanced at Jane.

"She was friendly," Jane said. "The chef was happy. It seemed like he was joking."

"We could barely understand him," Florabelle said. "He had a thick accent."

"So what have we learned about Mrs. Lorillard?" I said. "She's never even met you and she buys you new outfits and takes you to tea on your first day in town. That tells us she's not only generous but thoughtful and gracious. She goes out of her way to be nice to the staff. That tells us she's friendly and sympathetic to service workers. And you said she gave you each a strand of pearls to wear, right?"

Jane nodded. "White South Sea pearls. They're very expensive."

"That tells us she's rich," Florabelle said.

"Let's stick with generous," I said. "So what did the three of you talk about?"

"Ordinary stuff, really," Jane said. "It's so weird to have an old lady who seems more like a friend."

"That's good," I said. "What did you talk about that made her seem like a friend?"

"We talked a little bit about Jane's mom," Florabelle said. "Mrs. Lorillard knew who she was."

I looked at Jane. "What did Mrs. Lorillard say about your mom?"

"Not much."

"She was sorry she was dead," Florabelle said. "She admired her courage."

"But she thinks rich people don't pay enough taxes," Jane said. "She thinks we should do more to help poor people."

"So she's charitable and tenderhearted," I said. "Write that down, too."

Jane wrote in her notebook.

I surveyed the two girls. Florabelle kept nibbling at the chips, but she avoided the guacamole.

"Did Mrs. Lorillard say anything about her past or offer any advice about growing up?" I asked.

Florabelle studied an odd-shaped chip. She brought it to one eye, as if it were a pirate's patch.

Jane sat tall and looked at me. "She said you have to make your own future, that you can't rely on other people."

"Especially husbands," Florabelle said. She snapped the chip in half.

"So she's self-reliant and determined, not afraid of a challenge?" I said.

"But it wasn't always easy," Florabelle said.

I looked at her. "How so?"

"Umm…" Florabelle turned to Jane.

Jane took a small chip from her wire basket. "She said when she was younger, she went through some dark times. She did some things she wasn't proud of."

"Such as?"

Jane shook her head. "She never said." She sank the chip into her guacamole, took a crunchy bite, and chewed.

Florabelle said, "Maybe she felt her life was lame and wanted to kill herself."

Jane crossed her arms and turned to her friend. "She never said anything about wanting to kill herself."

Florabelle looked at me. "Maybe she felt like her brain was on fire and no one believed her."

"You know, girls, Mrs. Lorillard isn't the only one—most of us go through dark times in our lives," I said. "Sometimes we do things we're not proud of. You can be a good person, but a bad side can take over. It can be triggered by something hidden in your subconscious and totally out of your control… a deep emotional scar… a cry for help. It doesn't make you a bad person." I paused and fixed my gaze on Florabelle. "Last night, Wanda lost some things that were very important to her. They aren't worth a whole lot to whoever took them, but they mean a lot to Wanda and me."

Jane perked up. "What did she lose?"

"Doesn't matter. The items were taken from a drawer in her nightstand."

"A mystery for Sky and Cassidy to solve!" Jane said.

"This isn't sport, Jane. It's serious." I looked from Jane to Florabelle. "I want you to know that if you have these things, you can put them back or leave them somewhere where we'll find them—a counter in one of the bathrooms or on Pierre's bar, maybe. You can return them with no questions asked. You won't be punished, and you won't be asked to explain why you took them, unless it's something you want to talk about. Okay?"

Florabelle's face remained expressionless. Jane opened her mouth to say something, but I raised a finger, stopping her from speaking.

"Just sit with it," I said. "Finish your notes and wash up for dinner. I'll see you at the table."

IT OCCURRED TO ME THIS MIGHT BE some sort of divine test. My life had been plodding along normally—too often, things at the big house in quiet, tree-lined Hillsborough were borderline mundane—and then came the winter storm, and with its torrential rains and fierce winds, the call from Creighton School, and suddenly here I was, less than a week later, in Tucson, living in a railroad yard, caught up in a mixed bag of threats, lies, and suspects worthy of a Clue game. Wanda was pressing me to come to bed.

"I know too many things," I said. "Things that could put people in jail, that could ruin their reputations. Charles Lorillard is divorcing his wife and wants to have her lover killed. Bunny Lorillard appears to be having an affair. Your rings have mysteriously vanished. It's like I'm living in an Alfred Hitchcock movie." I stepped into the bathroom and resumed my vigorous toothbrushing. The clown in the mirror wore vertically striped pajamas. This annoyed me. In a Hollywood movie, dressed like this, I'd be one of the first victims. I stepped back into the stateroom. "I'll tell you something. Florabelle has those rings. I should go in there right now and turn that bedroom upside down—before that little kleptomaniac does something stupid."

Wanda looked at me from the bed, where she was perusing the latest issue of *Bon Appétit*. "Like what would she do?"

I leveled my frothy toothbrush at my wife. "Sell them, hock them. For all I know, she'd eat them."

"*Eat*, Majordomo?" Wanda sized me up dubiously. "You're saying she'd eat my rings?"

"Listen to me, Wanda. That kid's off. ADHD, maybe OCD, possibly even schizophrenia. It's a known fact. People with clinical mental illness eat weird stuff all the time." I returned to the bathroom sink, spit, and rinsed my mouth.

"You can't just accuse her willy-nilly."

"She did it, Wanda. Not a doubt in my mind." I extinguished the bathroom light.

"Maybe you brought the rings back here and got distracted. Have you double-checked your pockets?"

"Wanda, I'm positive I put your rings in the drawer. I remember because I was tired, and I thought about going back to sleep." I walked over to the bed, thrashed my pillow into sleep-shape, and pushed it against the headboard. I needed every inch of this bed. The mattress was a foot short.

"Maybe Mr. Lorillard did it."

"Mr. Lorillard's a billionaire. Why would he steal your rings? Besides, he never came all the way back here. He can barely walk." I stripped back the covers and climbed into bed.

Wanda closed her magazine.

"How about that trainman who came through to check the brakes?" she asked.

"I doubt he took the time to look through your nightstand."

"Maybe he has a panty fetish and got lucky, finding the rings."

"Check yourself, Wanda. Your low opinion of men is starting to show."

"And you're backsliding into your negativity, which is always such a wonderfully pleasant experience, particularly at bedtime. You've never liked Florabelle."

"Are you trying to pick a fight?"

"I'm talking about doing right by a child. When I want to pick a fight, you'll know it." Wanda put her magazine away and turned out the light.

Our stateroom had blackout shades. It was darker than death.

We both lay awake, listening to the persevering tick of a wall clock.

"Can I explain about Florabelle?" Wanda asked.

"Can we please sleep?"

"You said that, other than the accident, she did well today at brunch. Then with Mrs. Lorillard buying her clothes and taking her to tea … It's like we keep building her up, only to knock her down again …"

"Knock her down how?"

"I'm thinking about what she overheard … what you said about her before Disneyland. If we turn around and accuse her of stealing the rings, we're whipsawing her from one extreme to the other. It's a feedback loop she can't survive—no human can. I know because that was me once."

I sighed heavily. "Don't you want to get your rings back?"

"Not if it risks stigmatizing a child."

"You don't care about the symbols of our marriage?"

"We have insurance, right?"

I sat up on one elbow. "Yes, we have insurance. But is that really your answer—ignore all this, go back to our happy lives, and release the little monster to the world?"

"That's not what I'm saying at all—"

"And what's the lesson in this for Jane, by the way? What would you say to that?"

Silence. Then:

"I'd say we promised to take care of Florabelle on this trip, and that includes her emotional well-being. And I'd also say despite her issues, Florabelle has a right to feel good about herself and lead a happy life. Okay, so she might have taken the rings. But wouldn't it be better to stick to our plan, give her a chance to give them back, and then encourage her to get the help she needs?"

I let my head flop back onto the pillow.

"Why do you always come across as the most virtuous person on the planet and leave me feeling like some knuckle-dragging Neanderthal?"

I could sense Wanda turning toward me, moving closer. "You don't really want me answering that, do you, Majordomo?"

"SHE LOOKS CRACKING GOOD, SERGEANT," Horace said. "Tell the boys at the museum they've done a slap-up job."

The meticulously restored, black-and-white Tucson PD prowl car, a 1955 Ford Custom, was Horace Button embodied in Detroit steel: heavy-set frame, rounded fenders, brash chrome bumpers. On the sedan's curved roof were two forward-facing steady-burn red lights with a revolving red beacon centered between them. A chrome siren, shaped like a WWII-era bomb, was mounted on the car's front fender. Even the vintage police car's balloon tires, polished to gleam in the morning sun, resembled the shiny black lace-up oxfords Horace usually wore.

Something momentous was clearly going on in this block of South Stone Avenue, the block that housed the three-story concrete bunker that was Tucson Police headquarters. Long rows of orange safety cones made curbside parking inaccessible, and an enormous white party tent occupied the visitor's parking lot under a blue Arizona sky.

Cutting a handsome figure in his long-sleeved navy-blue uniform shirt, with his jet-black hair, Sergeant Jimenez led us up a concrete walkway, a Glock on his gun belt. The rock gardens around the building were thick with rosemary and marguerites growing in the dappled shade of pepper, olive, and palo verde trees.

"They worked hard getting that car ready," he was saying. "Dropped in a new engine, detailed it, just got the seats back from the upholstery shop in Mexicali."

"Mexicali, eh?" Horace said. He wore his leather duster with the silver police badge affixed to the breast pocket. The legs of his suit trousers were tucked firmly inside his red anteater boots, and he carried his Stetson in a liver-spotted hand. "That means the seats are stuffed with donkey hair and straw."

"I'll be sure and mention that to my father," Sergeant Jimenez said. "He was the upholsterer."

"How's your media turnout?" I asked.

Overlooking the double doors of the lobby entrance was an angled window of green glass—it resembled a bank teller's drive-up window. Sergeant Jimenez motioned to someone behind the glass, and there was a buzzing sound at the door.

"Turnout's even stronger than last year," Sergeant Jimenez said, holding the door for Horace and me. "All the TV stations and newspapers, lots of radio, some food and wine writers. Everyone's up at the Bloody Mary bar, getting bombed."

As the three of us entered the building, a metal detector sounded its loud alarm, which Sergeant Jimenez ignored. We crossed the spacious lobby, our heels clicking on the highly polished red stone. On the far wall, behind glass, were museum-quality exhibits of police memorabilia: tommy guns and truncheons, uniform hats and badges, crude handcuffs and elaborate prisoner restraints. An open concrete stairway led to a gallery on the second floor, but Sergeant Jimenez pushed the elevator button. He no doubt noticed Horace's face was already crimson after the short walk from the street.

Waiting for the elevator, Horace stepped forward and took stock of a framed, formal portrait. A brass plate declared the man's name: Chief Ralph Sandoval. The chief, posturing haughtily in front of an American flag, had rodent eyes and a ruddy complexion. His multiple chins sagged over the collar of his uniform shirt, crowding four silver stars.

"Your new chief doesn't miss many meals," Horace observed.

Sergeant Jimenez tried hard to hide his smile.

"The deputy chief wants a quick word with you," he said, ushering us into the elevator. "She has the keys to the parade car."

The second-floor gallery led to an open reception area, which served as the hub for a handful of private offices. A sign at the threshold said

Office of the Chief of Police. The place was as silent as a bank vault. Sergeant Jimenez knocked softly on an open door and escorted us into a corner office, where Deputy Chief Kimberly Earhart sat behind a heavy desk. She looked up from her papers and frowned, a stern governess interrupted by pestering children.

"Gentlemen, have a seat," she said to Horace and me. "Sergeant, you can close the door on your way out."

She sat stiffly in her ergonomic chair and waited for Sergeant Jimenez to leave. Her dark hair was pulled tightly into a braid. Beneath her uniform shirt, which sported three stars on the collar, the inflexible panels of a bulletproof vest concealed any suggestion of gender. She had an irregularly shaped mouth—as if she had too many teeth. She sat forward and placed her elbows assertively on the desk.

"You and I haven't met, Mr. Button. Last year, I was a lieutenant running the violent crimes section—"

"Earhart," Horace interrupted, reading the name placard on the desk. "There's a famous sausage puller named Earhart, hails from Kenosha, Wisconsin—"

"The thing I don't like about you, Mr. Button, is you're a distraction—"

"First name Heinrich. Specializes in all facets of the Bavarian wiener."

Kimberly's toothy barracuda mouth fell open.

"Don't suppose you're related? Or have any family in Kenosha?" Horace licked his lips. "No wiener pullers in the woodpile?"

Kimberly glared.

Horace shifted uncomfortably in his chair. "May I ask your first name, Deputy Chief?"

"It's Kimberly. But you can call me Deputy Chief Earhart."

Horace looked at Kimberly with wide eyes.

"This is a working police department, Mr. Button. We've had two officer-involved shootings in as many weeks. Most of us are operating on about four hours of sleep—"

"Yes, I understand. Everyone is busy—"

"We can't hire and train new officers fast enough. We keep losing personnel to higher-paying departments, which means our patrol divisions go out short-staffed day and night, which puts our people unnecessarily in harm's way. And now, because of you, Mr. Button, I've got a conference room full of frivolous media types more interested in drinking Bloody Marys and hyping the best chefs in Tucson than in the very real challenges of protecting and serving the residents of this city. Don't get me wrong. I appreciate all that Mrs. Lorillard and Los Picadores do for this community, but it galls me that we're taking assets off the street for this showboat circus parade you do, when we're already operating with a manpower deficit of thirty-five percent."

Horace worried his Stetson in his hands.

"If you could just give Jack the keys," he said, "we'll be out of your hair."

"The keys?"

"The parade car—that old Ford parked out front—"

"What about it?"

"It's my car for the jail-and-bail."

"*Your* car?" Kimberly opened a top desk drawer and took out a set of keys. She wiggled them at Horace. "No, Mr. Button. My car. And in this little fantasy of yours, who was going to be driving my car?"

Horace glanced at me and turned back to Kimberly.

"Jack, here," Horace said. "Jack's my driver."

"That would be Mr. John Vincent Marshall?" Kimberly opened a file folder and eyed me scornfully. "We did a background check on you, Mr. Marshall, when we heard you were coming." Her tone was triumphant as she read aloud from a paper inside the folder. "City of Los Altos, county of Santa Clara, California: misdemeanor driving under the influence. Blood alcohol content point-one-five. Property damage. Sustained major injuries to self. Pled guilty. Sentenced to $1,800 in fines, 90-day restricted license, three years' probation, community service, restitution to city for property damage..." She looked at me. "The famous football player who got drunk and crashed his motorcycle."

"College," I said. "We all make mistakes in college." My face burned.

"For the record, Mr. Marshall, under no circumstances will you be driving a Tucson police car, even one that's owned by the museum. Sergeant Jimenez will drive that car. In fact, if you so much as touch the steering wheel of any vehicle in our fleet, you'll be greeted by a phlebot-omist from our DUI task force who'll take you to a cold little closet and draw blood samples we're gonna test ten ways to Sunday." She trans-ferred her hard-eyed gaze to Horace. "One other thing. There'll be no drinking in that car—"

"We always drink," Horace said. "It's tradition."

"That tradition is over."

Horace stood. "Let's go, Jack. I've had enough."

I stood.

"Not so fast, Mr. Button," Kimberly said. "I called you in here today because there's something I need from you."

"And what is that?"

"Promise never to come back to Tucson. The next time Mrs. Lorillard asks you to do this fundraiser event, I want you to tell her no. And when this day is over, you'll turn in that badge."

Horace stared. "Turn in my badge?"

"You're an ordinary citizen. Seeing you wearing that shield offends me."

"This badge was a lifetime appointment—"

"Your appointment was the proclamation of another chief, a differ-ent city council. Half those people are dead. Chief Sandoval has asked the city attorney to revoke your declaration. He doesn't want you here any more than I do. Mark my words, Mr. Button. Your time as honorary police chief has come to an end."

ELEVEN

I'VE NEVER MET A GREATER OPTIMIST than Horace Button. He consumed at least two meals a day of rich sauces and fatty foods, and never gave a thought to heart disease or stroke. He quaffed wine and spirits with abandon and never cared a whit about cirrhosis of the liver or alcoholism. He ran a magazine and book publishing company in the age of the internet and never worried about business failure or insolvency. He doubled down on a mode of transportation—the vintage private railroad car—that could be eliminated with the swipe of an Amtrak bureaucrat's pen. His instincts were those of a heavyweight prize fighter. You could hit him hard and knock him to the canvas, but he'd always get up and come at you more fiercely than ever.

That Deputy Chief Kimberly Earhart had boorishly, viciously, deeply affronted Horace was a thing she'd soon regret.

The Bloody Marys, poured by two fun-loving Los Picadores volunteers, both attractive women in their forties, were decidedly high-octane. A lectern bearing the seal of the Tucson Police Department was situated at the front of the large conference room. A throng of reporters joked, laughed, and gossiped—word was spreading that the police union was about to cast a no-confidence vote on Chief Sandoval, and among the reporters who knew the department well, this news was met with a decided glee.

The doors suddenly burst open. Horace, wearing his Stetson and leather duster, strode confidently to the front of the room, Bunny and Sergeant Jimenez in tow. Sergeant Jimenez stepped first to the lectern.

The reporters gathered in a semi-circle and grew quiet.

"Thank you for being here this morning. My name is Sergeant Jimenez. I am with the public information office for the office of the chief of police, Tucson Police Department. The Best Chef Tucson Jail-and-Bail Weekend Gala is a charity fundraiser the Tucson Police Department is proud to have played a role in for many years. You should all have the schedule for today's events. This morning I'd like to introduce to you Mrs. Bunny Lorillard, chairperson of Los Picadores and co-chair of this event…" There was a smattering of polite applause. "And most of you know our honorary police chief, Mr. Horace Button, editor and publisher of *Sunshine Trails* magazine, which sponsors the Best Chef award. Chief Button tells me he just finished finalizing the latest edition of the magazine, which allows him to join us here today. Chief Button…"

To more light applause, Horace gave Sergeant Jimenez a pat on the back and stepped to the lectern. He scanned the assembled reporters with mirthful eyes.

Here we go.

"Thank you, Sergeant Jimenez," Horace said. "It's an honor to be back in Tucson as your chief of police, and I hope to return for many years to come." He turned to Bunny. "I want to thank my good friend Bunny Lorillard for always including me in this worthwhile event." He gazed at the reporters. "Over the years we've raised a lot of money to get juvenile delinquents off the streets, particularly from Tucson's poorest, least educated neighborhoods, and I'm pleased to report that today, thanks to our efforts, many of these dead-end hooligans are now successful, contributing members of society. Every day you see them expertly pushing your lawnmowers, washing your cars, and running your police departments…"

Titters of laughter and several groans arose from the crowd. Bunny looked down at her designer high heels and shook her head.

"But I assure you," Horace continued, "our work here won't be finished until they all vote Republican, right, Bunny?"

To more laughter, Bunny brought a hand over her eyes.

"I also want to thank the men and women of the Tucson Police Department," Horace said. "This fundraising event is a great example of

the fruit that can be borne from a far-sighted public-private partnership."
He hesitated. "At least any reasoned half-wit would think so, right?" He
firmly grasped the lectern with both hands and gave his audience a
self-satisfied smile. "By the way, has everyone met this preposterous
woman, Deputy Chief Kimberly Earhart? I just now ran into her. A real
charmer... I think you must get one star for each ex-husband."

The reporters laughed even harder this time.

"The department recently finished inventorying its air-support
assets," Horace continued. "Our Air Support Unit consists of three Bell
Jet Ranger helicopters, two surveillance drones, and Kimberly's broom."

The reporters howled.

"And how about this interloper, Chief Ralph Sandoval?" Horace said.
"It's barely coming up on a year, and already he's in trouble. He may be
the worst chief, ever. The rank-and-file hate him, half the city council
wants him fired, and the city manager won't give him a new contract.
The only things Ralph Sandoval grows faster than his enemies list are
his waistline and his wallet."

From the reporters there came peals of laughter and a lot of applause.

"I should be calling him *Fat Ralph*," Horace said. "We've all heard
that a grand jury would indict a ham sandwich. Well, as luck would
have it, there hasn't been a single criminal indictment since Fat Ralph
was named chief. Turns out he's eaten all the ham sandwiches."

The room erupted in laughter. Again, Bunny shook her head and
brought a hand over her eyes. The din made Horace smile.

"People often ask how my work as a food and wine writer prepared
me to stand in as Tucson's chief of police. The fact is it didn't. In one
job you spend more than half your time stiff as a plank, shaking down
desperate restaurant owners, eating like a pig, drinking for free, and
sleeping off the latest bender in your office behind a closed door. In the
other job I write articles about food and wine."

The reporters hooted and clapped. Sergeant Jimenez turned away
and framed his jaw with a hand, unable to suppress his broad grin.

Bunny gave Horace a hurry-up motion with her hand.

"All right, she's giving me the signal. It's time to announce the
winner." Horace glanced down at his notes and looked up again. His

expression turned serious. "As citizens of Tucson, you can rightly take pride in your culinary savoir faire. Your top restaurants credibly match up to the best in the country, anywhere, and this year's winner is no exception." He moved some papers around. "The time has come to issue an arrest warrant for the Best Chef Tucson, but before we embark on that foolhardy parade, I want to recognize our two finalists. This year's honorable mention goes to Chef Miguel Ramirez of El Whisky. El Whisky has been described as the convergence of bold Latin flavors with a progressive edge. Located in a converted bodega in South Tucson, El Whisky is also known for its extensive offering of exceedingly rare mezcals and top-shelf tequilas." He turned a page. "This year's first runner-up goes to chefs Tatiana Wong and Sebastian Root of Family Bone. Family Bone offers contemporary American cuisine served family-style on the grounds of a restored landmark mansion located in the city's El Presidio Historic District. Family Bone's food is simple, approachable, and seasonal, and their craft cocktails, served from two iconic bars, set the standard in cutting-edge mixology." He looked up at the reporters. "To the chefs of Family Bone and El Whisky, congratulations, all. A job well done.

"And now, as your honorary chief of police, and as directed by the steering committee of Los Picadores, I hereby issue an arrest warrant for this year's Best Chef Tucson, Jean-Claude Clemenceau, chef-proprietor of the restaurant Papillon. Papillon, the relative newcomer of this year's finalists, features traditional French cuisine served in an elegant dining room on the grounds of the Saguaro Mesa Resort & Spa. Papillon's wine list features more than 200 labels, each hand selected personally by Chef Jean-Claude. To the men and women of the Tucson Police Department, I hereby order that we apprehend Jean-Claude Clemenceau immediately, and that we seize his finest wines and brandies. By my order he will cook for me and my special guests until such time as he raises sufficient funds to post bail." He turned his steely gaze to the cameras. "Citizens of Tucson, remember my solemn pledge as your chief—Horace Button always gets his man!"

Horace delivered this last line with the grandiloquence of a veteran Shakespearean stage actor.

The reporters—and the volunteers of Los Picadores—answered with an enthusiastic ovation. At the back of the room, a few reporters glanced nervously at the doorway.

There, standing a foot or so beyond the threshold, was Kimberly, staring daggers at Horace.

TWELVE

"...FELLOW FANCIED HIMSELF THE PRINCE OF GASTRONOMY, had an ironclad attachment to beef," Horace was saying, a cigar in one hand and a double Jack Daniel's in the other. "Divorced his wife of fifty-one years when she developed spinal stenosis and could no longer lift a six-pound standing prime rib roast into the oven."

The fawning reporters roared with laughter. Seated at the long bar inside the Los Picadores hospitality tent, his leather duster unbuttoned down the front, one anteater boot propped up on the footrest of the adjacent barstool, Horace had been drinking whiskey and holding court since the food line opened.

Sergeant Jimenez pushed through the crowd.

"Mr. Button, there you are," he said. "You're wanted in the chief's office right away."

Horace spit his drink. The writers and reporters needled and jeered him.

"Tell him I've left town," Horace said.

Sergeant Jimenez shook his head. Barbecue smoke drifted across his face. "You need to follow me upstairs."

*   *   *

Sergeant Jimenez showed us into the police chief's windowless office and then shut the door, staying out with the secretary. The leather chair behind the expansive desk was empty. Kimberly sat in a visitor's chair in front of the desk, looking glum. Across the room, a black-haired Latina in a police uniform stood rigidly at parade rest, her hands clasped behind her back. Her eyes darted to the scrawny balding man who paced beside a small conference table.

"Mr. Button, please, have a seat," said the man, smiling grimly. His gray suit fit rather poorly in the shoulders. He indicated the second visitor's chair in front of the desk.

Carrying his Stetson, Horace crossed to the desk and sat. His nod to Kimberly went ignored.

The man hesitated. His meager tuft of blond hair and the way he pursed his lips into a thin line made him look like an ostrich. "I should introduce myself. I'm Irwin Atkinson, city manager. You've already met Deputy Chief Earhart. And this is Captain Gomez, chief of staff."

The black-haired Latina nodded tersely. She had captain's bars on her collar. The boldness of her red lipstick struck me as an act of aggression.

The city manager steepled his hands and brought them to his lips. "I don't know where to begin. This is rather an odd predicament—an unlikely series of events, as they say." His unctuous smile came off as a nervous tic. "The city attorney tells me we can easily handle this with a simple letter. In the meantime, on a purely temporary basis… well, there's something you should know… not that it's a permanent situation, but in my experience, with these darn attorneys, you can never be one hundred percent certain—"

"Oh for God's sake, Irwin," Kimberly interrupted. "Just tell him so he can sign the damn letter!"

The city manager raised an angry finger. "Kimberly, you flipping shut your big bazoo, okay? I'll tell him when I'm good and goddamned ready!"

Kimberly shook her head.

The city manager took a deep breath, focused his gaze again on Horace, and forced a smile. "See, Mr. Button, the city attorney says it's imperative I give you full disclosure before I get your signature on the document."

Horace's radar went up. "Document?"

"This whole thing came to light when Chief Sandoval asked the city attorney to look into revoking your status as honorary chief of police. It boils down to a clerical error… one little word, in fact. We checked the files. The proclamation said *honorary*, but the resolution didn't. It seems the attorney at the time did a find-and-replace on a real resolution to install a new chief of police, and that's what the council signed. And now this morning, when Chief Sandoval and I couldn't come to terms on a new contract, I had no choice but to accept his resignation."

Horace sat back in his chair. "So Fat Ralph resigned, eh? I say good riddance." He regarded the city manager with a hint of indignation. "But to hear this convoluted story, you pull me away from brisket and an open bar?"

The city manager's eyes met Kimberly's. He turned again to Horace. "Mr. Button, what I'm trying to tell you is that by law—at this particular moment in time and strictly on paper—you are Tucson's chief of police. You see our predicament? We need you to tender your resignation so Kimberly, here, can step in as interim chief."

Kimberly slid a piece of paper in front of Horace. "This is your letter of resignation. We need you to sign it."

Horace's expression hardened. "Why is it every time I see you, Kimberly, you're asking me a favor?"

"Sign the letter, Mr. Button."

Horace took the letter in his hands and skimmed it. He looked at the city manager. "And if I don't sign this thing, then what?"

The city manager traded a woeful expression with Kimberly, and then he turned back to Horace.

"If you don't sign the letter, then we'll have no choice but to get a resolution from the city council to remove you from office. But that takes time and paperwork."

Kimberly cut in. "All of it unnecessary if you do the right thing and sign the letter. Use this." She slapped down a pen.

Horace squinted adroitly at the city manager.

"Exactly how long to get this removal thing passed? Are we talking hours, days, weeks?"

For a moment the city manager's eyes bugged. He stabbed an index finger beneath his collar and did an ostrich thing with his neck. "Well, that's an interesting question. The council's on a business retreat through Monday. So I could theoretically have the resolution in hand, signed and legally binding, as early as close-of-business Tuesday. But that's a best-case scenario, I'd say."

"Jesus Christ, Irwin," Kimberly said. "Why are you telling him all this?"

Horace eyed the city manager shrewdly.

"But until then, you're telling me, I'm the bona fide chief of police?"

The city manager showed his empty hands. "Our problem in a nutshell."

"And Kimberly works for me?"

The city manager took a step toward Horace, waving his hands feverishly. "No, no, Mr. Button, that isn't —"

"And this is my office, this is my desk, and that pretty little girl out there is my secretary?"

"Well, technically, until you sign that letter."

Horace turned to Captain Gomez. "Tell me again, who are you?"

"Captain Gomez, sir, chief of staff."

Horace sat up eagerly. "*My* chief of staff?"

Captain Gomez glanced uncertainly at the city manager. "Uh, the police chief's chief of staff... whoever's chief at the time... uh, Chief."

"This is absurd," Kimberly fumed. "This man doesn't have the standing to be chief of police!"

Horace sprang from his chair and began pacing. "Clam it, Kimberly. I'm trying to get to know my chief of staff. Captain Gomez, tell me your first name, if you would?"

"Lucianna, sir."

"Lucianna. Beautiful name. And tell me, Lucianna, what does a chief of staff do?"

"I'm your right-hand man, sir. Anything I can do to assist. Special projects, reports, studies. Personnel matters..."

"A jack-of-all-trades."

"Yes, sir, Chief!"

"I have a favor to ask, Lucianna. There's a 1955 Ford parked out front—it's from the police museum, recently restored. I need it for this afternoon's jail-and-bail. Can you get the keys from Kimberly?"

"I'm certain it can be arranged, Chief," Lucianna said, snapping back to parade rest. "Consider it done."

"Excellent." Horace checked his watch. "I'm late. It's already 12:45. Have the jail-and-bail caravan meet us out front. Get the keys to Jack here. He'll be driving."

"Yes, sir, Chief!"

Kimberly jumped from her chair. "Oh my freakin' God! Irwin, you have to put a stop to this. This guy honestly thinks he can be chief of police!"

"Have him sign the letter, Kimberly," the city manager said. "Absent that, there's nothing I can do."

"Let's go, Jack. We have Chef Jean-Claude to take into custody." Horace had his hat in hand and was striding toward the door.

"Button, wait!" Kimberly called after him. "We need to talk about this!"

Horace stopped at the door and turned. "Not now, Kimberly. And from now on, it's *Chief Button* to you. It's time we started showing a little goddamned respect around here!"

THIRTEEN

"MORE CHAMPAGNE, DARLING!"

"Here you are, my dear. Bottoms up!"

In the back seat of the old prowl car, Horace and Bunny swigged champagne from tall crystal flutes, drinking at the pace of teenagers on their way to senior prom.

"To Fat Ralph," Horace said, clinking glasses with Bunny.

"To Chef Jean-Claude," Bunny answered, clinking again.

The wide vinyl bench seat was unusually slick. With every turn, Horace and Bunny slid wildly from side to side, knocking into each other, spilling champagne. They refused to wear seatbelts. To them, this run to apprehend the best chef in Tucson was little more than a time-honored, booze-saturated amusement park ride. As the driver, I did my best to stay with Sergeant Jimenez, who led the caravan in a marked black-and-white police Tahoe running with its lights and siren.

Horace whacked me on the shoulder with his walking stick.

"Faster, Jack. You're falling behind! And let's hear that siren!"

I tromped the gas pedal. Despite the restored Ford Y Block 272 engine and the added power steering, the old Ford accelerated like a freight train and handled like a shoebox full of mud. Pushing a red button on a switch box mounted below the car's spartan dash, I goosed the siren. It screamed up and down like an air raid siren, adding comic relief to the cacophony of modern sirens—the whoops, yelps, and wails—that were already blaring from the five cars that constituted our caravan.

Our escort of police motorcycles employed a leapfrog method

of zooming ahead and clearing intersections. Using Tucson's main thoroughfares, hitting speeds of 60 and 70 mph, we laddered our way east and north, skirting the University of Arizona campus and passing a succession of increasingly upscale retail centers, office buildings, and shopping malls.

Bringing up the rear of the caravan were two vans. The black-and-white CSI van would transport everything Chef Jean-Claude needed for the big dinner: the pots, pans, and personal cooking utensils; the wines and champagnes that would be poured with *l'apéritif* and with each of the main courses; and the cognacs, Armagnacs, and liqueurs that would be apportioned into large-bowled snifters and petite cordial glasses with each of the dessert courses. The white, unmarked prisoner van would ferry Jean-Claude's service team: the sous-chef de cuisine, a captain waiter, two servers, two bussers, and a sommelier. In order to keep the hired hands happy on the trip to the convention center, the van was stocked with a case of beer and several magnums of champagne.

We began to climb out of the valley.

*   *   *

Our caravan had passed through the resort's gate and the Saguaro Mesa Hotel was within sight when Sergeant Jimenez suddenly doused his emergency lights, slowed considerably, and came to a stop on the sandy shoulder at the side of the road.

I followed suit and brought the old Ford to a stop behind the Tahoe, glancing in my rearview mirror, looking for smoke.

Bunny sat up in the back seat. "What's going on, why did we stop?"

"Is it a flat tire?" Horace asked.

"No idea," I said. "If it's a flat, I sure didn't feel it."

Sergeant Jimenez alighted from the Tahoe. I cranked open my driver's window to talk to him, but he simply walked past me, his gaze fixed on the cars in the caravan behind us. I watched him in my side mirror. He said something to the police officer in the car behind us and gestured for the other cars in the caravan to start making U-turns. Finally, he came back to my window.

"Sorry about this, Chief... Mrs. Lorillard," he said, looking into the back seat, his face filling my window. "We need to secure the scene."

"What's happening?" I asked.

"You haven't heard?" He glanced down at the radio-less dash and smiled. "Oh, that's right. Something's missing from this old tuna boat." Four police motorcycles came rumbling up. He pointed them in the direction of the hotel lobby and turned back to my window. "So, here's the deal. The whole thing's off."

"Off?" Bunny said.

"It went out as a medical assist. But the paramedics pronounced your guy dead."

"My guy?" I said.

"Your chef, Jean-Claude what's-his-name. He's dead."

"Dead!" Horace exclaimed.

"What!" Bunny cried. "No, Sergeant, you must be mistaken!"

Sergeant Jimenez turned his empathetic eyes to Bunny.

"Afraid so, Mrs. Lorillard. They positively ID'd the body. They found him out by a dumpster, cold as a Popsicle."

In the back seat, a heavy bottle hit the floor.

"Bunny!" Horace said.

"Well, isn't this just about hysterical," Bunny said. She fumbled with the silver door handle, wrenching it up and down until the door swung open. She stepped out of the car.

"Mrs. Lorillard, you okay?" Sergeant Jimenez asked.

"Lordy." Horace took a gulp of champagne.

On rigid legs, bracing herself against the tail fins of the old Ford, Bunny stumbled her way around the trunk.

"Mrs. Lorillard, you goin' somewhere?" Sergeant Jimenez asked.

By this time Bunny was walking away from the car, striking out across the Saguaro Mesa Resort's desert landscaping, heading in the general direction of a manicured fairway.

Picturing her stepping on a rattlesnake or impaling herself on a looming saguaro cactus, I left the car and joined Sergeant Jimenez chasing after her.

"Mrs. Lorillard, you're gonna get hit on the head by a golf ball,"

Sergeant Jimenez called.

We caught up to her near a small mound of deer grass and boulders. Sergeant Jimenez and I stood by helplessly as the socialite, bent at the waist, vomited onto the neatly raked sand.

FOURTEEN

HORACE, BUNNY, AND I SAT ON BARSTOOLS midway down
the glittering white-granite bar, which was otherwise empty. It was a
good vantage point. The Lobby Bar overlooked the hotel's reception
desk and gift shop and sat across from the etched glass doors of Jean-
Claude's restaurant, Papillon. The restaurant was closed until further
notice. The entrance was safeguarded by a resolute young police officer. We couldn't hear his words, but we caught the anguished cries of
the employees as they arrived for work, were given the news, and then
turned away.

"Sergeant Jimenez, what's the latest?" Horace called out. His leather
duster was draped over a fourth barstool.

Sergeant Jimenez came over. "County medical examiner's on the
scene. That's half the battle."

"Heart attack, you suppose?"

"Or aneurysm, maybe."

"I'd like to see the body," Bunny said. She was sparing with her eye
contact. She tenaciously clutched an embroidered handkerchief Horace
had given her.

"Sorry, Mrs. Lorillard," Sergeant Jimenez said. "We can't do that
right now. Gotta give the medical examiner room to do his work."

An hour later we were still at the bar, passing time like passengers waiting in an airport lounge for a hopelessly delayed flight. This
opulent hotel bar was at least much more pleasant than a departure
lounge: the high, ornate ceiling, the walls done in marble, the half

dozen highly textured, backlit vertical panels that screened the bar from the Tea Court, the sunken salon where Bunny had entertained Jane and Florabelle the day before.

Horace swung his big horse's head about, testy over the pace of the cocktail service. His glass was bone dry. He flagged down our bartender, a slight, soft-spoken Asian man with dark features and a receding hairline. He wore a white shirt and black vest. His name was Johnson.

"I understand you're upset, Johnson, but we're the only customers in this doghouse," Horace said. "It shouldn't take an act of Congress to get this lady another martini. And I'll take another old-fashioned."

Johnson was apologetic. This time he was swift with the drinks.

"Did you know Chef Jean-Claude well?" Horace asked, after taking a sip of his new drink.

"Only who he was," Johnson said. "Chef was a very private man."

"But his employees come in after their shifts and often stay and drink after hours?"

Johnson regarded Horace with a willfully inexpressive face.

"I've been around the restaurant business all my life, Johnson," Horace said. "I know how these things work."

"Okay, okay," Johnson said. "Yes, boss. Sometimes after hours."

"It's a capital misstep to underestimate my powers of observation," Horace said. "I'll tell you a few things about yourself, Johnson. You left the Philippines at an early age. You went to sea. In your thirty years with the Cunard Line, you spent time on the *Queen Mary 2*. My guess is you tended bar in the Grills Lounge. You retired to Tucson because you like heat, but not too much of it."

Amazed, Johnson drew back. He gave me a high-spirited look and gestured with a thumb at Horace. "Magician! Psychic!"

"This isn't a cheap parlor trick, Johnson," Horace said. "I'm the chief of police. I've trained myself to notice these things."

"But they're all true!" Johnson said. "How'd you know all that?"

"It's rudimentary."

"I say it's a trick."

"Not a trick. I'll give them to you one at a time. First, about growing up in the Philippines. Even an imbecile could look at you and listen to your accent and know immediately you're a native Filipino. As for the part about going to sea, only a Cunard man ties together the fruit in an old-fashioned the way you've tied it here—a maraschino cherry on a cocktail stick, bordered by two knots of citrus peel. It was a detail insisted upon by Sir James Charles, commodore of the Line. And, of course, I recognize your tie pin—that golden orb and lion—as being a Cunard thirty year."

"Working the Grills Lounge… how did you know that?"

"When we first sat down, Jack, here, asked if you had any interesting drink recommendations. You suggested an *Amer Picon* with soda. That's the first aperitif listed on the drink card in the Grills Lounge on *Queen Mary 2.*"

"You must be a genius."

"Not a genius, Johnson. A logical thinker who thinks not-so-innocent thoughts about Angus calves and baby lambs. You and I have formed a bond here. But you should know I'm on official business. From now on, I expect you to be quick with the drinks. And I expect you to be discreet about anything you might overhear, got it?"

"Yes, boss, understand totally. I must be quiet as a kissing dog, silent as a nosebleed."

Horace narrowed his eyes at the back of the bartender's head as he stepped away.

Bunny turned to Horace. "I don't understand. What's taking so long? Why can't I see the body?"

"You heard the sergeant," Horace said. "They need to do their work. They don't want sightseers contaminating the scene."

"It's a dumpster. How can you contaminate a dumpster?"

"Trace evidence. Forensic engineering. The smallest detail might be the clue that cracks the case."

Bunny brought her martini glass to her lips. "It must be one immaculate goddamned dumpster."

Johnson hovered a few feet away, but the inquisitiveness remained on his face. He kept looking over at Horace.

"Yes, Johnson, what is it?" Horace asked.

"You said I came to Tucson because I like the heat, but not too much of it. How did you know this?"

Horace waited to answer. He took a gulp of his old-fashioned and then spoke.

"You come from the steamy swamps of Malay. Only people who like heat come to Arizona, and those with dignity and a modicum of taste settle in Scottsdale, unless they can't take the heat. In that case they move to Tucson."

Johnson's eyes brightened. "Yes, Chief, that's exactly right!"

Ignoring all this, Bunny brought her drink to her lips. "What am I going to do with all these people and all this money?"

"We'll reschedule," Horace said. "I'll come back in June. Pick any weekend."

Bunny looked at Horace with no small amount of gratitude. "Really? You'd do that?"

"Of course I will. We'll announce a new winner."

"No refunds?"

"Never. We postpone the gala weekend, that's all."

Bunny firmly gripped the stem of her martini glass, as if it were her tiller.

"But Miguel Ramirez and Tatiana Wong... and that other guy with Tatiana... Everyone will know they were finalists and not the real winner. We just told the world at our press conference."

"It doesn't matter. The new winner will reap the same benefit—recognition on the national stage. We'll give them a feature spread in *Sunshine Trails*. They'll have the title *Best Chef* on their resume. What is there to complain about?"

*   *   *

Bunny was halfway through a third martini when Sergeant Jimenez finally reappeared.

"Nothing too suspicious," he said, referring to his notepad. "A kitchen employee goes out back for a smoke, finds the body by the dumpster. Medical examiner says no sign of foul play. Death was pretty much instantaneous."

"Consistent with a heart attack," Horace said. "What else?"

"No known drug history or medical problems. Everyone's working in the kitchen, prepping for this big dinner. They say he seemed fine, healthy and in good spirits, stepped out for a cigarette. Smoking was a habit he kept hidden from the public, but all the guys in the kitchen knew about it."

Horace frowned. "Every French chef smokes. And they always do it out by the dumpster."

Sergeant Jimenez smiled. "Well, this poor guy was no exception."

Bunny squinted at Sergeant Jimenez. "I still don't understand. Why can't I see the body?" She slurred her words.

"Sorry, Mrs. Lorillard. Like I already explained, we can't let you do that."

"Oh, bunk!" She pressed her eyes shut and opened them again.

"Trust me," Horace said. "A body's nothing to see. Better to remember him as he was."

"No, blast it!" Bunny said suddenly, raising her voice, fixing Sergeant Jimenez with an angry stare. "I want to see the fucking body!"

People as far away as the hotel's front desk looked over.

"Mrs. Lorillard, maybe one of our officers can take you home?" Sergeant Jimenez said.

"Don't take me home," Bunny said. "Take me out to the dumpster and show me the fucking—" She started to collapse.

I caught her from behind. "Whoops!"

"... body!"

"Back you go, Mrs. Lorillard." I got her sitting upright again on the barstool.

Horace pulled Bunny's martini glass out of reach. "That's enough firewater for you, Mrs. Lorillard. Johnson and I are cutting you off." He turned to Sergeant Jimenez. "Maybe it's a good idea, getting her home. She lives right around the corner, you know—100 Staghorn Drive."

Sergeant Jimenez got face-to-face with Bunny. "Hear that, Mrs. Lorillard? Chief says it's time we got you home. We all want you safe." He addressed her in a firm, loud voice.

"What nonsense!" Bunny wobbled on her barstool and stared into the Tea Court.

Sergeant Jimenez gave Horace a knowing look, to which Horace nodded. Sergeant Jimenez turned away from the bar and keyed the microphone on the left-shoulder epaulet of his uniform. He said a few words over the radio.

Horace faced Bunny and took both her hands in his. "My dear girl, all the planning… all the effort… and now this unforeseen tragedy. The horror of canceling your gala has proved too much for your nerves. You must go home and go right to bed. Spend the afternoon sleeping it off. Promise me, will you do that?"

Bunny lowered her head and began to cry.

"Will you go home and go straight to bed?" Horace asked again.

She sniffed. "Yes."

"Don't talk to anyone until you talk to me first, all right?"

"I want to see the body."

"No, it's impossible. The medical examiner is conducting his investigation. Have some eggs for dinner. I'll see you in the morning, all right?"

"Tell me why, Horace." Bunny wiped her eyes. "Why? Why did this happen?"

"Things happen," Horace said. "Sometimes for no reason at all."

"I'm afraid this time there was a reason."

Horace reached out as if to stroke Bunny's hair. At the same time, he brought his mouth close to her ear. "Like I said, not a word to anyone. We'll talk about this in the morning."

Bunny became quiet. She rested her head against Horace's broad shoulder and planted her open hand on the lapel of his suit jacket. She closed her eyes.

"I love you, Horace. I hope you know that."

Two uniformed police officers—one female, one male—entered the lobby. Sergeant Jimenez went over and spoke to them. He brought them to the bar.

"Mrs. Lorillard, this nice young lady is Officer Frick, and this handsome young man is Officer Miller," Sergeant Jimenez said. "They're going to take you home. Would that be all right?"

Bunny sat up but appeared to be in a fog.

"Mrs. Lorillard, would that be okay?" Sergeant Jimenez asked again. Bunny shrugged.

Sergeant Jimenez turned to the officers. "Let's help her up."

Officers Frick and Miller got on either side of Bunny and held her elbows as she slid off the barstool and stood.

"Any purse?" Sergeant Jimenez asked. "Any personal effects?"

"Purse," Bunny said.

By this time, I had retrieved Bunny's purse from the hook under the bar counter. I gave it to Sergeant Jimenez. He followed Bunny and Officers Frick and Miller out of the bar. The last we saw of them, they were passing through the lobby, headed for the exit.

"I'm surprised at how quickly she fell apart," I said to Horace.

"Yet, not entirely unexpected." Horace signaled down the bar. "Johnson, I'll have a cup of coffee," he called.

I chuckled. "You? Coffee? In a hotel bar?"

"No choice, Jack. I must convey at least the illusion of being sober."

"Because you're the chief of police?"

Horace turned to me with a serious expression. "Because the name on that prescription I found in Bunny's guest bath was Jean-Claude Clemenceau. Don't you see? Bunny's reaction today was that of a lover."

My mind reeled. *Of course! Why didn't I see that?*

"Coffee, Chief," Johnson said, setting down a cup and saucer. "On the house."

"Excellent, Johnson. Thank you."

Johnson lingered a few moments—long enough to make certain the coffee was to Horace's satisfaction.

FIFTEEN

HORACE MARCHED THE LENGTH OF THE HALLWAY and muscled open the heavy door. We found ourselves standing in harsh sunlight at the back of the hotel. About thirty feet away was a pod of dumpsters. Sergeant Jimenez and a handful of police officers and city firemen were there. At their feet was a white body bag. The horse-laughs and lively banter told me death was about as sacred to these first responders as watching a traffic light change. Sergeant Jimenez saw us and peeled away from the group.

"We're about wrapped up here, Chief."

A slight breeze carried the whiff of a ripe, putrid stench from the direction of the dumpsters. I scrutinized the thick plastic bag, discerning signs of the human form I knew to be zipped inside: the peak of the nose, the swell of the belly, the pup tent formed by the feet that have taken their final steps. Was Jean-Claude still wearing his white cooking apron, chef's toque, and kitchen clogs?

Two field-team members from the medical examiner's office, both colorless as corpses themselves and dressed as if for a round of golf, wheeled a gurney over to the body.

"What about a homicide detective?" Horace asked Sergeant Jimenez. "Have you called one out yet?"

"No need, Chief. Medical investigator says there's no sign of foul play, and nothing's suspicious about the circumstances."

"Other than a man in perfect health suddenly drops dead," Horace noted.

Sergeant Jimenez turned to him. "Speculation on your part, Chief. There's nothing to say he was in perfect health."

"Someone must have that answer," Horace said.

The exercise of lifting the body onto the stretcher turned into high camp. In mid-lift, Jean-Claude jackknifed at the waist, as if intent on giving a cook one last, stern dressing down for a substandard plate of salmon en papillote that was about to leave the cooking line. The two medical examiners doing the lifting lost their handholds; the body bag hit the ground with a thud. The medical examiners leaned over, renewed their grips, counted to three, and heaved the body bag toward the stretcher, where this time it landed on target, settling like a side of beef on a butcher's block. The medical examiners fastened the body to the gurney with a series of straps.

"We're working on that, Chief," Sergeant Jimenez said to Horace. "We're trying to locate his next of kin."

The gurney exited stage right, leaving the grease-stained concrete pad in front of the dumpsters looking as though a large family had picnicked there—the plastic wrappers for the endotracheal tube and God knows what other disposable medical equipment that was used in the failed attempt to revive the chef; the pairs of latex gloves that had been stripped off and cast aside by the police officers, firefighters, and paramedics after Jean-Claude was pronounced dead; an open pack of cigarettes, one of which our victim perhaps was about to smoke; and paper products, food wrappers, and other kitchen and restaurant detritus that had never quite made it into the dumpster, left behind by careless employees to blow with the wind.

Horace watched the body go, then regarded the sergeant with uncloaked haughtiness.

"You should've asked me, Sergeant. I can tell you who his wife is."

Sergeant Jimenez stared incredulously at Horace. "You know his wife?"

"Odette Garin. She chefs at the Thunderbird Lodge."

"And where is this Thunderbird Lodge?" Sergeant Jimenez took a notepad and pen from his shirt pocket.

"Lake Tahoe. East Shore. It's the old George Whittell estate."

"They're divorced? Separated?"

"If they are, it's news to me."

Sergeant Jimenez made a note and raised intrigued eyes to Horace. "What else can you tell me?"

"Dick Peck hired them as a husband-and-wife team—he owns three or four casinos around the lake. But when Odette got the job cooking at Thunderbird Lodge, Jean-Claude started spending his winters in Tucson. He opened Papillon a few years back, and it became his year-round occupation. Odette's always stayed at the lake."

"Got a phone number for her?"

"Try the Lodge. She should be there. By the way, her coq au vin is world-class."

Sergeant Jimenez broke into a grin. "'Cock a' what?'"

Horace smiled. "You're no gastronome, are you, Sergeant Jimenez?"

"Not me, Chief. I'm just a dumb street cop. But I thank God every day for this job and the paycheck."

"You're no dumb street cop, Sergeant—you're a credit to this department. Tell me something. Off the record, what was the union's problem with Chief Sandoval?"

Horace huddled privately with Sergeant Jimenez for several minutes. Then he walked over and asked me to get Kimberly Earhart on the phone.

"Kimberly, I haven't forgotten you," Horace said, taking my phone, his face upturned. "Listen, I'm calling from a bar, and it's filling with boisterous happy hour customers. I have to make this quick..."

This made me laugh since Horace and I were still standing at the dumpsters with Sergeant Jimenez.

"I want you to run the department as if you were chief," Horace continued. "Do whatever you'd do. I'm tied up at the scene of a shocking death and can't say how long I'll be... that's right, Jean-Claude Clemenceau, the Best Chef Tucson... No, no one suspects foul play, but I owe it to Bunny Lorillard to monitor the situation closely... that's right, Kimberly, to monitor it from happy hour at a bar. By the way, if you ever feel like going on a whiskey bender, this guy Johnson makes a whacking good old-fashioned... Well, Kimberly, don't knock it until you've tried it.

Unless you're telling me you're some kind of stubborn, snake-eating Baptist..." Horace looked at me and rolled his eyes. "Well, even if that's the case, I wouldn't brag about it. No one cares about a reformed alcoholic. It's a tired, shopworn tale. I'll tell you something, Kimberly. Write about a heavy man getting skinny, and you'll get yawns, but write about a skinny man getting enormously fat, and that's something people will pay to read... Oh, and one last thing. For patrol, I want the department going back to a four-ten plan... that's right, four ten-hour days per week, none of this eight-hour, five-days-a-week crap. It takes people away from their families and their paid-under-the-table landscaping jobs. And from now on we pick shifts strictly by seniority, got it? We can't ask the old buzzards to work weekends and graveyards. They'll burn out and quit. Now be a good deputy chief, Kimberly. Run and get this stuff done. That's an order." He hit *End Call* and returned my phone.

Sergeant Jimenez gave Horace a smile. "Thank you, Chief. I appreciate that."

Horace frowned. "It was necessary." He surveyed the dumpsters. He turned to face the hotel. "Sergeant, I'd like to keep things undisturbed until we're certain about the cause of death. Can you keep some men here?"

"You suspect something?"

"Nothing I can point to. Just a precaution until we know more."

"No problem, Chief." Sergeant Jimenez canted his head. He was squinting into the sun. "How much of the area do you want secured?"

Horace hesitated. "These dumpsters and this back courtyard, for certain. And Jean-Claude's office. As I think about it, seal off the entire restaurant—kitchen, dining room, hostess stand. All of it." He gave Sergeant Jimenez a wry smile. "It's not like anyone will be eating at this malt shop anytime soon."

SIXTEEN

RIDING NEXT TO ME IN THE PASSENGER SEAT, his snobbish tendencies were on full display. Horace looked down his nose at the locals as if he were regarding street peasants in a third-world country. He winced at the cars around us—their sunbaked hoods, paint peeling, windows rolled down, squalling infants strapped into car seats. He stared with popping eyes at the storefront ethnic and casual-dining joints in strip mall after strip mall. He regarded with disdain the tracts of small flat-roofed houses tucked behind sand-blown masonry walls, their rock gardens shaded by straggly desert willows, their open carports occupied by brawny pickup trucks and absurdly small economy cars.

"That's our answer," I said. "Get a rush on the autopsy."

Horace followed a car with his eyes.

"This hooligan is gesturing at me," he said.

A restored '60s cruiser, a classic Chevy Impala with sparkling turquoise paint, was parallel to us in the next lane. The driver looked dangerous: shaved head, burly arms, colorful tattoos. A black Fu Manchu mustache sprang from his bulbous nose, concealing the sides of his mouth. He made a circular motion from his open window.

"He wants you to roll down your window," I said.

For a moment Horace's eyes widened. Finally, he gripped the silver handle and began rolling it counterclockwise, lowering the glass. Lively Mexican *Banda* music—peppy brass, thumping drums—blasted from the Impala's open windows.

"Sweet ride, grandpa," said the man with the Fu Manchu. "Beautiful.

You do the work yourself?"

Horace frowned at the impudence of the question—he held auto mechanics in low regard unless they worked for Rolls-Royce, in which case they were paragons of virtue.

"Certainly not," Horace said. "This is a company car."

"You a cop?"

"I'm the chief of police."

Fu Manchu laughed out loud. "The chief of police, for real?"

There was gridlock ahead. I braked to a stop. The Impala pulled up beside us. Horace studied the car's peculiar steering wheel—a chrome chain the diameter of a dessert plate. He looked at the driver.

"Got any liquor over there?" he asked Fu Manchu.

"You gonna cite me for open container?"

"Nope. I'm knackered. I need a drink."

Fu Manchu laughed. "You like tequila and grapefruit?" His lane began to move. He quickly pulled two or three car lengths ahead. We eventually caught up to him.

"That sounds pretty good," Horace said. "Maybe I'll ride with you."

Fu Manchu laughed again. This time it was our lane that pulled ahead. A moment later the Impala drew even with Horace's window.

"That thing supercharged?" Fu Manchu asked, his eyes drifting in the direction of our old Ford's rounded hood.

"Can't say," Horace replied. "But it might as well be a donkey, for Jack's despicable foot-dragging. He refuses to turn on the siren. I'm missing cocktail hour."

Fu Manchu eyed me with disapproval. "You must respect the Chief, Jack. He's a thirsty man. Get him out of this *mierda*."

The lane in front of Fu Manchu opened up, and he moved on.

"Charlie Lorillard is no murderer," Horace said, as if we'd never been interrupted. "He doesn't have it in him."

"Then there's no harm in asking, is there?" I kept my eyes trained ahead. Everything was coming to a stop again. In the next block, the Impala was bouncing up and down on hydraulics, performing for a crowd of drinkers on a second-floor bar balcony. The Impala appeared to hop in place: dropping, lifting, dropping, lifting.

"You're punishing me," Horace said.

"It's our duty to tell the police everything we know. Period."

Horace made a show of looking at his watch and shook his head in disgust.

"Tell you what," I said. "I'll make you a deal. Get a rush on the autopsy. Ask the medical examiner to check the scalp for a bullet wound. Do that, and I'll turn on the lights and siren, and we'll get you to your precious cocktail hour that much sooner." I reached into the side pocket of my blazer, fished out my cellphone, and placed it on the seat between us. "We need to know the truth."

Horace glanced at the phone and studied me analytically.

"All right, Jack, you've got yourself a deal." He picked up the phone. "Whom shall we call?"

"I'd start with Deputy Chief Earhart."

"Kimberly? Call her back?"

"Why not? She works for you."

He soon had her on the phone.

"One other thing, Kimberly," Horace said. "We just sent Jean-Claude's body to the morgue, and I need to get a rush on the autopsy." Horace listened for a minute. He turned to me and rolled his eyes. "Well, I'm sorry to hear that, because the sooner we get the results of that autopsy, the sooner I might sign that letter of resignation. Now, do you want to tell me again what is and isn't possible with respect to a rush?... Who's this, you say? Captain Zavala? Well, whomever you must go through, I really don't care to know the details. But have this Captain Zavala tell the autopsist to look closely at the scalp. We're looking for the entry wound of a bullet, most likely small caliber... no, ruling things out, is all..." Horace made eye contact with me and winked. "Yes, I need it done as quickly as possible, overnight, even. You're a resourceful gal, Kimberly. I have no doubt you and Captain Zavala can get this done for me..." He checked his watch. "I'm heading back to the *Pioneer Mother* now. I'll be there for the night, but have someone call this number the minute there's any news, I don't care what time it is. Will you do that?... Good. No, get that autopsy report first, then we'll talk about your letter. I'm losing you, Kimberly, losing the signal... Goodbye, Kimberly."

Signing off." Horace ended the call.

"*Autopsist?*" I said. "Is that even a word?"

SEVENTEEN

SEEING THAT IT WAS HORACE AND ME in the old patrol car, Jane and Florabelle scurried from the *Pioneer Mother*'s back platform for a closer look. A moment later Pierre followed, a silver tray stacked with hot towels in one hand and a pair of bamboo tongs in the other. Twilight was falling over the railroad yard.

Horace clambered out of the car. "Shake the hell out of a good martini, Pierre," he said, accepting a hot towel. "My nerves are foxed."

"What is this?" Jane asked, wrinkling her nose.

"It's our police car," I said, my left arm out the open window.

"Looks like something clowns would drive," Florabelle said.

Horace lowered the towel from his face and shot Florabelle a venomous look.

"Why are you driving it?" Jane asked.

"Long story. Crazy day."

Wanda came out to the *Pioneer Mother*'s back platform. She paused at the brass railing, drying her hands on her apron. She broke into a wide grin and came down the steps.

"Fitting ride for you two dinosaurs," she said, checking out the car. By now, thanks to my text message updates, she knew all about our day: about Horace's de jure appointment as chief of police, that Jean-Claude was dead, and even my strong suspicion Charles Lorillard had made good on his threat.

While I climbed out from behind the wheel and locked the car, Horace led Pierre across the gravel road and inside the old Pullman.

Jane stood at the museum car's front fender with her arms crossed. "This is so weird."

"What's weird?" I asked.

"That the chef-guy is dead. We were just talking to him yesterday."

I looked at her, surprised. "You were talking to Chef Jean-Claude?"

"When we had tea with Mrs. Lorillard. He was the chef who came over."

Florabelle grabbed Jane by the arm and stared at her with wide eyes. "Oh my gosh, that's the guy who was murdered?"

"Yes, didn't you know?"

I chastised Wanda with a scathing look.

"Don't say *murdered*, girls," I said. "The police think it was a heart attack."

Jane pressed her lips together and turned to me quizzically. "Then why were you and Uncle there all afternoon?"

"Your uncle is worried about Mrs. Lorillard."

"What's he worried about?"

"She's a friend. He wants to protect her."

"Protect her from what?" Jane asked.

"That's the million-dollar question."

"Maybe we can help."

I studied Jane curiously.

"There's a Ram Urban novel where Cassidy and Sky save a grandmother from a cold-blooded killer. She was riding on a train when she saw him murder his wife, only she had Alzheimer's and didn't remember what she saw."

I squinted at the sharp mountain peaks along the horizon. In the dwindling light they'd gone from purple to black. I returned my gaze to Jane.

"I don't get it. Where's the story in that?"

"Cassidy and Sky figured out why the killer wanted the grandmother dead and saved her life. Maybe we can help Uncle figure out who wanted the chef dead."

"Like I said, in this case there's no murder to solve yet." I began walking toward the *Pioneer Mother*. Jane and Florabelle followed me.

"Let's not make this guy's unfortunate death the focal point of our trip, okay? Sometimes people die for no reason. You two have your homework and your papers to write. That's enough on your plates."

As the girls scrambled up the steps of the railroad car, I looked for Wanda. She hadn't moved. She stood near the old Ford with her arms folded, looking north, giving the Kino Parkway overpass a stony stare.

"You coming?" I asked her.

She turned and glowered at me.

"You wanna talk about this?" she asked.

I glanced over my shoulder to confirm the girls had gone inside, then stared angrily at my wife. "You crossed a line, Wanda."

"Crossed what line?"

"You betrayed my confidence."

"I didn't do shit. What are you talking about?"

"They're kids, Wanda. They didn't need to hear this guy was murdered."

"You don't know the context."

"Tipping off two teenagers with hyperactive imaginations—getting 'em all worked up about a mystery to solve—I think I understand the context perfectly well."

"They're smart girls. They drew their own conclusion."

"Yeah? How come I think they had a little coaching?"

Wanda put her hands on her hips and exhaled scornfully. Her white cooking apron was stained. "God. You can be such an asshole."

At that moment I saw her at her worst: this self-righteous, uneducated, insular chef, this headstrong woman with a past that didn't seem to exist.

"You weren't the only one who heard Lorillard's threats," Wanda said, glaring. "I was there too, you know—twenty feet away in the galley. I think he had that guy killed as much as you do. Why shouldn't the girls know there's this kind of evil in the world?"

"Because they're kids, Wanda."

"You can fend for yourself. So can Mr. Button. But to be a woman and to hear those kinds of threats... it's terrifying." On the verge of tears, she pushed past me but stopped. She got right up in my face. "The girls were working on their essays, and they asked me if someone as old as Mrs. Lorillard could ever marry again, and that got us to talking about abusive relationships. I told them rich or poor, it doesn't matter. If you find yourself in one, get out, no matter what you have to do. Charles Lorillard is an abuser, there's not a doubt in my mind. There was a lesson to be learned, and I wasn't about to miss the opportunity. I did nothing wrong. In fact, I'd do it again. Every time."

She turned, mounted the steps of the railroad car, and went inside, slamming the door behind her.

When I got up on the back platform and put my hand on the brass doorknob, I discovered I'd been locked out.

EIGHTEEN

"YOU'VE GOT TO ADMIT, this chief of police thing is ludicrous,"
I said.

Facing me, seated in his favorite parlor chair, Horace puffed a big
after-dinner cigar. The railroad yard was quiet and dark.

"I think you should go first thing in the morning, tell the police
everything you know, and sign that letter for Kimberly—"

"Kimberly can go fly a kite."

Pierre came out from behind the bar with a crystal decanter of
vintage port. I waved him away. He topped off Horace's glass.

"People at home are depending on you to run the company," I said to
Horace. "So are your readers and advertisers."

"No, at this point it would be a grievous mistake to resign as chief
of police."

"How so?"

"The minute I do, they'll shut me out of the investigation."

"The city manager says you have until Tuesday. What can you possibly accomplish in that amount of time?"

Horace drew thoughtfully on his cigar but didn't reply.

"Answer me this," I said. "If the medical examiner finds a bullet in
Jean-Claude's hairline, what will you do?"

Horace gave me a shrewd smile. "I'll do whatever's right."

"Even if it means ratting out a friend?"

"Interesting assumption. You assume ratting out a friend is the right
thing to do."

"Meaning you'd protect Charles Lorillard?"

"Jean-Claude's cause of death was a simple heart attack—I'd bet money on it."

"If it's a heart attack, will you go to Kimberly and tender your resignation?"

Horace brought his glass to his lips and took a sip.

"I'll sleep on that one, Jack. The trappings of the office and political advantage… I might like being chief a lot better than publishing a magazine."

*   *   *

That night, around midnight, my ringing cellphone woke me from a deep sleep. In a fog of wine, port, and grogginess I did my best to sound lucid.

"Jack Marshall."

"Chief Button, please." It was a woman calling.

Chief Button?

I drew a blank, but then I remembered we were in Tucson living aboard these railroad cars, and Horace had been given the unlikely title.

"Deputy Chief Earhart asked me to call when we had news," the woman explained. Her voice sounded vaguely familiar.

I turned on the light. "Mr. Button went to bed a long time ago, I'm afraid."

Wanda lifted her head off the pillow and blinked at me incoherently.

"Who is this?" I asked.

"This is Captain Gomez, his chief of staff."

"Lucianna!"

"Yes, sir. I hope I didn't wake you?"

"Not at all… My wife and I were just thinking about going to bed."

Beneath the covers, Wanda kicked me. She pulled a pillow across her eyes.

Some hours earlier, penitential, humbled after regaining entry to the *Pioneer Mother* (Pierre let me in), I had worked my way back into my wife's good graces. My poor man's bouquet of trackside marigolds, their stems stuffed into a discarded bottle of Buffalo Trace bourbon, was so pitiful, and my apologies for second-guessing her parenting instincts were so sincere, that we'd gone to bed on good terms. *Very* good terms.

"What's your pleasure, sir?" Lucianna asked.

"My pleasure, Lucianna?"

Wanda looked at me reprovingly.

"How would you like to proceed?" Lucianna asked. "I'm happy to hold while you wake Chief Button—"

"I don't think that's a good idea—"

"Or I can give you a message…"

"That's probably best, Lucianna. I'll see that he gets it first thing in the morning." I scrambled for the notepad and pen that every aspiring writer keeps on his night table.

"Ten-four," Lucianna said. "Let me know when you're ready to copy."

"Ten-four," I said. When I had the pen and pad in hand: "Okay, ready to copy."

Thwack! Wanda hit me on the head with her pillow.

"Badge-banger," she whispered. "Pistol-sniffer."

I shushed her and pushed her away.

"I've got a preliminary on Jean-Claude Clemenceau," Lucianna was saying. "They finished the autopsy."

"Go ahead, I'm listening."

"Medical examiner found no bullet wounds in the scalp or the body. Point one."

"All right. Got that."

"Point two. Pretty sure cause of death is acute intoxication from a synthetic opioid—the deceased exhibited white foam in the lungs and a swollen brain."

I lifted my pen from the pad. "I can't write that fast, Lucianna. Can you give it to me in plain English?"

"Basically, a drug overdose, sir. Nothing conclusive until the blood tests come back, but we're seeing a lot of this in Tucson. Fentanyl, possibly carfentanil. Nasty stuff when an addict starts mixing it with heroin. You don't want to touch it, much less ingest it."

A heroin addict? Chef Jean-Claude?

A rush of adrenaline coursed through my body, clearing my head. I asked Lucianna to walk me through the details a second time, slowly, so I could write it all down for Horace. By this time Wanda sat cross-legged on the bed, her hair in her eyes, the collar of her gray sleep shirt hanging loosely off a shoulder. She tilted her head, trying to decipher my handwriting. She looked at me, puzzled. I shook my head at her—she wasn't going to believe this.

"What's next?" I asked Lucianna.

"Nothing much to do until the blood tests come back. Tell Chief Button we've asked for those code three."

"Code three?"

"Red lights and siren."

"Got it. Good job."

We agreed to touch base in the morning. I thanked Lucianna and ended the call.

"So what's the verdict?" Wanda asked.

I stared at my wife. "Get this. Chef Jean-Claude died of a drug overdose."

"What does that mean, exactly?"

"It means our weekend in Tucson just got a lot more interesting."

NINETEEN

"WHO IS IT, PLEASE?" Bunny asked in a cheerless voice.

Horace and I stood before the rustic door. The morning sun beat down on the spartan courtyard. The fountain was still.

"Bunny," Horace said, "can you let us in? I must speak with you."

"Horace?"

"Yes."

Behind the door came the sounds of a small chain coming loose and a dead bolt sliding. Bunny opened the door and blinked into the sunlight. In her blue silk kimono, without makeup, she looked much older. There were age spots on her face. Her eyes were red and swollen.

"I'm sorry, I don't look very presentable." She tightened the tie of her robe and ran a hand through her uncombed hair.

"We've come with news about Jean-Claude," Horace said. He held his derby hat in his hands. "Please, may we?"

Bunny stepped aside. "Of course."

I followed Horace into the tiled foyer of the duplex. In the living room, the blackout shades were drawn.

"It's cold enough to hang meat in here," Horace said.

Bunny took a pack of Marlboros from a Parsons table in the entry. She shook out a cigarette.

Horace eyed her closely. "I've never known you to be a smoker."

"An old habit," Bunny said, "coming back with a vengeance. Get you a drink? Bourbon or scotch?"

"No, nothing." Horace strode to the center of the living room. "It's been a shocking turn of events."

"I daresay the ladies of Los Picadores will survive." Bunny clamped the cigarette between her lips. She cupped a hand and lit the cigarette with a silver metal lighter. Inhaling deeply, she tilted her chin up and blew out a long stream of smoke. "But it's a damn shame they wasted all that money on hair."

Horace forced a smile. "There's always another party."

Bunny took a broody drag off her cigarette and slipped the lighter into the pocket of her robe.

"How are the girls?" she asked, looking from Horace to me.

"The girls are fine," I said. "They're hoping to see you again."

"I'd like that very much. They're sweet." Bunny crossed her arms, holding the cigarette between two fingers. She began pacing.

"The reason we're here," Horace said, "…it's disturbing news, I'm afraid. They did the autopsy last night. You should sit for this." Horace gestured with his hat toward the overstuffed sofa. "Please, Bunny, sit."

Holding her cigarette in the air, pinching her robe closed at the neck, fixing her wary gaze on Horace, Bunny drew alongside the sofa and sat.

"We don't believe Jean-Claude died of natural causes," Horace said. "The medical examiner thinks he died of a drug overdose."

Bunny's lips parted slightly, and her eyes went glassy.

"I need to ask you some questions."

Bunny turned sharply to Horace. "Questions as my friend? Or as chief of police?"

"Does it matter?"

Bunny sighed and turned away. "Jean-Claude and I were having an affair. But you already knew that, didn't you?"

"He was handsome and exciting, an international playboy. You found him irresistible."

"And now he's dead."

"It isn't your fault," Horace said. "You mustn't blame yourself."

"Our romance would stay as quiet as the falling snow—that was my promise to him. We made a good team. We hid it well, I have to say."

"You did," Horace agreed. "The citizens of Tucson are none the wiser."

Bunny looked at Horace pleadingly. "I'd like to keep it that way.

I hope you can respect that. I loved him very much, Horace."

"Enough to rig the outcome of the Best Chef award?" Horace studied Bunny's face.

Bunny gave a weak smile. She stumped out her cigarette in an ashtray on the coffee table. "The restaurant was failing. It needed a boost. I was in a position to help."

"Helping a friend is no crime." Horace moved to a wing chair facing the sofa, placed his hat on a glass side table, and sat. "Bunny, you can speak freely with Jack and me. It will never leave this room. Was Jean-Claude a heroin addict?"

Bunny turned away and shook her head faintly.

Horace leaned in. "Bunny, you must tell me the truth. Did he use drugs?"

Bunny stared defiantly at Horace. "No, absolutely not."

"Was he addicted to opioids, maybe—"

"No."

"Oxycodone from an old operation?"

"No, Horace, it's impossible!"

"Why do you say it's impossible?"

"Because I would've known. We've been living together for almost three months." Bunny fell silent. A smiled crossed her lips. "His thing was strictly wine. I couldn't even get him to smoke a joint with me in bed."

Horace glanced at me. He sat forward and took one of Bunny's hands solemnly.

"You understand what this means, what you're telling me?" he asked.

Bunny looked down. "I don't understand anything anymore…"

"It means Jean-Claude was murdered."

Bunny closed her eyes. "No."

Horace reached for her other hand. "Don't you see? That means he was deliberately poisoned. Can you be absolutely certain he wasn't an addict?"

Bunny looked Horace firmly in the eye. "I'm positive, Horace. How many times do I have to say it?"

"If there's a murder investigation, suspicion will almost certainly fall on Charlie."

"Charles?" Bunny started. She stared at Horace.

"He knew Jean-Claude was your lover?" Horace asked.

Bunny chewed her lip. "He hired a private detective. He had me followed."

Horace let go of Bunny's hands. "I'll tell you something incriminating. Three days ago, in Los Angeles, he threatened your lover's life."

Bunny gave a dismissive snort. "Sounds like Charles."

"Do you believe he's capable of murder?"

Bunny locked eyes with Horace. "Not in a million years. He's too self-centered and narcissistic to kill. He wouldn't put his freedom at risk—not for me, not for anyone."

"He talked of hiring an assassin."

Bunny looked over at me and back to Horace. She smirked. "Let me guess. A sparrow from the Philippines?"

Horace raised his eyebrows. "You know about that?"

"It was his stock answer to everything—a slow contractor, a greedy partner, every banker he ever dealt with. Empty words from a blowhard who can't handle his liquor or his temper—that's Charles for you. That's the man I was married to for all those years."

"So his was an empty threat? You give it no credence?"

"None whatsoever."

"What about Jean-Claude? Did he have any enemies?"

"Enemies? Don't be ridiculous. He spent every waking hour at Papillon, trying to make that place work. He didn't have time for enemies."

TWENTY

"Morning, Chief."

"Everything secure, officer?"

"Yes, sir."

"Good. We're going in." Horace turned to me. "Every chef has an office. We'll start there."

I followed Horace past the hostess stand and into Papillon's darkened dining room. What little light there was came from the open cooking line. We negotiated our way around the tables, which were draped in white and set for dinner service. Under the pall of Jean-Claude's death, the spacious restaurant—an extravagant build-out done in cut glass and high-gloss wood, with oversized modern art—had an eerie, portentous feel, like a museum locked after dark.

We zigzagged around the cooking line, pushed through a swinging door, and entered the brightly lit kitchen. Pyramids of chopped vegetables stood at intervals on the stainless-steel counters, along with mixing bowls, oils, and spices left abandoned by the kitchen staff. A dishwasher's station was piled high with pots and pans. We found Jean-Claude's office down that same long, shadowy corridor that led to the door marked *EXIT* and the pod of dumpsters outside.

I switched on the light. The small windowless room wasn't much larger than a walk-in closet. A five-drawer tanker desk was pushed against a wall, its surface concealed by a desktop computer, monitor, and printer awash in a jumble of catalogs, computer printouts, and assorted files, notebooks, and swollen three-ring binders. Taped to one wall, above a two-shelf bookcase, were shift schedules, event calendars, and colorful food shots cut from magazines.

The notion of tabulating all this clutter, combing through it for clues as to Jean-Claude's murderer—and doing it under Horace's insufferable scrutiny—made my eyes glaze over. I wanted to bolt.

"Don't touch a thing," Horace said. "Do you see what I see?"

"I see a pigsty—"

"Be right back. Don't move."

I scanned the office again.

What had Horace seen?

He returned a moment later with a long pair of stainless-steel kitchen tongs. He stepped around the desk's mesh-back roller chair and went to the bookcase, and only at that point did I fathom the objects of his attention: on the bottom shelf were two colorful Chow-Bella shipping cartons, each about the size of a nine-quart Igloo cooler.

Tucson's best chef orders from other restaurants?

Horace kept his gaze fixed on the Chow-Bella food boxes. Using the tongs, he pushed away the lid of the first box and peered cautiously inside.

"Anything in there?" I asked.

"Only this."

Clamped in the tip of the tongs was a piece of paper. Horace set the paper carefully on the desk. He used the tongs to pull an identical slip of paper from the second box. He looked from one paper to the other.

"Interesting."

"What do you see?"

"Packing slips, each a Chow-Bella order. I can't say I'm surprised."

"Why? What did he order?"

"A tamale combo pack here, and a ribs-and-sausage sampler platter here."

"I don't get it. What's the significance?"

"One from El Whisky, the other from Family Bone."

"Our first and second runners-up. That can't be coincidence."

"Certainly not." Ruminating over the raised tongs, Horace had a faraway look in his eyes.

"Are you thinking poison?" I asked. "Resentment over the fact Jean-Claude was named winner?"

Horace looked at me. "Not beyond the realm of possibility. Chefs can be a cruel, vindictive bunch. Get Kimberly on the phone. Tell her we've got a break in the case and we're coming in. And be careful not to touch anything. This could all be evidence."

TWENTY-ONE

"THAT'S THE STUPIDEST THING I EVER HEARD," Kimberly said. "Poisoned by a rival chef?"

Horace kept walking. The open door of the chief's office was within sight.

"Become useful, Kimberly. Step into my office. Bring a pen and a notepad."

Kimberly balked at the command. "Only if you're going to sign that letter."

Horace stopped at the door. "I want you to put a homicide detective on the case and test those food boxes for drugs."

Kimberly's face hardened. "Not my job."

"Your job is to do what I say." Horace disappeared inside the office.

I followed him in. The big desk, the bookcases, the credenza—all the workspaces had been stripped clean. On the whiteboard were two words written in red: *Fuck you.*

"You're asking the wrong person," Kimberly said from behind me. "Captain Zavala runs our Central Investigations Division."

"Well, get him in here."

"Her."

"*Her?*"

"Captain Zavala's a woman."

"I don't care if she's an Irish goat with hookworms. Get her in here."

About ten minutes later there came a tentative knock on the open door. Lucianna peered around the corner.

"Chief Button?"

Horace stood quickly and beckoned Lucianna with an open hand.

"Yes, yes, Lucianna, come right in!"

I stood.

"Chief Button," Lucianna said, "meet Captain Zavala."

Trailing Lucianna was a petite woman with lustrous black skin, her full lips screwed into a scowl. Her loose-fitting uniform shirt was smartly pressed, and her Ray-Ban Aviator sunglasses were parked high over her pronounced forehead. Like Lucianna, she carried a Glock in the holster on her leather duty belt. She glared at Horace.

Horace did a double take.

"Valentina," he whispered, horror-stricken. "The midnight croak of the raven…"

Captain Zavala bridled.

"You calling me a croaking raven?"

Horace leaned forward and shamelessly studied the features of Captain Zavala's face—her high, hollow cheekbones, her lovely brown doe's eyes.

"It's uncanny," he said, as if in a dream. He started suddenly, licked his lips, and smiled woodenly. "Please, sit. Everyone sit."

Captain Zavala glanced warily at Lucianna. We all sat at the table. Horace couldn't take his eyes off his visitor.

"Please, Captain Zavala, tell me your ancestry. Dominican Republic, I'd guess?"

Captain Zavala hesitated. "That's right. My parents—"

"I once met a woman in Santo Domingo," Horace interrupted. "Her name was Valentina."

"Common enough—"

"You could be her daughter. Her specialty was a seven-meat stew called sancocho."

"I know sancocho…" Captain Zavala crossed her arms. The receding cuffs of her long-sleeved uniform shirt revealed her delicate wrists.

"When I complained of finding fish fins and chicken feet in the broth, we had words. She invoked the croak of the raven and cast a voodoo spell I'd as soon forget."

"A *what* spell, Mr. Button?" Captain Zavala asked defiantly.

"Voodoo, Captain Zavala." Horace turned a knowing gaze upon her. "Surely you're no stranger to the practice?"

"Sir, I am a career law enforcement officer. I assure you, I do not practice voodoo."

Horace's face flushed. He forced a smile.

"That comes as a tremendous relief. You have no idea. Can you tell me about your mother and father?"

Again, Captain Zavala looked questioningly at Lucianna. She turned back to Horace. "My father was Dominican. My mother was Cuban."

Horace slapped the table and looked at me triumphantly. "That explains it."

Captain Zavala narrowed her eyes at him.

"Explains what?"

Horace turned back to her.

"How a coat-check girl rose through the ranks to become a captain in this department. The police DNA is in your blood—blackjacks and rubber hoses administered at midnight in the cane fields of a rum-bum island." Horace looked proudly about the table but was met by down-cast eyes and a mortified silence. He flashed a nervous smile at Captain Zavala. "I meant that as a compliment, you know... an expression of my admiration for the way you've managed to shed the indolence and lassi-tude so engrained in the typical Island Carib." He cleared his throat. "You no doubt have a lazy uncle or two?"

Captain Zavala stared into the distance, shaking her head in disbe-lief. "I have a degree in criminology from George Washington University. I have an executive MBA from USC..."

"Chief Button," Lucianna said, "you have Captain Zavala to thank for the expedited autopsy."

Horace turned to Captain Zavala and brightened.

"Is that so! Tell me everything."

"This death has all the characteristics of an unattended, self-inflicted drug overdose," Captain Zavala said, placing her hands atop the file folder she'd carried in with her. Her fingernails were painted that dark shade of purple I've always associated with Mardi Gras. "We're seeing a lot of this on the streets. Heroin laced with fentanyl. Counterfeit prescription painkillers. The accidental deaths have medical examiners backed up all over the country."

Horace shook his head. "I don't buy it. Chef Jean-Claude, a drug addict?"

"Drugs are rampant in the restaurant business. Everyone knows that."

"In this case it's counterintuitive. A topflight French chef dying like a common street bum. His hare plates and frogs' legs were too well-informed."

Captain Zavala scoffed. "As far as this department is concerned, the investigation is closed. Unless the medical examiner says otherwise."

"Tell me, Captain Zavala, if certain food items were laced with this fentanyl, could it kill a man?"

"It could kill an elephant."

"But a man—how much would it take?"

"A few flecks of powder comparable to a few grains of salt, no more than that."

"And he wouldn't taste it?"

"Not necessarily. It can be odorless and tasteless."

The worry lines deepened in Horace's forehead. He looked from Captain Zavala to Lucianna.

"I must tell you something in strict confidence. May I have your word? I say this only because it might have a bearing on reopening the investigation."

Captain Zavala eyed Horace skeptically. "You know something?"

"I do."

"And what might that be?"

Horace leaned in. "My editors felt the Best Chef Tucson award should go to El Whisky or Family Bone. They thought Jean-Claude merited a distant third, at best."

Captain Zavala glanced at Lucianna, then looked back at Horace.

"I don't follow," she said.

"It's very simple," Horace said. "We may have a jealous, maniacal, killer chef on our hands, possibly even a murder conspiracy involving the two runners-up."

Captain Zavala raised her face contemptuously at Horace.

"And for this you want to open a formal homicide investigation? Because your editors say there are better restaurants in town?"

"Precisely."

"Forget it, Mr. Button. It's a preposterous theory. We don't have the manpower to chase ridiculous ideas."

Horace sat back in his chair.

"We have a crime lab up on Miracle Mile, yes?"

Captain Zavala shook her head. "I'm not listening to this—"

"Surely they have the means to test for a drug like fentanyl?"

"We don't deal with poisoning deaths. They're handled by the medical examiner's toxicology lab."

"But in our lab we have machines that can detect the presence of fentanyl?"

Captain Zavala glanced at Lucianna before turning back to Horace.

"Honestly, Mr. Button, a resentful cook?"

"I want you to assign a homicide detective and test those boxes—"

"Impossible. I won't do it! And besides, we'd need a warrant."

"Get a warrant if you have to. But get a CSI team out to Papillon in the Saguaro Mesa Hotel. On the bottom shelf of the bookcase in Jean-Claude's office they'll find two Chow-Bella food containers. Tell the lab to test those containers for traces of this fentanyl, as you call it."

Captain Zavala stared at Horace, fuming.

"What about fish fins and chicken feet, Mr. Button? Shall we test for those, too?"

Horace eyed Captain Zavala wrathfully.

"Ridicule me at your peril, Captain."

"This isn't television, Mr. Button. Deputy Chief Earhart asked me to attend this meeting to humor you. Otherwise, I wouldn't give you the time of day. You're an affront to our profession and a mockery to this badge. We have specific investigative protocols and operating procedures. You need to let my people do their work without your knee-jerk civilian interference."

Horace's face reddened. He sat forward, making his chair groan, and stood. He raised his broad shoulders and planted his hands palms-down on the conference table.

"Captain Zavala, what's my title?"

"Your title?"

"This morning, this minute, right here and now at this department?" With each word, he drummed a thick fingertip on the table for emphasis.

Captain Zavala's eyes widened. She drew back in her chair.

"You're chief of police, sir."

"That being the case," Horace said, "assign a homicide detective and get a search warrant. Send out a CSI team. Test those food containers for drugs. Do it *now*. That's an order!"

*   *   *

Horace and I sat alone in the chief's office, drinking coffee, awaiting a call from the newly assigned homicide detective. My cellphone rang. It was Wanda.

"Hey," she said, "I just hung up with a guy looking for Mr. Button, says he's an old friend flying in from Reno. Wants to know if Mr. Button can meet his plane at the executive jet center when he lands around 11:30—something to do with Chef Jean-Claude. Can I give you his name and number?"

I reached for a yellow legal pad on the table.

"Sure, go ahead."

I wrote down the guy's name and number and looked at Horace.

"Dick Peck?"

Horace nearly spit his coffee. "What about him?"

"He's flying in. Wants to meet. Says it has something to do with Jean-Claude."

Horace frowned.

"Dick Peck can go sit on a sharp tack."

TWENTY-TWO

WE WERE BACK IN THE OLD PROWL CAR, making our way to the airport. The flat, colorless scenery was a mix of sandy, overgrown lots and run-down commercial establishments: corner gas stations, cinder-block motels converted to studio apartments, tire shops with their open garages and yards full of discarded clutter.

"I've been thinking about this thing with Captain Zavala," I said. "Now that you've got a homicide detective assigned, you'd better be prepared for what might come."

Horace raised an eyebrow at me.

"Come to whom?" he asked.

"Charles Lorillard, for one. What if he hired a sparrow who kills with fentanyl? Have you thought of that?"

Horace looked away.

"Or what if Mrs. Lorillard is the killer?" I asked. "What if her relationship with Jean-Claude took a bad turn? He found another woman, so she exacted her revenge…"

Horace turned back to me. "Speculation without fact. That either one is capable of murder—it's an absolute crock."

"How can you be so sure?"

"Because." Horace tugged on a shirt cuff. "Charlie's a mogul of the first chop. And everyone knows Bunny is gentle as a kitten."

"That's it? One's a mogul and the other's a kitten?"

"That's it."

"Those are two pretty stupid reasons." Exasperated, I blurted this out. When it came to his playfellows, Horace's Pollyanna perspective defied logic. "Do I have to point out Bunny Lorillard has already lied to us twice?"

Horace looked at me askance.

"About living alone and not taking a lover," I said.

"She was protecting a friend. Don't hold that against her."

As we neared the airport, the city blocks turned dense with covered long-term parking lots, fast food restaurants, and chain hotels. The street medians showcased a wide variety of cactus under the speckled shade of pruned palo verde trees. A sign said *Visit Again Soon*.

Playing devil's advocate inspired me. Pressing Horace to the limits of his reason, I figured, was part of my reporter's research.

"How about if we go back to the police station," I said, looking at him. "You sign Kimberly's letter—"

"Forget it—"

"Then you and I return to our normal lives. The police close the case as a self-inflicted drug overdose. Bunny and Charles Lorillard both walk free, whether either one was involved or not. What do we care?"

Horace frowned but didn't reply. He assumed a posture of stiff resolve and stared out the window as if mesmerized. The grass-lined entrance to the Four Points by Sheraton, with its grand palms, appeared to be the most interesting façade on Earth.

*   *   *

Majestic Flight Support was housed in a sand-colored hangar at the end of a service road off East Airport Drive, adjacent to Tucson International Airport's main taxiway. I parked the old Ford in a visitor's space beneath a shade structure. On the other side of a cyclone fence, perhaps 200 feet away, a United Airlines Boeing 737 was making a sharp turn, getting into takeoff position. Its engines howled.

"Dick Peck is a scoundrel," Horace said, after the plane had gone hurtling down the runway. The air was tinged with the biting tang of jet exhaust. "Tell me again why I'm doing this?"

"You're doing this for your friend at the Thunderbird Lodge," I said.

"You extol her French cooking, and Dick Peck signs her paycheck."

At the entrance to the lounge, a good-looking brunette staffed a formal reception desk. On the wall behind her were a bank of closed-circuit TV monitors and clocks showing the time in four different time zones. Looking out the two-story corner windows, a smallish, white-haired man meditated on a row of gleaming corporate jets parked on the tarmac outside, his hands clasped behind his back.

We walked over to him.

"One of those yours?" Horace asked.

The man turned.

"Horace."

"Dick Peck."

"My old friend. So good of you to come. It's been too many years."

"Has it?"

Dick extended a hand to Horace. His pallid skin was speckled with sunspots. He wore the collar of his yellow Polo shirt turned up. The two men shook hands.

Horace's smile wavered. "How's Odette holding up?"

"It's been tough on her, Horace. She couldn't bring herself to deal with it."

"She didn't make the trip?"

"No."

"I'm sorry. I was hoping to extend my condolences in person."

"She told me you were here. I called because I thought you might be able to help."

Horace's expression turned guarded. "Help, how?"

"With claiming Jean-Claude's remains. It's the weekend, and I don't have a lot of time."

"What's the hurry?" Horace asked.

"Business obligation. We need to be back in Reno on Monday."

Horace gave Dick a quick look.

"We?"

From behind me, a fit-looking man in his fifties joined our huddle. His head was smooth-shaven and pink as a thumb. He had lively eyes and a carefully groomed box-shaped goatee.

"Have you met Wayne Clark?" Dick asked Horace.

Horace turned to Wayne. "Don't believe I've had the pleasure."

Dick took the time to make introductions. They were an odd pair, Dick Peck slight and frail with age, Wayne Clark handsome and powerfully built, with a crushing handshake.

"Do you have time to chat?" Dick asked Horace.

Horace touched the face of his wristwatch. "Not a lot. We have an appointment with a detective."

"In that case let's sit right here."

The four of us settled into a grouping of low leather armchairs. The executive jet center was busy—crew members and passengers coming and going through the automatic doors, followed by valets wheeling carts loaded with luggage.

Horace was distracted by the private jets.

"Those things have always struck me as artifacts of sorcery." He turned to Dick. "Which one's yours?"

"The first one. The Gulfstream 450."

We all admired the first jet in line. Its windows were oval-shaped and it was by far the biggest. Horace looked back at Dick.

"You like flying?"

"The only way to go."

"How many hours from Reno?"

"Two."

Horace's mouth fell open. "Two? It took me three days by train."

"You should try flying. You might like it."

Horace turned his gaze again to the jet. "How many in your crew?"

"Two pilots. I keep it simple."

"No stewardess? No chef?"

"What's the need? I have every restaurant in the country at my beck and call. I can be in New Orleans for brunch, Denver for dinner, and back in Reno for a nightcap. You really ought to try it, Horace. Once you do, you'll never travel any other way."

"Ha!" Horace waved a dismissive hand. "All you need is twenty-five million to buy the damn thing."

"You can always charter one, you know, if you need to get

somewhere fast."

Horace leaned back in his chair and smoothed his tie. "I'm an old railroad man, Dick. I don't need to get anywhere fast."

"How's Jane?"

Horace's face filled with pride. "Heir to a fortune, destined to be a grande dame of the world, a patroness of the arts."

"Taking after her uncle."

"Her uncle is a patron of trifles."

Dick shook his head. "We followed Ruth Pepper's funeral coverage on TV, start to finish. Very sad. But I must say, Horace, I envy you. That child will keep you young." He stopped and blinked, as if something shocking had passed in front of his face. He turned to Horace. "One thing I want to start with. I'm sorry things went the way they did between us."

"A casino operator who puts friendship before business misconstrues his calling," Horace said.

"Kind of you to say, even if you don't believe it." Dick spread his elbows to the armrests of his chair and put his palms together. "So what the hell happened to Jean-Claude, anyway? Was it a heart attack?"

Horace leaned forward.

"I have news about that. We have privileged information from the police. There are… shall we say… suspicious circumstances surrounding the death."

Dick snapped his head back.

"Suspicious?"

"The medical examiner says it was a drug overdose."

"Jean-Claude? A drug overdose? That's absurd."

"I agree," Horace said. "That's why I've asked the police to investigate his death as a homicide."

Dick's mouth dropped open and he stared at Horace without blinking. Wayne turned quickly away, and then looked hard at Horace.

"Seems odd," Wayne said. "Cops don't generally work at a civilian's disposal."

"These cops do." Horace outstared Wayne.

Wayne turned to Dick. "Not in my experience."

"And what's your experience?" There was an edge to Horace's voice.

"Wayne's ex-law enforcement," Dick said. "He understands how these things work."

Horace gave Wayne the once-over. "Is that so?"

"A rookie out of college." Wayne settled back in the chair and crossed his legs at the knee. He wore leather loafers and colorful socks. "A few years on a small force, until I met Dick. He convinced me there were better opportunities in the private sector."

Horace's eyes warmed. "Any experience as a detective?"

"A little bit at the end. I worked property crimes—burglary, theft, fraud, that sort of thing."

Horace touched his fingertips together. "I'd like to tell you about the case. Things aren't adding up."

Wayne removed a piece of lint off his slacks and flicked it to the floor. "Yeah? What kinds of things?"

"It appears Jean-Claude was deliberately poisoned."

Dick's expression went dark. "My god, that's shocking. Who'd do a thing like that?"

"That's what we intend to find out."

Wayne looked at Horace. "What makes you think he was poisoned?"

"The medical examiner performed the autopsy last night. Knows an overdose when he sees one."

"A heroin overdose?" Dick asked.

"Fentanyl," Horace said. "The telltale signs are unmistakable."

Wayne stared off in the distance and shook his head. "Fentanyl. Jesus."

"Fentanyl?" Dick asked Wayne.

"A synthetic opioid, more lethal than heroin," Wayne said.

Horace turned to him. "Sounds like you know something about it."

"Like I said, I was a cop before I met Dick. We're seeing a lot of these same overdoses in the casinos. It's so damn pathetic and heartbreaking. But I don't get it. What makes you suspect foul play?"

Horace eyed Wayne. "Ask me, this thing stinks like a five-day mackerel. I'll be interested in your expert opinion, but—" He looked quickly at his watch and turned to Dick. "I can explain, but we're already late for our meeting. Where are you staying? We'll come find you later."

Dick looked at Wayne. "Great question. Where are we staying?"

"The Arizona Inn," Wayne said. "Near the University."

"I know where it is," Horace said. "Eat in the Main Dining Room. Try the French onion soup and the braised short ribs."

"I'm impressed," Wayne said with an easy smile, looking from Horace to Dick. "Your friend knows his town."

"Horace knows everyone and everything," Dick said. "I'm sure that includes the powers that be at city hall."

"You might be surprised," Horace said with a self-deprecating grin. "I may have met my match this morning in a cutthroat pirate named Captain Zavala." He stood. "If you'll excuse us, gentlemen…" And then, as we all shook hands: "We'll give you a call when we finish our business. The Arizona Inn has a good bar. We can meet there, and I'll fill you in on what we know."

TWENTY-THREE

THE BLACK FORD CROWN VICTORIA SEDAN, with its generic silver hubcaps, parked in a red zone in front of the Saguaro Mesa Hotel, all but shouted *cop car*. Parked in the same red zone was a marked Tucson PD CSI van. As Horace and I passed through the lobby, a dark-haired man left the hotel gift shop and hurried after us.

"Chief Button," he called. "Chief Button, hold on!"

Horace and I stopped and turned.

"I'm Detective Ivanovich, homicide."

The detective appeared to be in his early forties. His face was heavily pockmarked. He held a Day of the Dead skeleton mask that he'd carried with him out of the shop, but Horace paid no attention to the mask. He gaped incredulously at the detective's sports coat—a purple-and-red-checkered job that looked like it came from the cast-off pile at Goodwill.

"We spoke on the phone," Detective Ivanovich said, offering his business card to Horace. "I've been assigned to the case."

Horace regarded the detective mistrustfully. "Tell me, Detective, did you pay for that hideous thing?"

"No, I guess I didn't." The detective glanced at the open door to the gift shop and turned back to Horace. "Just killing time, you know, until you got here."

"I was talking about your sports jacket. I wouldn't touch that thing with fire tongs." Horace snatched the detective's card and pressed on toward Papillon's glass doors, which were sealed with yellow crime tape.

Detective Ivanovich gave me a baffled look and fell in behind Horace.

"Captain Zavala said you have some particular evidence you'd like to collect for the crime lab?"

"That's right," Horace said. "And you're welcome to look over my shoulder while I do it." He nodded at the lanky, older police officer who sat in a swivel chair, guarding the restaurant's entrance. "Officer."

"Afternoon, Chief!" The officer sprang to his feet, causing the chair to clatter away on its rollers. He looked sideways at Detective Ivanovich and me, but his eyes kept returning to Horace.

"Everything battened down tight?" Horace asked.

"Tight as a drum, sir."

"Excellent." Horace reached for the sleek steel pull handle of the nearest door, ignoring the crime tape.

Detective Ivanovich stepped forward. "I'm afraid you can't do that, sir."

Horace froze and looked truculently at the detective.

"Going in there like that," the detective explained. "You'll have to suit up first."

"Suit up?"

"A full hazmat suit, Chief. Regulations. I have to insist."

Horace raised his eyebrows. "Spacesuit and booties? For two Chow-Bella food cartons I can pick up with my hands?"

"Fentanyl can be transmitted transdermally. A few specks of powder absorbed through the skin can be fatal. That's why our crime scene specialist is getting into protective garb."

Horace quickly let go of the door and said, "On second thought, you can give me a full report after you've finished." He took the pocket square from his suit jacket and vigorously wiped the palm of his hand.

Detective Ivanovich gave Horace a reassuring grin.

"No worries, Chief. We'll fully document the scene. Food cartons, lollipops, pills, patches… if our victim died of a fentanyl overdose, it shouldn't be all that difficult to figure out the source."

Horace did a double take.

"Did you say 'lollipops'?"

"I did, sir. A common delivery method. They suck it."

"Suck it?"

"Yes, sir."

Horace looked longingly toward the bar. "I need a drink."

"Of course, Chief. I'll see you back at headquarters this afternoon. I'll have an accounting of all the personal effects and paraphernalia we remove from the scene."

Horace started for the bar and then stopped.

"Detective, one other thing."

"Yes, Chief?"

"You understand why I want those food boxes?"

"Captain Zavala mentioned your theory. Something about rival chefs protecting their turf?"

"And what do you think of my theory?"

"A curious proposition. Interesting on a certain level."

"You're ducking my question, Detective. I asked what you think."

Detective Ivanovich hesitated. "I think if Captain Zavala were a competent investigator, she might have deserved her promotion to captain."

His eyes shimmering with delight, Horace stared for a moment at the detective.

"What's your first name, Detective?"

"Igor, sir."

"Igor Ivanovich." Horace smiled. "Good Irish kid, huh?"

"Something like that, sir."

"May I call you Igor?"

"Of course you may, sir."

"Tell me, Igor, this fentanyl… how does it kill?"

"The victim essentially chokes to death, sir."

"But technically, why? What happens to the body?"

"Physiologically, the fentanyl binds to vital receptors in the brain, gumming up the works. The lungs stop getting signals to breathe, and boom, the respiratory system shuts down. It's a gruesome way to die."

"But for the addict there's got to be some payoff, some high?"

"Without question. A flood of endorphins lets loose when the fentanyl binds to the receptors. That's what makes it such an insidious drug. You get addicted to this great high, and the next thing you know, you wake up dead."

Horace looked asquint at Igor. I could picture the editor in Horace's head rising to take the bait. Igor returned a deadpan expression. Horace glanced at the skeleton mask.

"I suggest you pay for that mask or take it back to the shopkeeper," he said, "before someone calls the police."

*   *   *

In the Lobby Bar, there were a few active lunch tables and a smattering of day drinkers. Horace and I settled onto two barstools near the cash register.

Smiling, his eyes glowing, Johnson came over and dealt us cocktail napkins like cards in a game of blackjack. "Back for more old-fashions, boss?"

"I should say not, Johnson," Horace snapped. "Yesterday my nerves were jangled, and brown liquor was unavoidable. Today I find myself matching wits with Chef Jean-Claude's murderer. Make it a double Tanqueray martini, extra dry with olives. And be quick about it."

"Holy moly!" Johnson said, his eyes wide. "Chef was murdered!"

Horace flapped his arms and glanced around the room.

"For the love of heaven, Johnson, be discreet about it. Don't announce it to the world."

"But you said *murdered*—"

"I'm confiding in you, you nitwit. Now get my drink. And act as though nothing's amiss."

"*Nitwit*," Johnson said, turning away, parroting Horace's words in a mocking, singsong voice. "*Get my drink, nitwit.*" He reached for a martini shaker.

"I may have a job for you," Horace said to Johnson's back.

Johnson turned quickly.

"A job?"

"You know most of Papillon's restaurant staff, am I right?"

Scooping ice from the bin below the bar, Johnson grinned. "They drink here. We're one big happy family—a family of nitwits." He packed the shaker with ice.

"I didn't mean to offend you, Johnson. I'm an unwavering acolyte of the Cunard Line and hold you in the highest regard, but I also count on your discretion. Lives may be at stake."

"You can trust me, boss." Johnson pulled a squat green bottle from the well. "I'm trustworthy as a nut."

Horace rolled his eyes in my direction and turned back to Johnson.

"I need to find someone, and I have a feeling you're the right man for the job."

"Glad to be of service, Your Excellency. What can I do?"

Horace hesitated, scrutinizing the largesse of Johnson's pour—it was considerably more than a double.

"You've heard of Chow-Bella, the food delivery service?" Horace asked.

Johnson nodded as he stirred the martini with a bar spoon. "Yes, yes, chicken wings from Buffalo, pizza from Chicago—"

"The point is—"

"Italian hot dogs from New Jersey—"

"The point is—"

"Bourbon balls from Kentucky—"

"All right, Johnson, enough! The point is that Jean-Claude received two Chow-Bella food boxes the day he died. I need you to find an employee who was with him when those packages arrived... cook, dishwasher, doesn't matter. I need to talk to him."

"Okay, boss. I can ask around."

"Make no mistake, Johnson. This is no favor I'm asking. By power of *posse comitatus*, as Tucson's chief of police, I'm deputizing you as my secret detective. I need you to find this person for me, do you understand?"

Johnson gave him a wiseass smile. "Big tips, this detective job?"

Horace castigated the barman with a scowl. "Don't be flip about it, Johnson. Fail me and I can have you dragged screaming off the premises and thrown in the slammer."

"Yes, Your Royal Highness. For you, I will journey into fire, swim through shark-infested waters, drag my king-size salami across broken glass—" Johnson pierced two fat queen olives with a fancy toothpick and arranged them in a bridge across a pre-chilled martini glass. "Jump into a volcano to appease the gods if I have to, but I will find this person who was with Chef when the Chow-Bella packages arrived." Using a strainer, he poured out the Tanqueray.

"Be inconspicuous about it," Horace said, eyeing the cocktail that was taking shape. "Don't say anything about murder."

"Mum's the word. My lips are sealed. I keep my mouth shut. I'm like the grave. Here you go, boss. Special for you." Johnson set the martini in front of Horace. He turned to me. "A drink for you, Mr. Jack?"

"Sparkling water, thanks."

I waited until Johnson had moved down the bar to tend to the other customers, and then I gave Horace a look.

"*Posse comitatus?*"

"These are desperate times," Horace said, lifting his martini. "A chief of police can do what he must." He took a sip. "I'm going to drink this fast. There's someone we need to see."

"Who's that?"

"A day barman. Knows the chatter on every buffalo wallow in town."

Horace downed his martini before my sparkling water ever arrived. I left cash for the drinks and a big tip for Johnson.

TWENTY-FOUR

"THERE IT IS," Horace said, pointing. "That's it!"

The whitewashed, flat-roofed cinder-block building resembled a munitions bunker. In the dirt lot around the building, late-model Mercedes Benzes and BMWs vied for space with big-tired, candy-colored pickup trucks. The sun-blistered sign said *Mermaid Bar and Grill.*

"There?" I asked, dubious about where Horace was pointing. He wasn't one to frequent dive bars.

"Yes, that's it. Pull in there and park."

We left the paved avenue, jounced through the lot on the old prowl car's spongy springs, and parked as close as we could get to the bar's front door, which was peeling paint and sported a tarnished brass porthole.

Inside, we were greeted by the aroma of mesquite smoke intermingled with sizzling beef and stale beer. In the crowded dining room, natural sunlight poured in broad shafts from skylights above the tables. On one wall, a mannequin mermaid was enmeshed in fishnets and glass floats.

Horace went straight to the long bamboo-faced bar that was tucked beneath a faux thatched roof. The bar, like the dining room, was busy with lunch customers, but we managed to snag two seats together.

"What differentiates this place from every other Polynesian trap," Horace said over the frantic steel guitar of *Wahine U'i* blasting from overhead speakers, "is their filet mignon with pepper cream sauce. We featured it one month in the magazine, and it put the joint on the map."

The bartender came over. An older man in a Brooks Brothers button-down shirt with a soiled white apron, he was tall and thin, his head squared to right angles by a crew cut and horn-rimmed glasses. Seeing Horace, the bartender's eyes lit up.

Horace rewarded him with a big smile. "Truman, what do you know?"

Truman grinned. "Wondered when you'd come around."

"I see you're still passing off fish heads and boiled newspapers as island delicacies. One of these days county health's gonna shut you down."

"I wish they would," Truman said, planting the sole of his shoe on the stainless steel well and resting a hairy forearm on top of his knee. "I'm too old for this shit."

"Ha!" Horace said. "What's special today?"

"Buffet's all-you-can-eat shrimp linguini Alfredo and breaded clam strips. Soup is ginger chicken noodle. Other than that, I plead the fifth."

"And your drink of the day?"

"Trust me, you don't want to know."

"Try me. I'm sitting down."

"Chi-chi."

Horace made a face. "God help you. Pineapple juice and cream of coconut—your clientele has the palate of babies."

"The usual?"

"Make it a double."

Truman looked at me. "Double martini for you, too?"

"Thanks, I'll have an iced tea."

"You guys staying for lunch?" Truman asked, turning to Horace.

"Can't," Horace said. "But I need a minute of your time. It has to do with Chef Jean-Claude's death."

Truman glanced down and hesitated before speaking. He took a bar towel and swatted at a fruit fly.

"Yeah, shame about that guy," he said. "No one saw it coming. Blew up your big gala weekend and all."

Horace leaned forward. "Is there somewhere we can go? To talk confidentially... everything off the record."

Truman surveyed the back of the dining room. The last row of tables was relatively open.

"For you, Horace, anything. Let's go to a booth." He called to the other bartender, who was working the far end of the bar. "Kenny, cover for me. And send me a double Tanqueray martini, extra dry, up, and two iced teas."

We followed Truman through the dining room to a corner booth on the back wall. Near us, a row of silver chafing dishes infused the air with the pungent odors of shrimp and clams. We made small talk until a petite brunette arrived with our drinks.

"Who gets the martini?" she asked. She had tattoos up and down her arms. Piercings graced her eyebrows and nostrils.

"Goes to Mr. Button," Truman said.

The girl flashed Horace a pretty smile. "I should've guessed," she said, blushing.

Horace stared at the waitress's piercings with unabashed, open-mouthed revulsion. As soon as she left our table, he turned accusingly to Truman. His distaste for body art was widely known—he once famously wrote that the sight of tattoos made him physically ill.

Truman shrugged it off. "What can I say? It's a bar. She's a nice kid, doesn't steal. So what can I do for you, Horace?"

Horace put his elbows on the table and made a ball of his fists. "I need the quick and dirty on two local restaurants. Not to be quoted, but Jean-Claude's death is being investigated as a homicide."

Truman looked away. "Criminy."

"I need to know. What was the word on the street about Jean-Claude?"

Truman turned back to Horace. He opened his mouth to speak, stopped abruptly, and cut his eyes toward me.

"Jack's all right," Horace said. "You can tell him anything you'd tell me."

Truman lifted his glass of iced tea, studied it thoughtfully, and set it on the table.

"Jean-Claude Clemenceau… where do I start? Guy was a social climber, a total snob. Staffed his kitchen pretty much exclusively with Europeans. The joke about Papillon is you have to have a Michelin star just to wash dishes in the place."

"Anything about Jean-Claude and drugs?"

Truman shook his head. "Couldn't tell you. Guy never really plugged into the local scene. The scuttlebutt was he stayed busy chasing women and awards."

Horace gave the martini a quick sip. He turned his gaze back to Truman.

"What about the restaurant Family Bone? What can you tell me about this woman who runs it, Tatiana somebody—"

"Tatiana Wong. They call her the dragon lady."

"Why's that?"

"She rules the place with an iron fist. Her partner chef, Sebastian Root, manages the day-to-day kitchen, but Tatiana's the force behind the restaurant."

"Anything illicit in the operation?"

"Maybe some illegals in the kitchen, stiffed a couple of vendors in disputes. Nothing too out of the ordinary."

"What about Miguel Ramirez at El Whisky, any rumors?"

"I've only heard one thing: drugs."

"What about drugs?"

Truman looked down and toyed with his silverware. He lowered his voice. "Word is they run stuff out the back."

"Interesting. What are they running?"

"The usual smorgasbord… pot, coke, maybe a little China White."

"China White? What's that?"

"It's all the rage in the industry these days. Pure-grade heroin mixed with a little fentanyl."

"Bingo!" Horace made eye contact with me and knocked once on the table—knocked so hard it made our drink glasses jump.

I looked at him with amazement. Wanting to play it cool in front of Truman, I reached for my glass of iced tea and took a long sip. My mind raced.

Is Horace a master detective, a crime-solving savant?

"One last thing, Truman," Horace said. "You know of any connection between Miguel Ramirez and this so-called dragon lady?"

"Like, are they friends?"

"Work, play, wild orgies—anything at all that connects the two of them?"

Truman turned his gaze skyward, thought a moment, and blew out a deep breath.

"Look into a group called Tucson Native Restaurants."

"Why, who are they?"

"Ever heard the term *culinary justice*?"

"Never."

"It's the concept that you have to have been born in it to profit off your heritage. Only Mexicans can cook Mexican, only Thais can cook Thai, and so on. Only African Americans can do chicken and waffles. Guy like me, I put moo shu pork and Mandarin pancakes on my menu, and I'm guilty of appropriating Chinese culture."

"Oh, for God's sake."

"We're talking a group of radical chefs. They operate way outside the chamber-of-commerce norm. They claim they're there to promote the local food scene, but they're all about keeping out the corporate chains—On the Border, PF Chang's, Dickey's Barbecue Pit. They call it *economic imperialism*."

"Here I thought I'd heard everything."

"Crazy, huh?"

"And where did Jean-Claude land in this idiot business?"

"Word is he was starting to experiment with Southwestern fusion—Mexican, Native American, Spanish—"

"A snail-eating Frenchman exploiting the local cuisine," Horace said, interrupting. "Must be stopped by any means necessary."

Truman shook his head. "No, Horace, that's not what I'm saying. These people aren't crazy enough to kill. In fact, they're both pretty respectable restaurant operators, if you ask me. I'm just saying take a look at the organization. That's your connection. Tatiana Wong's either president or secretary, and I'm pretty sure Miguel Ramirez is on the board. I'll tell you this, though. For these two local chefs to come in second to an outsider like Jean-Claude in this Best Chef thing—it had to jack their wires."

Horace turned to me. "Which takes us back to our original motive:

jealousy." He looked at Truman as if to admonish him. "When you're dealing with radical actors, never discount their capacity for violence. My sister was killed by terrorists. Now, where can I find out more about this Tucson Natives group?"

"They probably have a website," Truman said. "I'd say start there. Sorry I can't be more help, but that's all I know."

Outside, in the dirt lot, the old Ford spit and coughed and finally chugged to life. I rolled down my window for air.

"Where next?" I asked.

"El Whisky," Horace said. "It's time we paid Miguel Ramirez a visit."

TWENTY-FIVE

SHE WALKED AWAY FROM OUR CORNER TABLE, her long black hair undulating across the back of her loose embroidered top. She'd introduced herself as Carmen. A tall, captivating Latina in her late thirties, she strutted the length of the enclosed porch in tight jeans and sharp heels. Stopping at an alcove wait station, she whispered something to our ponytailed waiter. The popular Mexican restaurant, in a decaying South Tucson neighborhood, had been converted from an old meat market.

"I don't trust her," Horace said, collecting tortilla chip crumbs with one hand and sweeping them onto the floor. He leaned toward me. "I'll bet Ramirez is right here."

Caught looking at us, Carmen flashed her bright smile and disappeared around the corner.

I used the lull in service to text with Wanda and check that Jane and Florabelle were doing their homework. I also let her know Horace and I were eating lunch; that we had a meeting at the police department and then planned to see Dick Peck and his associate for drinks before returning to the *Pioneer Mother* for a late dinner. I put my phone away when our waiter surprised us with shots of a smoky mezcal. He also brought several ripe avocados, which he proceeded to mash, garnish, and whip into a generous bowl of guacamole. Staff members from the kitchen, wearing black chef's coats and pill-box hats, delivered samples of the restaurant's signature starters: bowls of pozole verde and a sizzling cast-iron skillet of queso fundido with chorizo.

We were working our way through this first course when Carmen came by again. Based on the confident way she placed a hand on my shoulder and looked pridefully at Horace, it was apparent the kitchen was firing on all cylinders.

"How is everything so far?" she asked.

Horace had a mouthful of food. His big horse's head was canted downward, and the question made his eyes pop. He nodded vigorously and made the A-OK sign.

Keeping her hand on my shoulder, Carmen watched Horace as he strove mightily to contend with the Mexican bliss that tied his tongue and puffed his cheeks. He chewed and chewed and finally swallowed, chasing the bite with a gulp of mezcal.

"Such an honor to have you on the premises, Mr. Button," Carmen said. "First time dining at El Whisky?"

Horace nodded again and pressed a napkin to his lips.

"It is," he said, looking up at Carmen. "My editors raved, you know, and finding myself in Tucson, I thought I'd see what all the fuss was about."

Carmen smiled. "I remember your editors well. Lovely people. The food photographer, too—she was a hoot. Is there anything in particular you'd like from our menu?"

Horace lifted his eyebrows and looked at me. I shrugged. My frame of reference was Tex-Mex from a fast-food carryout joint in Midland—yellow cheese nachos and fat bland burritos, all served in a grease-stained cardboard box. Wanda rarely cooked Mexican. What did I know about Sonoran-style sit-down dining?

Horace turned back to Carmen.

"I'd like to try the roasted carnitas enchiladas, and I wouldn't mind a sampling of your various tamales. Plus a Sonoran hot dog, of course. Bring it all for the table. Whatever else you'd recommend."

"You've heard of our famous carne seca—angus beef, shredded and dried in the sun and treated with our special spices?"

"Oh, yes, of course. Bring some of that, too."

"I've already asked the kitchen to set aside two helpings—served on our chili rellenos. It's generally the first thing to sell out."

"Excellent. And anything else you'd recommend."

Carmen took her hand off my shoulder, smiled, and gave us a wink. "Maybe I'll surprise you."

I watched her go, staring at the back pockets of her well-formed jeans.

"Rather an ominous comment," Horace said, loading another tortilla chip with guacamole. "You see what I mean? Solicitous and overly friendly... obviously hiding something."

"I see a restaurant manager who appreciates the value of good press," I countered.

Though we'd hardly eaten a thing—a blueberry muffin as we passed the *Pioneer Mother*'s galley in our rush to reach Bunny hours earlier— our voracious appetites were no match for the bombardment of sizzling, steaming, vibrant food that arrived at our table: tamales, enchiladas, fajitas, those carne seca chili rellenos Carmen had praised, along with salsas, tortillas, refried beans, and Sonoran rice. Horace followed his shot of mezcal with a string of house margaritas and several bottles of Tecate beer, which came in a pail of ice.

"Beer? You?" I asked.

"Only with Mexican food. But I mustn't overdo it, or it'll trigger my gout."

Miguel's venerated Sonoran hot dogs appeared at our table. Given that our stomachs were already stretched to the point of bursting, the dish came off as the work of a cruel chef. The dogs were wrapped in bacon, served over refried beans in a crusty roll, and topped with avocado, tomato, jalapeños, and onions. Mine was delicious. As I pushed away that final plate, groaning, and as Horace reached for another beer, Carmen orbited, watching us out of the corner of her eye.

"Carmen, come sit with us," Horace said. "Tell us more about your restaurant."

This brought a radiance to her face, but to me, it sounded like a spider inviting a fly into his trap. She drew up a chair and Horace began by asking Miguel's whereabouts.

"He's gone to Mexico," Carmen said. "To visit his sick mother."

Horace studied Carmen's eyes. She gazed back at him without blinking.

"Not a grave illness, I hope?"

"It was very sudden. We're saying our prayers."

"I'm sorry to miss him. My editors were right. El Whisky is the gold standard of upscale Mexican dining. And I'm talking the whole of Arizona."

Carmen smiled warmly. "I happen to agree."

Horace leaned back and took in his surroundings. By this time, he and I were the last customers left on the porch.

"The splashy décor, the old-school dishes, a menu the size of a horse blanket," Horace observed, "the restaurant must have an interesting story."

"It does. It all began with Miguel's mother. She ran a small Mexican restaurant over in Benson. Everyone loved her food. Miguel grew up in the kitchen and learned her ways. For his own place, he wanted to create a new dining experience—Mexican classics served with a progressive edge: fresh local produce, organic meats and poultry, all fused with Latin flavors. The small-batch tequilas and rare mezcals were his idea, too."

Horace lifted his beer bottle. "To Miguel and his red-hot reputation. Cheers."

As Horace drank, Carmen raised her face slightly, showing her long, handsome neck.

Horace gestured at an oil-on-velvet painting that depicted a psyche-delic, robe-clad skeleton wielding a scythe. "We're seeing a lot of those skeletons in Tucson. Is that supposed to be the Grim Reaper?"

"She's Santa Muerte, Our Lady of the Holy Death," Carmen explained. "She's said to protect the working class, also those who live on the fringes of society—the drug dealers and prostitutes. When death comes, she delivers her believers to the afterlife."

"A personal escort."

"You could say that."

Horace eyed me shrewdly and turned back to Carmen. "You're a follower of this Santa Muerte?"

"Not me. Miguel. He keeps a shrine in the kitchen. He believes embracing death heightens the experience of living, just as hunger heightens the experience of dining, abstinence the experience of… well, you know." Carmen smiled coquettishly, glanced at me, and blushed.

"And dispatching one's enemies to the afterlife? Does Miguel believe in that?"

Carmen thought a moment. "It's a prayer our White Lady might have sympathy for. You must understand, Mr. Button. By American standards, it may seem blasphemous to worship death. But followers of Santa Muerte can be taunting, even playful, when it comes to passing to the other side. You see a lot of painted skulls around Tucson, around the Southwest in general, because her believers are growing. They're everywhere."

"Tell me something," Horace said. "How did Miguel react to Jean-Claude Clemenceau winning Best Chef Tucson?"

Carmen looked down and brushed something off her arm. "He couldn't have cared less." She raised her eyes and stared solemnly at Horace. "Miguel doesn't cook for recognition. He cooks for his soul."

Horace took another sip of beer.

"I'm curious about this organization Tucson Native Restaurants. Miguel's a member?"

"He's on the board and chairs the community outreach committee."

"Community outreach?"

"They partner with local charities to provide food for their fund-raiser events."

"Charities like Los Picadores?"

"Among many others. It's all about giving back to the community."

"I've been told there's a militant component to the organization."

Carmen narrowed her eyes at Horace. "Militant?"

"A tension with outsiders, with the corporate chains."

"The mission is to cultivate and advance Tucson's independent restaurants. We're an endangered species. Food is in the fabric of this community. We're trying to preserve a rich cultural heritage. It has nothing to do with corporate chains."

"Disrupt their operations, deny their approval permits, keep them out of the Valley by any means possible—these tactics don't ring a bell?"

Carmen shook her head. "That sounds far-fetched to me. These are decent, fair-minded people you're talking about."

"Tell me about Chef Jean-Claude... did Miguel consider him an outsider?"

Something flickered across Carmen's face, and then her expression warmed. She shifted in her chair and squared her shoulders to Horace.

"Let's do a reset, Mr. Button. We seem to have wandered off topic. We were talking about El Whisky and the source of Miguel's success."

"Yes, but I believe this could make an interesting cover story for *Sunshine Trails*—portraying Miguel's success in the kitchen within the broader framework of culinary justice. He's a role model for food entrepreneurs, for anyone who wants to leverage the cultural value of their ethnic traditions into a profitable operation."

Carmen studied Horace with an astonished earnestness.

"You surprise me, Mr. Button. I always thought of you as an old fogie."

Horace smiled acerbically.

"Things aren't always as they seem. I'm old, but maybe not so much the fogie. How soon can I talk to Miguel?"

"As I said, he's in Mexico. It may be some time before he returns."

"But can you call him back? We're talking a cover story, here, Carmen."

"I'm afraid it's out of my hands." She smiled sadly and held Horace's gaze.

TWENTY-SIX

"I CAN DEFINITIVELY SAY Miguel Ramirez has fled to Mexico," Horace said.

Captain Zavala listened with her arms crossed. "And how do we know this?"

"Because his restaurant manager passed on a cover story in *Sunshine Trails* magazine. No manager in her right mind would do that unless the owner was really out of the country." Horace turned to Igor. "And you're telling me there were no pills, no patches, and no lollipops to be found at Papillon, either inside or out by the dumpsters?"

Across from me, Igor peeked up from his notebook.

"None," he said to Horace.

Horace gave Captain Zavala a what-did-I-tell-you look. "That means the Chow-Bella deliveries were spiked."

"Unless the victim happened to purchase a counterfeit pill on the street—that would explain the fentanyl in his system," Igor said.

The four of us sat around the small conference table in the chief's office. The spiteful note remained written on the whiteboard.

"Ramirez belongs to some sort of death cult," Horace said. "He keeps a shrine in his kitchen. He worships a female deity, a skeleton called Santa Muerte. She's a religious folk saint—"

"We know who Santa Muerte is," Captain Zavala interrupted. "You can't accuse someone of murder based on how they worship."

Igor studied his notes, keeping his eyes down and his face impassive.

"It's time we put the squeeze on Tatiana Wong over at Family Bone,"

Horace said suddenly.

"Another of your jealous chefs, Mr. Button?" Captain Zavala posed the question in a tone that was decidedly sarcastic.

"She's a part of the cabal at Tucson Native Restaurants."

"I know exactly who she is. She does a lot for this community."

Horace glanced sideways at Igor. "We can send in our ace homicide detective. Ask her a few pointed questions, see if she cracks."

Igor looked up slowly, his face filled with dread.

Captain Zavala regarded Horace with impatience. "What would you have him ask? What would you like to know?"

"I'd like to know if she and Ramirez laced the food in those Chow-Bella boxes. I'd like to know how she feels about Ramirez going on the lam, leaving her holding the bag for murder."

"You're getting way ahead of yourself here, Mr. Button. We haven't even tested the boxes yet. On what factual basis do you suspect Tatiana Wong of murder?"

"Her radical views are well-known. She detested Jean-Claude as an outsider and resented the fact he was being named Best Chef. More than that, he was starting to try his hand at cooking Southwestern fusion. He may as well have been signing his own execution order."

"Have you actually talked to her about this?"

"These are readily observable facts—"

"This is America, Mr. Button. People have a right to their opinions. It's called the First Amendment. And the idea that a model citizen like Tatiana Wong would murder a man over recipes is not only far-fetched, it's idiotic."

Horace scooted to the edge of his seat, his eyes fixed on Captain Zavala. "How about this for a coincidence: word on the street is that Miguel Ramirez might be running drugs out the back of his restaurant, including pure-grade heroin and fentanyl. Let's ask Tatiana Wong what she knows about that."

"Are you serious, Mr. Button? Do you know how many possible drug dealers we have here in Pima County? Knowing a drug dealer doesn't make you a murderer. It makes you someone who knows a drug dealer." Captain Zavala turned to Igor. "You'll continue to treat this as a self-inflicted, unattended drug overdose, as the medical examiner has said. Start with the widow. Find out about the decedent's medical history—a recent surgery or medical procedure that might have left him hooked on pain killers, any known recreational drug use."

"Yes, ma'am," Igor said, avoiding eye contact with Horace.

Captain Zavala looked at Horace and me and said, "If we can establish the victim was an addict, we can close this case without wasting any more time."

Horace managed a forbearing smile.

"You aren't hearing my wishes, Captain. I'd like to concentrate on questioning Tatiana Wong."

"Go back to California, Mr. Button. You're interfering with this department."

"I'll remind you I'm chief—"

"A day or two more, and then you'll be history—"

"Oh, for crying out loud!"

"Look, I've done as you've asked. I've assigned an investigator and we're testing your food boxes. At this point, I need you to stop playing cop. This department has a clear chain of supervision. Our trained investigators know what they're doing. Your interference is not only highly inappropriate, it's also dangerous. I don't want you going anywhere near Tatiana Wong. Accusing a prominent citizen of murder is a guaranteed way to get this department sued."

The rebuke left Horace red-faced. He turned away. His eyes searched the ceiling before his gaze returned to Captain Zavala. "An innocent chitchat session… We're only brainstorming here, comparing notes—"

"The 'chitchat session' is over. We don't have time for this." Captain Zavala turned to Igor. "How soon can you talk to the widow?"

Igor shook his head. "I just got assigned the case this morning. I haven't even seen the preliminary autopsy report yet."

"We'll get that to you."

"I'd like to see a copy of that, too," Horace said.

"Of course, Chief." Igor made a note.

Captain Zavala turned to Igor. "So when can you follow up with the widow?"

"Hard to say, I'm pretty snowed under right now…" Igor perused his notebook. "Maybe next week sometime…"

Horace looked at me with saucer eyes.

"Don't appear so shocked, Mr. Button," Captain Zavala said. "As I said, this isn't television. It's the pace of actual police work. Get used to it."

TWENTY-SEVEN

HORACE WAS SILENT ON THE ELEVATOR RIDE DOWN, but his eyes schemed. Outside police headquarters, in the shadow of the concrete building, the temperature had cooled. The vintage patrol car was parked on the street, directly behind our rented Cadillac Escalade, which we hadn't touched in more than twenty-four hours. I missed its quiet leather cabin, agile handling, and powerful air-conditioning system. Pushing through traffic in the old Ford with that crazy siren screaming—it would get on your nerves, I don't care who you are.

"Move back to the Escalade?" I asked, fingering the Cadillac's heavy key fob in my coat pocket.

"This is no time to give up the ship, Jack—not as long as I'm chief." Horace went to the old Ford, pulled open the passenger door, and looked at me wistfully over the car's roof. "It's like going back to the golden days of law enforcement. The cops were Irish, they drank on the job, and they were all crooked as hell."

*   *   *

We found Dick Peck and Wayne Clark seated at a four-top in the Arizona Inn's Audubon Bar. It was a convivial, plantation-style room with tile floors and rattan furniture arranged around a tall potted palm in the center court. This particular Saturday, on the cusp of nightfall, every table was taken. The middle-aged women with their layered scarves and sweaters, the white-haired men with their bow ties and horn-rimmed glasses—the clientele would have looked at home in a faculty lounge at the nearby university.

"Gentlemen," Horace said, "may we join you?"

"By all means." Dick gestured at the two open armchairs.

On the table were several empty cocktail glasses and a small carafe of snack mix. Horace and I sat. Dick asked what more we'd learned from the police.

"Not much," Horace said, pulling the snack carafe close. "They've put our homicide detective on a short leash."

"Homicide detective?" Wayne eyed Horace with amazement. "They actually assigned one?"

Horace gave the hint of a smile. "Fellow dresses like a bad-check artist from Belarus, but his heart's in the right place." He shook out a handful of bar mix and glanced around the room for a cocktail waitress.

"You said earlier you suspect foul play," Wayne said. "What makes you think so?"

"I have it on good authority Jean-Claude was no drug addict," Horace said.

Raising his eyebrows, Dick looked at Wayne.

"The only logical conclusion is murder," Horace continued. "If I'm right, he was poisoned by toxic tamales or a deadly ribs-and-sausage sampler pack, possibly both."

"Are you serious?" Wayne asked. "Toxic tamales and deadly ribs?"

Horace nodded. "Sent by the killer."

"You know who sent it?" Dick asked.

"We have our suspicions," Horace said.

"*We?*" Wayne asked.

Horace nodded in my direction. "Jack and I."

"What about your homicide detective, what's he saying?" Wayne asked.

"His captain's kissing it off as a self-inflicted, unattended drug overdose. Period. She's telling him to talk to Odette before he does anything else. That's why I need your help getting to the bottom of this—you're a trained investigator."

Wayne shook his head. "These are hard cases to prove. You're talking about an equivocal death … self-inflicted versus homicide. These investigations take a lot of time and resources."

"And we've got neither." Horace made eye contact with a waitress across the room and flagged her down. "Jack's booked us out Tuesday night on the westbound Sunset Limited."

Dick regarded Horace fondly and gave him a smile. "The police chief is skipping town."

Surprised, Horace turned to Dick. "How'd you know?"

"Talked to a cop this morning at the county morgue, while we were waiting to fill out forms. You're a legend among the rank and file."

The waitress came over and got our drink orders. Dick and Wayne happily partook of another round.

"By the way, that cop didn't say anything about foul play," Wayne told Horace after the waitress had left our table.

"The suspicious circumstances aren't broadly known," Horace said. "They only assigned the homicide detective this morning at my insistence."

Dick and Wayne traded uncomfortable looks.

"Take my advice," Wayne said. "Give it a rest and let the professionals handle it."

Horace looked solemnly at Wayne.

"Since the police are determined to go down this dead-end of a self-inflicted drug overdose, I need you to put the squeeze on our prime suspect. She's chef-proprietor of a place called Family Bone, over in the El Presidio District. First thing tomorrow. Interview her, see if you can build a case—"

"Whoa!" Wayne said, holding up his hands. "I'm not interviewing anyone. Dick and I are playing golf tomorrow, and we're out of here Monday, the minute we get the ashes."

"Ashes?" Horace shot Dick a look of incredulity. "You're having the body cremated?"

"It's what Odette wants," Dick said. "It isn't my call."

"She gave you proper legal authority?"

"I have her power of attorney."

"And you're doing this Monday?"

"Yes, Horace. First thing in the morning. As soon as they release the body to the funeral home. It's all arranged. What do you suppose we've been doing all day?"

Looking sick, Horace turned away. "I am stunned to learn they're releasing the body."

"You're showing your civilian stripes," Wayne said. "Morgues these days are backlogged everywhere. The coroner has his blood and tissue samples. What do you care if they release the body?"

"What concerns me is bureaucratic inertia—out of sight, out of mind. Once they release the body and I'm no longer chief, they'll dispense with any further investigation. The clock is ticking, gentlemen, and if we don't solve this soon, someone will get away with murder."

"Again, let's let the police handle it," Wayne said with a hint of exasperation.

Horace glared at him.

"Did you know Jean-Claude?"

Wayne gave Horace a tepid smile.

"Horace," Dick said, "Wayne's our executive vice president for people operations. He's the one who brought Jean-Claude and Odette into our organization fifteen years ago."

Horace opened and closed his mouth. He eyed Wayne cynically. "*People operations?* What the hell is that? Sounds like you do gall bladder surgery."

"It's what we used to call human resources," Dick said. "It means Wayne's in a position to know certain things about certain people." He nodded at Wayne. "Go ahead, tell Horace and Jack what you told me."

Wayne hesitated.

"It's okay," Dick urged. "You can talk freely."

Horace studied Wayne without blinking.

"I'm breaking a gazillion privacy laws telling you this," Wayne said. "But it's in my mind there were some issues awhile back with this guy—I'm talking about Jean-Claude—drugs, maybe heroin. I'm pretty sure we referred him to at least one EAP."

Horace looked puzzled. "EAP?"

"Employee assistance program. Treatment for drug abuse."

Horace stiffened. "You're saying Jean-Claude was an addict?"

"The idea is you deal with it like a disease," Wayne said. "Get the guy healthy and back being productive in the workforce as soon as possible."

"But you're telling me he had a history of drug abuse?"

"I'm not telling you anything for the record. He cooked for us for a long time, executive chef at—" Wayne turned to Dick. "Where was it, the Golden Mantle? Or was this after that?"

Dick shook his head. "God, don't ask me. I can't remember what I had for lunch."

"Anyway, the point is, much as we all liked the guy, he was no Boy Scout. And in the drug world, chronic relapses aren't exactly front-page news."

The cocktail waitress appeared over my shoulder. We watched in silence as she set down our drinks.

"Probably better if you don't mention this to the police," Wayne said, after the waitress was gone. "It'd be double hearsay, as far as they're concerned, and if they try to follow up with me on Jean-Claude's treatment history, I wouldn't be able to cooperate without a court order. Our legal department won't allow it."

Horace closed his eyes for a long moment, and then he focused his piercing gaze on Wayne.

"This isn't what I was expecting," Horace said. "I came here expecting your help in tracking down Jean-Claude's killer."

"Leave it alone, why don't you?"

Horace gave a heavy sigh. "Will you at least speak off-the-record to the detective? This is somewhat personal for me. His name is Detective Ivanovich. Anything you can tell him may exonerate a friend, were it to come to that."

Wayne stared back icily at Horace. "Sorry, I can't and I won't. And if this guy Ivanovich asks me anything about it, I'll have to say I don't recall."

Horace smiled in defeat. "Any other answer and you risk a lawsuit?"

"Not my choice," Wayne said. "It's the world we live in nowadays."

TWENTY-EIGHT

ON THE OTHER SIDE OF THE PICTURE WINDOWS, a long train of low black tanker cars passed through the half-light of the railroad yard. Tchaikovsky's Sixth Symphony played on the satellite radio, and the hearty aroma of Wanda's beef Bourguignon wafted from the galley. Horace and I were in the *Pioneer Mother*'s observation lounge, situated in opposing parlor chairs, contemplating our next move. I drank red wine. Tucson's chief of police was on his third martini.

"You have to admit he has a point," I said to Horace. "An addict who relapses isn't exactly headline news."

Horace had turned his attention to a charcuterie board on the side table beside his chair.

"You overlook the obvious," he said, constructing a sandwich of rye crackers, prosciutto, and brie. "Of utmost dignity, held in great esteem, respected as all get-out—a woman of Bunny's standing would never lark about with a heroin addict." He stuffed the sandwich into his mouth and chewed forcefully.

"Wayne Clark is a senior executive," I said. "Why would he lie?"

Horace licked his fingers.

"You talk about him as if he's Cardinal Richelieu at Lourdes. It's clearly a matter of faulty memory. All those hotels and casinos... Dick Peck must've employed hundreds of chefs over the years."

I remained silent, watching the final tanker car pass. The red strobe of a flashing rear-end device—called a *FRED*, Horace had once told me—blinked above the car's coupler.

"You revealed something this evening," I said. "You still consider Charles Lorillard a suspect."

Horace contemplated this.

"I don't consider him a suspect. I just don't want a friend descended upon by a lynch mob out for blood." He sat back in his chair and wiped his fingers with a cocktail napkin, which he then brushed over his lips. "We're nearly out of time, Jack. If you and I don't force the issue, Jean-Claude's killers will get away with murder."

"What do you suggest?"

"Tomorrow we'll pay a visit to Family Bone."

"That's a terrible idea."

"Why do you say that?"

"Because Captain Zavala specifically warned us to stay away."

"Pay no mind to her hand-wringing. I run the show here."

"But you have no evidence—"

"Identify the person who benefits most—that's the first rule when investigating a capital crime. In this case, that person is Tatiana Wong. Make or break, shoot the works, put it all on double zero—we'll go it alone, and we'll do it first thing in the morning.

"Don't worry," Horace added, reacting to my look of dismay. "I have a plan. And I'll do all the talking."

From the narrow corridor of our railroad car there came a flurry of teenage verve—Jane and Florabelle walking side by side, their elbows interlocked, their hands prodding and slapping at each other as they came before us and stood at attention.

I set my wine glass on a side table.

"Okay, girls, what are you up to?"

Florabelle turned and slugged Jane on the shoulder.

"Go ahead, dum-dum. Ask."

Jane was quick to retort. "You're the dum-dum, monkey face."

"Monkey face yourself."

"Girls," I said, interrupting. "We're in the middle of a conversation. What do you want to ask?"

Florabelle whispered something into Jane's ear, and Jane answered with a hockey check that sent her friend reeling into the wall. Florabelle quickly rebounded, returning to Jane's side.

"Come on," Florabelle urged Jane. "Ask!"

Jane turned to me. "Mrs. Lorillard invited us to spend the night tomorrow night. Wanda said we should ask you. We were wondering if that would be okay?"

I pictured Bunny as I'd last seen her: disheveled, pacing in her robe, grieving the death of her secret lover, who may have been murdered.

"I don't think that's a great idea," I said.

Jane's face fell. She looked at me with disbelief.

"But it would be so much fun!"

I glanced at Horace. "It's really up to your uncle."

Jane turned imploringly to Horace, who at first said nothing.

"Please, Uncle. She's such a sweet lady, and we need to interview her more for our papers!"

Horace interlaced his fingers and studied Jane thoughtfully. "I'll make you girls a deal. Do some detective work for me tonight and in the morning, and you can spend tomorrow night at Bunny's as your reward."

With open mouths, Jane and Florabelle traded wide-eyed stares.

"Sit down, the both of you," Horace said. "I've got a story for you—a mystery to solve as a sort of warm-up."

The girls lowered themselves into parlor chairs. Horace ate the last of his cracker.

"This happened years ago at Lake Tahoe, at a place called Thunderbird Lodge. Picture little Maggie Peck, ten years old, flaxen hair, alabaster skin, the only child of a man who owned several hotels and casinos around the lake. Maggie's father was regarded with universal contempt. If it meant putting an extra penny in his pocket, there wasn't a grandmother he wouldn't swindle, a dog he wouldn't kick. Maggie lived with her mother, who by this time was divorced from Maggie's father. Little Maggie attended public school on the Nevada side of the North Shore. She rode the bus every day—it stopped at an intersection quite close to her house. One winter afternoon, as Maggie made her way home from the bus stop, a woman in a van pulled to the side of the road and said she was looking for her lost dog, and would Maggie help her find it? The woman showed a picture of a small dog, and as Maggie stepped in for a closer look, someone threw a blanket over her head and forced her into the back of the van, kidnapped."

Jane gasped. Florabelle's eyes grew large.

"But the mystery isn't in the kidnapping," Horace said, pausing to take a sip of his martini. "In fact, the kidnappers were never caught. The mystery is in the remarkable way they took their ransom and made their escape. Shall I go on?"

"Yes, please!" Jane and Florabelle said in sync.

Horace set his glass aside and looked at the girls. His eyes shone with impishness. "Maggie's father, being a casino operator, had no trouble raising the ransom. The kidnappers demanded a quarter million dollars in small, unmarked bills, but they could easily have asked for a million. Maggie's father would have paid any price. In his mind, you see, Maggie hung the moon, and he wasn't about to risk her life by going to the police. The kidnappers directed Maggie's father to take the ransom—a suitcase full of cash—to the Thunderbird Lodge, an abandoned estate on Lake Tahoe's East Shore.

"Now picture an alpine retreat in the old-growth forest, soaring pines all round, the massive lodge snowbound, perched at the lake's edge. The estate was laid out roughly like a triangle: the Main Lodge your first point, the Card House your second point, and the Admiral's Cabin your third. The Card House and the Admiral's Cabin were smaller outbuildings with the same architecture as the Main Lodge—that is to say, random stone siding, steep gable roofs, and whimsical rock chimneys. Each structure lay within plain eyesight of the other two. This is an important detail when it comes to solving the mystery.

"Maggie's father arrived at the Main Lodge. He tromped through the freshly fallen snow and found the front door unlocked. The giant living room was empty, but there was a crude note telling him to take the money to the Card House, a short walk up a narrow stone pathway. Inside the Card House, another note directed him to leave the money on the poker table and to proceed to the Admiral's Cabin, which was a small one-bedroom guesthouse near the Main Lodge. There he was to await further instructions.

"The time went by... thirty minutes, forty minutes, an hour. Sitting alone in that cold deserted cabin, Maggie's father smelled a rat. He feared Maggie was dead, and that he'd been played for a sap. Suddenly, all he could think about was the money. He raced back to the Card House, but the suitcase had vanished. He thought he was going mad because he'd been watching that house the whole time. Not a soul had entered."

"Where did the money go?" Jane asked.

"That's the mystery for you two junior detectives to solve. But here's the rest of the mystery: When Maggie's father returned to the Main Lodge, in utter despair, certain he'd lost the two things in life that mattered to him most, there sat Maggie in the middle of the living room, blindfolded and bound, yet alive and unharmed. As I said, in all this time shuttling between cabins, keeping an eagle eye on the pathways and doors, Maggie's father never saw another human being. The only footprints in the snow were his own. Where had the money gone? And how did Maggie wind up in the Main Lodge?"

"I can't imagine," Jane said.

"Sounds like ghosts," Florabelle said.

Horace turned to her. "The place is reputed to be haunted, but these kidnappers were no ghosts. They were very real."

"They must have hidden in a closet," Jane said.

"The walls of the Card House are solid stone. There are no closets," Horace said.

"Or hiding behind trees?" Florabelle guessed.

"Remember, no footprints in the snow, other than those of Maggie's father."

"Maybe drones," Florabelle said.

"No drones—this happened decades ago."

Sounding the dinner chime, Pierre came into the observation lounge. Behind him, on the dining table, the silver candelabra was lit.

"Dinner is served."

Horace downed the last of his martini. He set the glass aside and turned to Jane.

"Do you give up?"

Jane looked at Florabelle and turned back to her uncle.

"Tell us, how did they do it?"

"The Thunderbird Lodge has a series of tunnels, you see, dug through the granite. This network of tunnels connects the Main Lodge to the Card House and to a boathouse beyond that. The kidnappers used the tunnels to collect their ransom and to release their victim. A secret stairway leads to a false door in the Card House's powder room. They took the suitcase into the tunnel and counted the cash. When they were satisfied all the money was there, they led Maggie through the same tunnel back to the Main Lodge, where her father eventually found her."

"And Maggie's father never called the police?" Jane asked.

"The police were brought in, but the case soon went cold."

"How did they find the tunnels?"

"Maggie, being blindfolded, had the audible memory," Horace said, standing. "She helped them piece it together. Then, some years later, the Thunderbird Lodge came up for sale. Maggie's father bought it. He wanted to turn the cursed old estate into a force for good. That's enough of the story for one night. Our dinner is getting cold."

Not long after that, my cellphone rang. I took the call.

"Johnson?"

Horace's eyes met mine.

I stepped away.

"What's up?" I asked.

"I found him," Johnson said. "A restaurant employee who was with Chef when those food boxes arrived."

"That's great news, Johnson." I gave Horace the thumbs-up. "When can we talk to him?"

"Here, tomorrow. He's working the hotel dining room, Sunday brunch."

*   *   *

On the lower level of the *Alaska*, just past the stateroom Wanda and I shared, tucked beneath the steep staircase that led to the vista dome, was a cozy alcove—Wanda's favorite spot on the train. She often napped on the upholstered bench seat, pulling an afghan over her shoulders, placing her legs under the stairs. The built-in nautical bookcase, made of mahogany and cherry, held her traveling library of cookbooks. An elegant stainless-steel rod along their spines kept the books in place. At the end of the bench seat was a drop-down butler's desk upon which Wanda wrote out her menus in longhand. She warmed her cups of herbal tea in the alcove's microwave. A second workstation held the MacBook Air that Jane used for her schoolwork. A laser printer was hidden away in a cabinet.

Now the cozy nook looked like an assembly line. Jane was at the computer, sending pages to the printer. Florabelle snatched up the sheets as they came off the printer and arranged them in neat little stacks on the bench seat. It was nearly midnight.

"Weren't you two supposed to be doing math and history after dinner?" I asked.

"Jack, look what we found!" Jane said, eager to show me a page printed from the internet. "Tucson Native Restaurants. Tatiana Wong is founder and president. Miguel Ramirez is a co-founder and board member. Their mission is to preserve, promote, and champion iconic, locally owned, independent restaurants."

Florabelle pushed in between us, reading aloud from another print-out. "'While China is the primary source of illegal fentanyl entering the United States, most of the drug shipments come into the country through Mexico...'"

Jane looked at me. "And listen to this from the *Wall Street Journal.* 'Miss Wong is considered a leader in the culinary justice movement. "We are warriors in this fight," says Ms. Wong, standing in the pristine kitchen of her flagship restaurant Family Bone, in Tucson. "When the privileged white chef, trained at a tony school like the Culinary Institute or Le Cordon Bleu, comes in and rips off the quintessence— and recipes—of the Mexican, Asian, or African-American chef, without compensation, and makes a fortune, that white chef is robbing the others of their historic identity. It's cultural appropriation, and it's morally reprehensible."'"

"She had a clear motive," Florabelle said with the confidence of a prosecutor.

"Should we wake up Uncle?" Jane asked me. "This is exactly what he was looking for."

Initially proud of their exuberance for research, I cringed inwardly at their rush to judgment.

"I think you should tuck everything in a folder and go to bed," I said, "before your imaginings keep you awake all night. These are all intriguing facts, girls, but nothing here makes anyone guilty of murder." I hushed their protests. "Remember, this is America. You're innocent until proven guilty."

TWENTY-NINE

AFTER BREAKFAST, HORACE WALKED EVERYONE through the plan one last time. Pierre, Jane, and Florabelle, wearing their ridiculous tourist garb, stood around Horace's parlor chair, listening intently.

An Uber was summoned and soon departed with the trio.

For the next thirty minutes, I was Horace's bartender, taking him a succession of vodka tonics with lime. Waiting for our cue from Pierre, he said little. His face inexpressive, his gaze averted, he drummed the fingers of his right hand against his thigh to the stirring notes of "The Battle Hymn of the Republic" as it played on the satellite radio—he often had me dial in this channel of patriotic marches in advance of an important public appearance.

Using the pass-through window that connected the galley to the bar, Wanda kept making eye contact with me and shooting me woeful looks, as if to ask, *And you're okay with this?*

It was maddening to be assumed an accomplice to Horace's foredoomed, harebrained scheme of entrapment, especially by my own wife. I was as concerned for Jane's and Florabelle's safety as she was.

"The two girls are in no danger," Horace kept assuring me. "And their observations are critical to my plan."

At 10:10 a.m., Pierre texted that everything was in place. The Disneyland tourists were seated at a table in Family Bone's main dining room, and their food had arrived.

Pierre sent a follow-up text: "Dragon lady beware!"

I replied that we were on our way, and we quickly were.

The vintage black-and-white Ford, its lights flashing, the air raid siren caterwauling high and low, its gaudy chrome bumper riding their tail—the rare sight bewildered the Sunday drivers, who were maddeningly slow to yield. I could see their eyes in the rearview mirrors, first the delight, then the confusion, as they tried to decide if this was a joke, or what.

The staff must have been watching from one of the large, rectangular windows of the lavishly half-timbered Tudor-style mansion that housed Family Bone. Horace and I no sooner had alighted from the old squad car and stepped onto the red brick walkway than the front door swung open, and a party of restaurant employees gathered to greet us under the gable-covered entry. Leading the bunch was an attractive, feline-faced woman. She wore a white double-breasted chef's coat over a floral-print *crepe de chine* skirt. Her black hair was straight and long, with red highlights. Heavy makeup emphasized her exotic eyes.

"Tatiana Wong," she said, shaking hands with Horace. She cast a smiling glance at a crimson-faced man in a white apron who stood at the front of the group. "And this is my business partner, Sebastian Root."

Sebastian stepped forward and shook Horace's hand.

"I don't know how to properly thank you," he said. He had sincere blue eyes and a receding hairline. Like Tatiana, he was in his thirties. "We couldn't believe when you called to say you were coming over. A write-up in *Sunshine Trails* means the world."

Tatiana passed us champagne flutes brimming with sparkling wine.

"Come meet our employees—at least, these are the ones we could pull away." Cutting through the knot of people, she looked at us over a shoulder. "Most are inside working. Sunday brunch is consistently our highest guest count of the week. We absolutely kill it."

Horace had a murmured greeting and handshake for each server, manager, and bartender on the porch.

Tatiana marched us through the front door. "And now, meet Family Bone."

The shadowy foyer had a hostess stand and an imposing wooden staircase. Guests waiting to be seated stood in groups or sat on two long benches. The floorboards creaked. Woodsmoke sweetened the air.

"The two bars, main dining room, and kitchen are all on the ground floor," Tatiana was saying. "Offices and storage are upstairs. We'll start our tour in the kitchen."

Horace made a grumpy face. "I write about food, Miss Wong, not kitchen appliances. Take me to your dining room. Let's get this show on the road."

Tatiana appeared taken aback by the crusty response, but she recovered quickly—with an accommodating smile for her celebrity guest.

"Yes, of course. We have a table waiting. Sebastian and I will join you if that's all right?"

"In fact, I insist on it." Horace gave Tatiana a brusque nod. "Please, show us the way."

The baronial dining room had a high ceiling and molded plasterwork on its cornices and walls. The centerpiece was an enormous brick hearth. The noise level was high. Several people stopped eating and gawked as Tatiana led Horace and me to a long farmer's table in front of the hearth. I spotted Jane, Pierre, and Florabelle right away. They sat at a four-top across the room. In their ridiculous tourist outfits, they blended seamlessly with the Tucson locals. Sebastian brought up the rear of our little parade, talking as we all sat.

"Our food is simple, approachable, and seasonal. Grilled meats, magnificent vegetables. I keep a culinary garden on the terrace."

"We source whole animals from local family farms," Tatiana was saying. "Farms that treat their animals humanely. We do our own butchering."

She and Sebastian were tag-teaming us, talking over each other. I looked around the restaurant. The room's quirky ambiance felt forced. Interspersed among the traditional dining tables were period armchairs, overstuffed Victorian sofas, and Tiffany floor lamps. The artwork was a hodgepodge of multicultural mosaic art and animals in semi-abstraction: cows, bison, roosters, pigs. Near the hearth, a massive iron bin overflowed with firewood.

"By receiving the whole carcass, we can customize our cuts of meat and reduce waste," Sebastian said, looking earnestly at Horace.

As if Horace Button ever gave a damn about waste in his life.

Tatiana turned to me.

"Full transparency from farm to fork—that's our philosophy. Every cut of meat can be traced back to an individual farm, ultimately to a single animal. The entire menu is available day and night."

Horace focused his penetrating gaze on Tatiana. "Your food should be as remarkable as your cunning."

Tatiana appeared baffled—or to have completely misheard her visitor.

"Excuse me?"

"If you can trace a cut of meat back to a single animal, wouldn't it follow that a good detective could trace a package back to its original sender?"

Tatiana glanced questioningly at Sebastian, then looked again at Horace and said, "I'm afraid I don't—"

"Pestilence in a pizza box, Miss Wong. You're a preferred Chow-Bella shipping partner, do I have that right?"

Tatiana tilted her head coyly. "We are. Proudly so."

"Chow-Bella runs the website and markets the service, but it's you, the restaurant, that packs and ships the food?"

"A few signature items, the ones we can ship without losing quality. It helps our bottom line and gives us a little extra brand recognition. Sebastian can tell you about the logistics, if that's what you're interested in."

Horace turned to Sebastian. "Please. Tell me the process."

"It's quite simple, really," Sebastian said. "Chow-Bella forwards the orders daily. In the lull between lunch and dinner, we pack and ship the meals, usually for next-day delivery."

"You keep a log? All orders received and shipped?"

"Sure."

"You've got a record of last week's shipments?"

"Upstairs in the office. In a file."

A gaggle of servers surrounded our table, their arms heavily laden with platters of food.

Tatiana ignored the servers. She leaned in toward Horace. "Forgive me for asking, but you're here to write a review of our restaurant, right?"

Absorbed in resolve, Horace stared at Tatiana. He pushed back from the table and stood theatrically.

"No, Miss Wong, I am here to spare you death by lethal injection!" he thundered.

The servers stepped back. The dining room fell silent. All eyes were on Horace.

Puzzled, Tatiana turned to me. "Is he drunk?"

"The review was a false pretense," Horace said, speaking to everyone in the dining room. He showed his badge. "I'm here this morning in my capacity as chief of police." He turned back to Tatiana. "I have enough to charge you with a capital crime. I'll give you one chance to save yourself, but you must tell me everything."

The color drained from Tatiana's face. Her mouth dropped, and she looked at Sebastian, who appeared equally horror-struck.

"I don't…" she said to Horace. "What are you talking about?"

"You know exactly what I'm talking about, Miss Wong. Or shall I say *dragon lady*?" Now Horace was backpedaling through the dining room, dodging tables effortlessly, the circus ringmaster working the crowd, keeping the audience on the edge of their seats. "Ladies and gentlemen, forgive the interruption of your Sunday brunch, but a serious crime has been committed, and justice must prevail…" He came to a stop at Jane, Pierre, and Florabelle's table. Without making eye contact he scooped up the platter of ribs and sausages that awaited his arrival like a stage prop. "This innocent sampler pack—a staple of American barbecue. Who'd believe it could bring the kiss of death?" He raised the platter to chest height and approached our farmer's table. "Shall I take a bite, Miss Wong, or are there house rules against foaming at the mouth and seizing in your dining room?"

In a panic, Tatiana looked from Sebastian to me. Her eyes welled.

"I don't understand. Why is he being such a butt?"

"Not a heinie, Miss Wong. Your worst nightmare." Horace dropped the platter on the table with a *bang!* "I know every vile thing you've done, and I don't intend to let you get away with it!"

The sausages went rolling across the table. One fell into Tatiana's lap.

She looked up at Horace. Two streams of black mascara began coursing down her cheeks. She quickly brushed away the tears.

"Are you *arresting* me?" she demanded, her voice trembling, looking both fearful and indignant. "In my own restaurant in front of my *customers*?" She turned to Sebastian. "God, what's happening? I don't even know what I did!"

"You couldn't stand it," Horace said. "It's anathema to your pedigree. You don't finish second to anyone."

"Tatiana, honey, don't you see?" Sebastian reached across the table for his partner's hand. "It's the jail-and-bail weekend. Mr. Button is here to arrest you." He gave her a reassuring smile. "Play along, girl. You've gone from first runner-up to being named Best Chef Tucson."

Tatiana gasped. Her eyes went wide, and she covered her mouth with both hands.

"No, wait—" I said, but Tatiana paid me no mind. She sprang from her chair and turned enthusiastically to Horace.

Expect nothing. See the good. Accept what is.

"All right," she said, raising her hands in surrender. "You found me out. I confess, I did it!"

For a moment Horace was speechless. He appeared flabbergasted.

"You did?" he asked.

"Of course I did!" Tatiana said, looking about the room, playing to her patrons. She turned to Sebastian. "Shouldn't we be taking pictures here?"

"I don't need pictures, Miss Wong," Horace scolded. "These people are all my witnesses. And now the facts, in front of God and everyone. I'm guessing your ancestors have a factory in China?"

Tatiana glanced at Sebastian. He nodded eagerly.

"A factory, that's exactly what they have!" Tatiana said.

"A clandestine chemical lab, probably hidden away on a reeking, rat-infested junk bobbing in the black waters of Hong Kong harbor—"

"A rat-infested junk, that's it, yes!"

"Made in China, smuggled through Mexico. Miguel Ramirez specializes in a lot more than tamales and Sonoran hot dogs. He was your conduit, wasn't he?"

"Yes, our conduit, so true!" Tatiana's eyes gleamed. She brought her fists together under her chin. "Oh my god, are we sharing the award with Miguel?"

"Who else was involved?" Horace shifted his gaze to Sebastian. "What about this bootlicking flunky with the pasty skin? Come clean, Miss Wong. He's up to his eyeballs in this sinister plot, isn't he?"

"Yes, Chief Button, you are so spot-on right. Up to his eyeballs." Tatiana leveled an accusing finger at her business partner. "No one deserves jail time more than that man sitting right there!"

"Ah-ha!" Horace said. "You see, in the end, the truth comes out, and justice prevails. The lot of you couldn't stand to see an outsider win, couldn't stand to see that filching frog expropriating your precious recipes. And now you'll rot in jail for it!"

"Or until we're bailed out by our fellow Tucsonians…" Beaming with pride, Tatiana disengaged from Horace and began walking the length of the dining room, addressing her brunch customers. "I don't know how many of you get what's happening, but this is an epic event for Family Bone. There could be no higher honor for Sebastian and me than to be arrested on this special weekend by Chief Horace Button."

A ripple of polite applause passed through the dining room.

Horace stood there a moment. He squinted at Tatiana, then looked at me, mystified. I gestured urgently toward the exit.

Horace turned back to Tatiana.

"There won't be any arrests this morning, Miss Wong. I'll give you twenty-four hours to put your affairs in order. You and your business partner will surrender to police headquarters by noon tomorrow, or you'll be considered fugitives from justice."

To a new wave of applause, Horace and I made for the doorway.

A handful of brunch patrons stood. Their eyes followed Horace.

"Bravo! Bravo!" they shouted.

"This is such a thrill," Tatiana was saying. "I hope you can all pitch in for our bail. No dollar amount should be considered too small…"

THIRTY

"MAKE IT A DAIQUIRI," Horace said, sitting back, closing his eyes, resting his head against the top rail of the parlor chair. "But shake it, don't blend it. Crushed ice in this kind of heat will only make my head-ache worse." He lifted his head and looked at me. "Those people can't be serious. You're telling me they really believe they're being named Best Chef?"

"That's what they think." I stood behind the bar, searching Pierre's well for light rum. I brought up a bottle of Bacardi. Wanda was on the other side of the pass-through, not making a sound.

"I thought the dragon lady's confession seemed a bit peculiar," Horace admitted. He rested his head again on the back of the chair and spoke with his eyes shut. "They'll figure it out soon enough when they're sitting in the hoosegow."

I poured the rum with a heavy hand.

Horace suddenly opened his eyes and raised his head again. "You disagree with me. You don't believe they're guilty of murder?"

"I found them both credible and lacking obvious guilt." I squeezed a cut lime over the drink and then added a tablespoon of simple syrup and several ice cubes.

"You would, being a rank amateur. The telltales were all there: the fast talking, the furtive glances, the way she went wide-eyed when I mentioned Miguel Ramirez. She was like a firebug caught with a spent match. You didn't see all that?"

"What I saw were two restaurant partners eager to impress the editor of *Sunshine Trails* magazine. And suddenly everything went batshit crazy." I capped the mixing glass with a metal shaker tin and shook it hard over my shoulder, not stopping until my fingers were numb. I poured the daiquiri through a strainer and garnished the drink with a sprig of mint.

"That scarecrow Sebastian is every bit as guilty as Miguel and our dragon lady, who I assume is the ringleader," Horace said. "Did you see the panic in his eyes when he realized we were onto them?"

"Honestly, no." I came out from behind the bar with the cocktail on a tray.

"Oh, look, you've made a drink!" Horace said brightly. "For all the time it took, I thought you were back there carving a totem pole."

As I set down the cocktail, the platform door opened. In a flurry of excitement, Jane and Florabelle entered the observation lounge and went straight to Horace's chair.

"You did it, Uncle!" Jane cried. "You uncovered two murderers!"

"You think so?" Horace looked pleased.

"Yes!" Jane said.

"It was so obvious," Florabelle agreed.

Pierre came in behind the girls, his black sunglasses parked in his hair. Lagging at the door, he made eye contact with me and shook his head. By this time Wanda had come out of the galley. She listened with a chef's towel over a shoulder and her arms crossed.

"Tell me," Horace was saying, "what did our dragon lady do after we left the restaurant?"

"She called for champagne on the house," Florabelle said, though she hadn't been directly addressed.

"And then she went back to the kitchen," Jane said.

"We followed her."

"Excellent." Horace looked from Florabelle to Jane. "And how did she behave? Did she start throwing pans?"

Jane wrinkled her nose. "Not really."

"She hugged a lot of people," Florabelle noted.

"But listen to this," Jane said. "She left the kitchen and went upstairs to one of the little rooms—"

"Her office, we think."

With a straight-arm, Jane pushed her friend back. "You won't believe this. She made a call—"

"We pretended we were looking for the restroom," Florabelle said. "We followed her up the stairs—"

"Let me guess," Horace said, shifting his gaze to Jane. "She telephoned her lawyer?"

"No, Uncle, she said, 'Carmen, where is Miguel?'"

"She said that into the phone?" Horace arched his eyebrows. "*Carmen, where is Miguel?*"

"Yes!" Jane exclaimed.

"And then she saw us and kicked us out," Florabelle said.

Horace steepled his hands with a studied detachment.

"Trying to reach Ramirez," he said. "To warn him we were hot on the trail."

I glanced at Pierre. He again shook his head. I turned back to Jane.

"I hope you're telling us what really happened and not what you think your uncle wants to hear."

"It really happened, we swear!" Jane said.

Florabelle nodded emphatically.

I turned. "Pierre, how'd it look to you?"

Pierre responded thoughtfully and with his usual dry grace.

"I watched Tatiana and Sebastian closely after you and Mr. Button left. It was a party atmosphere. Not a speck of anxiety or fear. Every interaction they had showed an ecstatic state of mind. These are happy, hardworking entrepreneurs, not cold-blooded killers." He flashed his snaggletooth smile. "I say not guilty."

"Any chance they knew who you were?" I asked. A thumbnail of Pierre's headshot appeared with his monthly *Sunshine Trails* column, Etiquette Advisor.

"Not a chance," Pierre said. "They were all too busy celebrating to notice who was in the restaurant."

Horace gave Pierre a calculating look.

"We've never mentioned the name *Carmen* in front of the girls. It means they're telling the truth. Tatiana Wong made that phone call."

"I'm sure she did," Pierre said. "But it might have been perfectly innocent—trying to get hold of Ramirez to spread the good news."

"There's one way to find out," Horace said, turning to me. "Johnson has that witness waiting. If he tells us Jean-Claude wasn't expecting those Chow-Bella food packages, and if we find traces of fentanyl on the boxes, the dragon lady and her conspirators will hang. Start the car, Jack. We need to get to the hotel before our witness changes his mind about singing." He drew his snub-nosed revolver from the holster that was concealed under his jacket and flicked open the cylinder, inspecting the bullets.

"Uncle, can we go with you?" Jane asked.

Wanda stepped forward. "No, girls," she said quickly. "I want you to stay here."

Horace closed the cylinder with a sharp click.

"She's right, it's too dangerous," he said, looking at Jane. "A key witness in a murder case and the chief of police gaining on the prime suspects—anything could happen." He rose from the chair, holstered the gun, and started for the door, leaving his daiquiri untouched.

THIRTY-ONE

WE CROSSED THE LOBBY of the Saguaro Mesa Hotel, cutting through a logjam of hotel guests in line with roller bags, waiting to check out. The Tea Court was busy with late Sunday brunch patrons, but the Lobby Bar was suitably quiet. We found Johnson working alone, pouring a row of mimosas.

Horace scooped one of the mimosas from the line and gave it an appraising swirl.

"Where is he, Johnson?"

Johnson nodded toward a booth in the center of the lounge, where a red-haired man sat with his back to us. He was looking down, as if engrossed in reading a book. He wore a white crewneck T-shirt.

"What is he, a cook?" Horace asked.

"Server," Johnson said. "Splits his time between Chef's restaurant and the Tea Court."

Horace narrowed his eyes at the server.

"What's his name?"

"Gerald."

Horace scrutinized the back of Gerald's head and then looked at Johnson.

"Is he trustworthy?"

"Sure, everyone likes him."

"For your sake, Johnson, I hope this goes well. If so, you'll be amply rewarded." Horace quaffed the mimosa and planted the empty champagne flute back on the bar. "Nice drink. Put it on the city's tab."

I followed Horace over and we slid into the booth on either side of Gerald. He was in his mid-twenties, a bit overweight, and heavily freckled. A black button-down shirt and a conservative-patterned tie lay in a heap on the table, next to an open magazine. He regarded me with alarm—my physical size and the scar on my face often leads strangers to take me for a henchman—before he turned and looked anxiously at Horace.

"Relax, son. You're in no trouble," Horace said. "I only have a few questions." He glanced at the magazine. "What's that you're reading?"

Gerald gave Horace a self-effacing smile.

"*S-s-Sunshine Trails.* January i-i-issue."

At Gerald's pronounced stutter, Horace raised an eyebrow. He paused a moment, then he pressed an assertive fingertip to the open page of the magazine.

"'A Gastronome's Napa Valley Tour.' They showered us with Kumamoto oysters, kilos of truffles, and smoked mallard breasts. We dined all over Yountville. Tasted up and down the valley."

"Sounds a-a-amazing. I'd love to do that someday."

Horace's gaze swept the shirt and tie. "I took you away from your duties at Sunday brunch."

"It's all right," Gerald said. "They were already c-c-cutting the floor."

"Tell me. Does the hotel still serve the smoked salmon eggs Benedict?"

Gerald grinned. "Every day."

"The supple eggs with their hint of vinegar… the salmon with its silky texture… that salty slab of latkes on the side—I've written about it often and dreamt of it even oftener. Johnson tells me you also work at Papillon. You must know your French foods and wines?"

"Most everything I know I learned from Chef. He sort of took me under his wing."

"A father figure to you."

"A mentor, I'd call it. I was s-s-scheduled to work the big dinner Friday night."

Horace smiled. "In other words, I'm sitting face to face with a rising star."

"Hardly." Gerald blinked back tears. "I'm sorry, Mr. Button. It hits me in waves. He was very good to me. I can't believe he's gone."

Licking his lips, Horace leaned in and regarded Gerald with prying eyes.

"Tell me the menu."

"The menu?"

"Friday night's dinner. What was Jean-Claude planning to serve?"

Gerald glanced around the lounge. He sat forward and sniffled.

"Oysters with sea urchins and caviar, lobster thermidor, veal shank in a sorrel cream sauce, stuffed shoulder of lamb in a red wine sauce. Assorted cheeses and hot apple crepes for dessert." He counted each item on a pale finger.

Horace listened closely.

"And the wines?"

"Krug Grand Cuvée, Puligny-Montrachet Sauzet, Château Latour, Château Lafite Rothschild, a Darroze Armagnac from the '60s."

"Was it by chance the '64?"

"The '61, I believe."

"The '61." Horace looked heavenward. "My god, we've been cheated out of our destiny!"

Gerald faced Horace with a sad expression. "We all feel the same way. We were s-s-superstoked for the weekend. Was it a heart attack or did something bad happen?"

Horace hesitated. "Why do you ask?"

"There's rumors. We're seeing lots of police."

"Johnson says you were there when the Chow-Bella food boxes arrived?"

Gerald nodded.

"This was what day?" Horace asked.

"Thursday."

"I believe you mean Friday, the day Jean-Claude died?"

"No, the food arrived Thursday. I'm positive. Because it was the day before the big dinner—the same day Mrs. Lorillard brought your niece and her friend to tea."

"All right," Horace conceded. "The food boxes arrived Thursday.

And the look on Jean-Claude's face when he saw those boxes—he was supremely surprised."

"Surprised?"

"Surprised to be receiving these Chow-Bella deliveries, because he knew nothing about them."

"Oh, he knew—"

"But you're saying he didn't touch that food until Friday, at which point he dropped dead on the spot, like a sack of potatoes—"

"I'm sorry, Mr. Button, but that isn't how it happened. I ordered that food. We ate it for dinner on Thursday night."

"Dammit, Gerald, focus! I'm talking about the Chow-Bella deliveries from El Whisky and Family Bone, the tamales and ribs and—"

"Exactly, Mr. Button. Chef asked me to place those orders."

Horace's eyes grew wide. His mouth fell open. "He *asked* you?"

"He was c-c-curious about his competition. So he asked me to order a few things."

Horace sat stock-still, staring at Gerald without blinking. He slammed a fist onto the table.

"You deviant! Why are you lying? What are you hiding!"

The color rose in Gerald's face. His flaccid mouth opened and closed.

"Please, Mr. Button, I'm not lying. I'm not hiding anything!"

"That food was laced with poison!"

Gerald glanced at me. He turned back to Horace.

"Poison?"

"A lethal dose of fentanyl, courtesy of the dragon lady and Miguel Ramirez. That suck-up Sebastian was in on it, too."

Gerald shook his head. "Mr. Button, there was nothing wrong with that food. L-l-look at me. I'm still here. We both ate the same food, and neither of us got sick. It wasn't until the next day that Chef died."

Horace raised his face and looked down his nose at the young server. "You'd swear under penalty of perjury that you ate those same tamales and ribs with Chef Jean-Claude?"

"I'd swear to it. Anytime. But why?"

Horace eyed Gerald with hatred. Suddenly, without uttering a word, he rotated his broad shoulders, put his hands on the table, scooched gut-first out of the booth, and went straight to the bar.

Gerald and I sat in silence, ruminating on what had just transpired.

"He seems upset," Gerald said.

"Man doesn't like surprises," I agreed.

"I need to turn in my tips. Am I free to go?"

"Of course."

Gerald gathered his shirt and tie from the table. He put a hand on the magazine and hesitated.

"Crap. I meant to ask him to sign this."

I looked across the lounge. Horace sat slouched over the bar. Johnson was getting him a drink.

"Maybe another time," I suggested.

THIRTY-TWO

DICK PECK STEPPED UP TO THE BAR TRIUMPHANTLY. He had Wayne Clark in tow.

"We were just coming off the eighteenth green when I spotted that old squad car out front. I told Wayne we'd find you here," he said to Horace. "What's the matter, my friend? You look positively sick."

"Fate has made a horse's behind of my wicked soul," Horace said, staring numbly into his rocks glass full of whiskey. He brought it to his lips and drank resolutely.

Dick looked at me and raised an eyebrow.

Wayne settled onto the barstool next to mine and gave me a faint smirk.

"How's the crime-solving business, Jack? Any luck?"

"We're reassessing the case. Taking a little break from police work." I had a big iced tea. I managed a long sip.

"Jack's driving me over to Tombstone in a bit," Horace said. "I'm going to get one of those drugstore cowboys at the O.K. Corral to shoot me in the heart."

"That bad, huh?" Dick said. "Mind if I sit?"

"Help yourself," Horace said. "Have a drink. It's on the city."

Wayne turned to me. "We're gonna squeeze in another nine. Got a three o'clock tee time if you guys want to make it a foursome."

"Thanks," I said, "but Mr. Button doesn't play golf."

"I specifically avoid anything that requires bug spray, steady nerves, and antivenom medication," Horace said.

Dick placed a comforting hand on Horace's shoulder. "Gotta get our minds off this gruesome business somehow. I'm sorry about the cremation, Horace."

Horace clutched his glass with both hands. "It's whatever Odette wants."

"I was hoping you and I might get our friendship back on track," Dick added. "But with you, it seems I'm always using the wrong fork."

I studied this delicate white-haired man and pictured him much younger, trudging through snow, a suitcase full of money in hand, desperate to rescue his kidnapped daughter, who was about the same age as Jane when Wanda and I had first met her.

But what had happened between Horace and Dick?

"You can make amends," Horace said, turning to Dick. "When you fly out of Tucson tomorrow, take me with you."

"You'd go?" Dick looked surprised.

"Anywhere," Horace said. "Anything to get away from this nightmare."

Dick transferred his curious gaze to me. "Must've been terrible, whatever it was."

"I merely took a cannon and flattened the personal reputations of three up-and-coming chefs," Horace said. "I can never show my face here again."

"Talking about your murder suspects?" Wayne asked.

"Cataclysmically, yes. The facts don't bear out my theory." Horace hung his head and took another long pull of whiskey.

"Like I told you, the police generally know what they're doing in these things," Wayne said. "Call me fatalistic, but given his history, Jean-Claude's outcome was preordained."

Johnson stood on the other side of the bar, polishing a wine glass, looking from Dick to Wayne.

"Any drinks, gentlemen? Slippery Nipple? Sex on the Beach? Screaming Orgasm?"

Wayne listened to Johnson with a growing irritation, then looked at Dick and said, "What do you say, skipper? Do we want to check in to our rooms before we hit the course again?"

"Check in?" Horace asked.

"We're moving," Dick explained. "Gonna test out the Saguaro Mesa Hotel for one night."

Horace stared at the casino mogul as if he'd spoken in tongues.

"You'd forsake the charm of the Arizona Inn for the sterile monotony of the Saguaro Mesa?"

"Wasn't our call. The Inn somehow screwed up tonight's reservation." Dick grinned. "I was just getting out of the shower. Next thing I know, Wayne's banging on my door and telling me we have to pack up and move."

Wayne looked amused. "What can I say? No room at the Inn."

Horace glanced at Wayne and shook his head. "The world's gone mad. Nothing makes sense anymore. This whole day has unfolded like a hideous street accident."

Dick smiled amiably at Johnson. "I'm intrigued with your drink menu. Maybe we'll see you after golf." He turned back to Horace. "Any chance you'd join us for dinner?"

Horace had taken a mouthful of ice with the last of his drink. He slowly shifted the ice around with his tongue and spit the cubes back into his glass.

"I'm unavailable," he said. "I have an irrevocable plan to get stiff as a plank with Johnson, here, and then crawl on hands and knees back to the *Pioneer Mother* for a nightcap, a cigar, and a suitable length of rope." He tapped the rim of his glass. "Keep them coming, Johnson. This is no time to lollygag."

Dick had a twinkle in his eye. "All right. We're wheels up at eleven tomorrow morning if you really want to hitch a ride."

"Eleven?" Horace asked. "What's the rush?"

"I need to get up to the lake—our annual Chairman's Dinner at the Lodge. We're hosting our governing board and twenty of our biggest contributors."

"Odette is doing the cooking?"

"She insists. You know how she is. Come as my guest. The folks would be thrilled."

"She isn't too distraught?"

"Don't ask me. Maybe it keeps her mind off Jean-Claude."

"But a party of twenty or thirty? All by herself?"

"We bring in help to set up and do the serving. It's like an army of ants. Trust me. Thunderbird Lodge will be crawling with people by three or four in the afternoon."

"I'll let you know," Horace said. "May be a fitting end to my weekend—to wind up splattered on a jagged peak in the High Sierras."

"You're talking about flying into Truckee or South Lake Tahoe. I always go in and out of Reno. The runway's longer and the weather's more reliable."

"Still, I'll put my money on the Grim Reaper. The sinister aspects of going by private jet must be heightened tenfold when the cargo is an urn full of human remains."

Wayne looked at Dick. "Not so sure I want to fly with this guy," he quipped.

THIRTY-THREE

WE PICKED OUR WAY THROUGH THE WEEDS and rocky ballast of the railroad bed, the scent of creosote oil and sage rising around us as the sun dropped. I helped Horace up the steps to the *Pioneer Mother*'s back platform. Holding open the door, I steered him inside.

"He's all yours," I said to Pierre, who sprang out from behind the bar.

"Oh, my," Pierre said, taking Horace by the arm. "You've had quite the party. Let's get you cleaned up and put to bed."

Horace's suit jacket was powdered with dust and there was a line of dried blood on the back of his hand. Pierre turned to me.

"Did he fall?"

"Only getting into the car and getting out," I said.

"A largely innocent scuffle," Horace insisted, through slurred words. "A smashed opera hat, the smudge of an exploding cigar. Donkey Teeth dancing the hootchy-kootchy at the Poodle Dog."

Pierre looked at me with knitted brow and mouthed, *Donkey Teeth?* I shrugged.

While Pierre took Horace up the hallway, I stepped over Jane's and Florabelle's roller bags and set Horace's badge and the .38 snub-nosed revolver on the bar. I had snapped up those two goodies early.

Wanda came out of the galley.

"Haven't seen him that bad in a while," she said. "Guess he won't be needing dinner tonight?"

"No, he had a ribeye and fries with his whiskey."

She placed a sealed Tupperware container on the bar next to the gun.

"Take this with you to Mrs. Lorillard's. The girls made brownies for the sleepover."

*   *   *

I had no sooner slid behind the old Ford Custom's steering wheel, started the engine, and buckled my seatbelt than a siren yelped. From the back seat, Jane's and Florabelle's heads popped up like lawn sprinklers, and they looked around. In the twilight, an unmarked Ford Explorer, black, filled my rearview mirror, a blanket of chalky dust settling on the trackside road behind it. Red and blue strobe lights flashed urgently. I transferred my gaze to the small round side mirror and watched as the driver's door swung open. A uniformed policewoman stepped out and marched toward us, vigorously motioning a throat slash. It was Kimberly. I couldn't hear what she was saying. I rolled down my window.

"Cut the engine," she was shouting. "Turn it off!"

I quickly put a foot on the brake and turned the key to the *off* position. The engine fell silent.

I smiled. "Deputy Chief Earhart, what a nice surprise."

Kimberly positioned her face in my open window, a hand on a knee, and scanned the Ford's interior. She had a dire expression. Making eye contact with Jane and Florabelle, she nodded.

"Ladies."

Jane stared back, wide-eyed and mute.

"Hello." Florabelle gave a little wave.

Kimberly took a step back and looked at me.

"Chief 502—where is he?"

"Mr. Button?" I asked. "Indisposed would be a polite way to put it."

"Indisposed or not, I need you to get him. I have something important to tell him."

"You'll be wasting your breath. He's in his stateroom, sleeping off an all-day bender. He couldn't tell you what planet he's on."

"Does this have anything to do with this morning at the restaurant?"

"You know about that?"

"We're the police. We know everything. You crossed the line, Mr. Marshall. Captain Zavala specifically told you to leave Tatiana Wong alone. You can't just show up at a place of business and start accusing people of murder."

"Trust me, Mr. Button regrets what happened. Can I tell you something, Kimberly, between you and me?"

She cocked her head warily. "What's that?"

"He intends to resign as chief of police."

With parted lips, Kimberly considered this. She glanced at the horizon. A hungry callousness showed in her eyes.

"When?" she asked.

"Sometime tomorrow. As soon as he sobers up."

Kimberly hooked her thumbs into her gun belt and leaned in my window.

"Call me the minute he's ready. I'll bring the letter over myself. You've got my cell?"

I nodded. "It should be before eleven. He's got a plane to catch."

Kimberly smiled, showing those barracuda teeth.

"That's the best thing I've heard all weekend. Let me know if he needs a ride. I'll drive him to the airport."

"I'm sure you would."

Kimberly gave the old prowl car a possessive sweep with her eyes.

"Can I ask where you're going? I'm sorry, I'm holding you up."

I told her about the sleepover.

"Mr. Button likes to promote the maternal influence whenever he can," I added.

Kimberly looked again into the back seat.

"Mrs. Lorillard's a nice lady. You're lucky girls. Which one of you is Jane?"

Jane raised a hand. "I am."

"I met your mother once when she came through town. I was on her security detail. She gave me a pin, which I treasure to this day: *Don't tread on me.* It's an honor to meet you."

"Thank you." Jane offered the Tupperware container. "Would you like to try a brownie?"

Kimberly initially declined, but after Jane peeled off the lid and showed her the stacked brownies, she changed her mind and took one.

"So what's the important news you were coming to tell Mr. Button?" I asked.

"The food boxes tested negative for fentanyl," Kimberly said, talking between bites. "But you probably already figured that out by now."

THIRTY-FOUR

THE WATER IN THE CORNER FOUNTAIN trickled pleasantly. A bronze entry light cast a web of tree shadows against the courtyard wall. Bunny answered our bell promptly, throwing open the rustic door, greeting Jane and Florabelle with hugs. She led us inside and directed the girls to set their roller bags and pillows in the second bedroom down the hall. The living room was brightly lit and cozy with its crammed mélange of gilded mirrors and heavily upholstered furniture.

"Here, the girls made brownies. And this is for you in case things get dicey." I offered Bunny the Tupperware container and showed her the bottle of Pouilly-Fuissé that Wanda and I had picked out from Pierre's wine chiller.

"Well now, isn't that kind?" With a slightly trembling hand, Bunny took the brownies and fixed me with her cheery gaze. "I hope you don't have to rush off."

"I can't stay long. Wanda's making dinner."

"Aren't you the lucky fellow? Wanda. Come, let's get that bottle of wine into the refrigerator."

Bunny locked arms with me, and we walked to the kitchen. She wore a long, white Bohemian dress.

"We can't thank you enough for doing this," I said, "for everything you've already done for Jane and Florabelle."

"Don't be ridiculous. I'm doing this entirely for me. There's nothing like a hen party to restore an old girl to Zen." She took the wine bottle and placed it in the refrigerator. "Okay if I keep them till noon?"

"You want them that long?"

"Oh, I do indeed. We have big plans. Call for pizza. Make popcorn. Watch *Gone with the Wind*. S'mores on the patio. Stay up until all hours, talking boys and careers and life. And there's our service project, of course."

"Your service project?"

"A sleepover needs a service project, or it's nothing more than an exercise in sleeplessness and self-indulgence."

I gave her a smile. "I see. And what's your project?"

"School supplies for disadvantaged children. We'll fill the backpacks tonight and drop them at the charter school in the morning." Bunny turned to the doorway. Jane and Florabelle stood there with an air of anticipation, as if eager to take orders from a beloved captain. Bunny obliged. "Girls, the school things are all on the dining table. Can you start unpacking them from their boxes? I want to have a word with Jack."

Jane and Florabelle scampered off, making Bunny smile. She looked at me but stayed silent until the girls were well out of earshot.

"I may have been hasty the other day. I've done some research on the internet." She hesitated. "Jack, may I be frank with you?"

"Of course."

"Jean-Claude and drugs—I don't know what to think. I may have missed some signs."

"Signs?"

"Mood swings, bouts of uncontrolled anger—I assumed it was anxiety over the state of affairs at Papillon. He blamed the bad numbers on the isolated location. He couldn't raise the revenue line, and he refused to cut expenses. He was afraid it would affect quality and ruin his reputation. We argued about it. He was becoming more and more withdrawn. I'm wondering now if he was turning to drugs."

As Bunny described her dead lover's foundering life, I studied her firm, striking mouth—a fleck of red lipstick had affixed itself to a front tooth, and I couldn't help but stare. The whole thing made me feel uncomfortable and slightly embarrassed.

One of her closest friends is Tucson's acting chief of police. Why tell me?

"Jean-Claude and I had a big fight the morning he died," Bunny continued. "I suppose that's one element of my guilt. He'd figured out I steered the Best Chef award to Papillon, and it hurt his damned Parisian pride."

"I can see where it might."

Bunny turned away, and the next moment she was crying and reaching for a roll of paper towels.

"I feel like a traitor. Jean-Claude loses his life, and here I am accusing him of being a drug addict."

Her bout of quiet weeping quickly died away. She dabbed the scrunched paper towel to her eyelids.

"You should go to the police," I said. "They need to hear this."

"You don't understand. I'm the chairman of Los Picadores. Having an affair with a married man."

"I guarantee you, the police have heard it before. I'm sure they'd be discreet."

Bunny opened the roll-out drawer for an under-counter trash compactor and jettisoned the paper towel. "I can't take that chance. My status in the community—my reputation—it's all I have left." She slammed the drawer shut and gave me a grim smile. "If Jean-Claude could figure out I'd rigged the award, you can bet the ladies of Los Picadores will figure it out, too. I'm begging you, Jack. Don't mention this to anyone."

I was by no means prepared to swear unconditional loyalty to Bunny Lorillard. Telling us she lived alone and lying about her affair, bilking the finalists out of the Best Chef Tucson award, and now changing her story on Jean-Claude's possible drug use—she was no exemplar of honesty and trustworthiness. In fact, the more she pressed the point, the more suspicious I became.

What's changed so suddenly?

"Mr. Button, I know, will handle this any way you want. What would you like me tell him when I see him in the morning?"

Bunny appeared to consider the matter carefully. After a long silence, she gave a sigh of resignation. "Tell him to let bygones be bygones. There's nothing more any of us can do."

"You know that'll be Jean-Claude's epitaph: he died of a drug overdose?"

Bunny's face was full of anguish.

"And you're okay with that?" I asked, pressing the point.

"Jean-Claude is at peace," Bunny said. "What does it matter what's written on a scrap of paper?"

THIRTY-FIVE

AN EASTBOUND TRAIN of double-stacked containers made its way through the 22nd Street railroad yard. Overhead, high-pressure sodium lamps cast the scene in a jaundiced light. Beyond the parking lot of the Union Pacific offices, on the trackside road, a black Crown Victoria sat parked near the *Pioneer Mother*. I knew that car.

I found Igor in the observation lounge, seated at the bar, drinking gin and tonic, wearing that same checkered sports coat that made Horace shudder. Wanda and Pierre stood behind the bar, smiling as they listened to the detective's story.

"He's just come from the Mexican restaurant," Igor was saying, "and he sees this framed portrait of Chief Sandoval hanging in the lobby, which, like, royally ticks him off. He tears the picture off the wall, screws and all, and takes it up to the second floor, where we're supposed to be meeting with the captain and where he runs into Deputy Chief Earhart, who keeps getting in his face, saying, like, 'Get out of here. You're wasting my people's time,' and he says, 'Here, Kimberly, tell Fat Ralph I brought him a going-away present,' at which point he chucks the picture at her feet. He throws a perfect strike—it lands right between her tactical boots, Chief Sandoval looking up with that smarmy grin, and the deputy chief looks like frickin' Godzilla she's so pissed off, her eyes buggin', spitting fire out her mouth. Am I right, Jack?"

I threw my coat over a parlor chair and joined Igor at the bar. Two days knowing Horace and already he had stories. He sipped his cocktail. At his elbow was a plate of portobello bruschetta with rosemary aioli, our starter for the night.

"I blame it on the mezcal," I said. "Generally, Mr. Button would never be that rude."

Pierre guffawed.

"*Generally*," I repeated.

Igor grazed on the bruschetta, seeking out the largest pieces of toast.

Wanda watched the detective eat. She turned to me and raised an eyebrow.

I nodded.

"Won't you stay for dinner?" she asked. "It's only the three of us. I've got more truffled squab with red-wine sauce than we can ever eat."

"Love to," Igor said, "but I'll have to take a raincheck. It's wham night for the squirrels."

I looked at Wanda and Pierre and turned back to Igor.

"Wham night for the squirrels?" I asked.

"My vegetable garden's overrun with the sneaky little buggers. I've got a system and I can't deviate from the routine. For two nights I set out a buffet of popcorn and nuts—all you can eat, no strings attached. They bring all their friends. Then on the third night, *wham!* The trap slams shut. I can get five or six at a time in the cage."

"Yikes," Wanda said. "What do you do with them after that?"

"It's illegal as all get-out, but I load the cage in the back of the company car and drive over to Reid Park. I let them loose at the duck pond, usually around midnight."

"Impressive game plan," I said. "The squirrels don't stand a chance."

"I can't take too much credit. They say a squirrel brain's about the size of a walnut."

"In other words, smarter than most humans," Pierre said, catching my eye and giving me a smile. He watched Igor drain his drink. "Freshen that up for you?"

"No, I need to hit the road." Igor checked his watch. "By now I've probably got a cage full of furry friends chittering for a ride to the park." He reached for a file folder at the end of the bar and turned to me. "This is the copy of the preliminary autopsy report I promised the Chief. I'd like to walk you through it so you can explain it in the morning."

"Please do," I said.

As Igor opened the folder, Wanda made the face she makes with spiders and turned for the galley. "This is where I go check on my truffled squab."

"Wait for me, darling," Pierre said. "The thought of a human brain hanging on a meat scale makes me woozy." He followed Wanda around the corner.

Igor leafed through the loose pages of the report. "Guess you've already heard the food cartons tested negative?"

I nodded. "This hasn't been the easiest day for your chief."

"I gather. Pierre gave me the tour when I got here, and I could practically smell the Jack Daniel's coming through his bedroom door."

I smiled. I was starting to like this guy.

"All right, let's go through this thing." Igor took up several pages of the report. "'Circumstances of death: A fifty-one-year-old male owned and operated a restaurant... last seen alive leaving the kitchen, snacking on cookies... Twenty minutes later an employee found him fully clothed, collapsed near a dumpster, not breathing. Called 911. Paramedics and Tucson Fire responded... pronounced dead at the scene. No evidence of licit, illicit, or intravenous drug use... One freshly burned cigarette butt, Marlboro brand, consistent with a half-smoked Marlboro in the victim's hand, was noted nearby on the ground.' Blah, blah, blah." He turned the page. "'External examination: Body a well-developed, well-nourished male. Head: Brain edema... froth in the airways... Heart: Normal shape and weight... Aorta: No measurable plaques.' Blah, blah, blah." He flipped to the next page. "'Lungs: Strong evidence of pulmonary edema. Cut surfaces exuded a white foamy liquid.'" He glanced at me over the pages. "There's your red flag for fentanyl, right there." His gaze returned to the report. "'Gastrointestinal system: Stomach contained approximately 750 milliliters of yellow liquid with partially digested brown and bright green food fragments... consistent with food fragments found lodged in victim's pharynx...' Probably one of those damn cookies, which the ME thinks was a chocolate-mint sandwich, that type of thing." He flipped the page. "'Onset of death appeared to occur rapidly. Presumptive cause: Fatal intoxication of fentanyl, administered orally, the manner of death accidental.'" Again, he looked at me. "Translation: Our chef had a big night ahead. He was looking for a little euphoria to get him through the stress of the event, took a pill, I'm guessing one he thought was on the order of a Percocet or a Xanax but was actually a counterfeit. They're popping up all over the place these days. He was camped out by the dumpsters, smoking Marlboros, snacking on cookies, when the fentanyl hit his system. He suffered respiratory depression. They found him too late for the Narcan to do any good, and that was that—adieu, Chef Jean-Claude."

"So the medical examiner's sticking to his story: this was a self-inflicted drug overdose…"

"Unless you have other ideas. These MEs are pretty good at connecting the dots."

I shook my head and smiled. "No, I've learned my lesson about second-guessing the experts."

Igor studied me, tilting his head.

"You're holding back. There's something else you want to say."

"Not really."

"Come on, Jack. I'm trained to read people."

"I'm only offering this because it might save you time…"

The detective laughed good-naturedly. "I appreciate the consideration."

I hesitated. "Just so you understand—we promised confidentiality."

"Fair enough. No names. What's the gist of it?"

"Two different people told us recreational drug use may have been a factor. Both knew the chef personally, one of them quite well, actually."

Igor nodded. "Not exactly a shocker, is it?"

"Probably not. There's another thing we learned: the restaurant was failing."

"So money problems, maybe?"

"Plenty of stress, you can be sure. We heard that through the grapevine, too."

"Not by chance from the chef's wife, was it? The lady up at Lake Tahoe?"

"No, Mr. Button hasn't even talked to her, as far as I know. I doubt he sees the point."

The growing cast of characters in our little drama appeared to engage the detective's imagination. He looked out the window a moment and turned to me.

"Anything else?"

Again, I hesitated. "There's a lot more I could tell you, but Mr. Button promised pretty much blanket confidentiality there, too. I hope you understand. Maybe he'll open up down the road."

"Right." As Igor stood to go, he handed me his card. "This has my cell. Tell him he can always come to me, whether he's chief or not." He showed me where he'd taped a USB flash drive inside the file folder. "If Chief Button is interested, these are the photos taken at the death scene."

Igor looked into the galley and said his goodbyes to Wanda and Pierre before I walked him out to his car.

He started the engine and lowered his window.

"I'll tell you something, Jack. Murder theories are fun and exciting, but real life is rarely that interesting. As an investigator, you learn to trust your gut. When it looks like an accidental overdose, it's probably an accidental overdose."

The admonishment was unnecessary. In my mind, I'd already moved on to another crime.

"Tell me this," I said. "How do you search a room?"

"Search a room?"

"Is there a process, a methodology you learn in detective school?"

"Depends on what you're searching for. A suspect, a weapon—"

"Let's say a piece of jewelry."

"No methodology, per se. Work systematically. Start at the door. Break the room into quadrants. Don't skip a thing—look for altered wallboards, floorboards, hidden compartments in dressers, false panels on furniture or in closets. Why, is something missing?"

BEING MARRIED TO WANDA, raising Jane, interacting daily with Horace, and serving as sole trustee for the David and Ruth Pepper Family Trust—I led an interesting life, but in my time working for Horace, no project was more fascinating to me than overseeing the renovation of the half-domed observation car *Alaska*.

Horace purchased the car from the BNSF Railway, where it ran in the consist of one of the railroad's special passenger trains, which are used primarily to entertain freight-customer executives. Horace had the car moved to a shop outside the Lake Superior Railroad Museum, in Duluth, Minnesota, where its interior was gutted—*tunneled*, they called it—and reconfigured according to a plan of Horace's design. Where once there was seating for forty-five executives from companies like UPS, Federal Express, and Genstar Container Corporation, there were now four bedrooms, one of which I was digging through inch by inch. I knew that double bedroom. If Wanda's wedding rings were in there, I'd find them.

"Wouldn't you rather come to bed?" my wife asked. She stood in the doorway, wearing a frown over a pink satin camisole set. Her arms were crossed.

"In a minute," I said, tearing back the blankets and sheets on Florabelle's upper bunk. The ultrabright light came from a portable halogen work lamp behind me. The search was methodical and slow going: empty each dresser drawer, put everything back exactly as it was, clear the furniture away from the walls, check for loose panels and boards, lift the carpet, tear apart the bunks.

"You've been at it for almost an hour," Wanda said.

"They have to be here somewhere."

"What makes you so sure?"

"I'm trusting my gut." I raised the mattress with one hand. With the other hand I felt for cuts or lumps in the top of the box spring.

Wanda sighed and turned away. "All right, Majordomo. See you in bed."

A minute later my cellphone rang. Caller ID said it was Jane. I experienced a split second of both guilt and confusion.

Does she know I'm tearing her room apart? And why is she calling so late?

"Jack, help us!" Jane cried.

I could hardly make out her words. A girl was screaming.

"Jane, what's going on—"

"Someone just tried to break in!"

The girl in the background kept screaming.

"Into Mrs. Lorillard's house?"

"Yes!"

"Who was it?"

"I don't know. Florabelle saw him."

"Is he still there, is he still trying to get in?"

"I'm not sure. Maybe."

"Well, can you see him?"

More screaming.

"I don't see anyone. He was at the sliding glass door, but no one's there right now."

"Is that Florabelle screaming? Is she hurt?"

"I don't think so. Florabelle, are you hurt?"

For a moment the screaming broke off. It started up again, even more shrill and hysterical than before.

"I'm scared, Jack. Please, can you come over right away?"

"Where's Mrs. Lorillard?"

"She's on the phone. She's calling 911."

"Good. Keep the doors locked. Don't open anything for anyone other than a uniformed police officer, got that? You and Florabelle stay close to Mrs. Lorillard. I'm on my way."

"Just please hurry!"

I told Wanda as much as I knew as I grabbed my wallet and car keys from the briarwood box I kept atop the bureau in our stateroom. From her place sitting on the bed, her back against the headboard, Wanda looked at me, horrified.

"Should I go with you?"

"No, I'd rather you stay here and put those beds back together. I'm bringing the girls home." My eyes swept the top of the bureau and settled on Horace's gun and badge.

Of course. Tucson Police.

I called Kimberly. She answered on the first ring.

"Is this the call?" she asked.

"Sorry to bother you at this hour," I said, "but I just got a call from Jane." I quickly told her about the attempted break-in at Bunny Lorillard's place, that she'd already called 911, and that Jane thought the intruder might still be trying to get inside the house.

"Is there any way you can accelerate the response?" I asked. "I hate to think what this guy has in mind."

"What's the address, do you have it?"

I gave her the address.

"Give me a second. Let me check."

"You can do that?"

"Magic. Hang on." I could hear her fingers pecking away on a keyboard. "Here it is: 100 Staghorn Drive. It's gone out as a priority two."

"Which means?"

"Which means... wait." I heard more typing. "All right, I've bumped it to a priority one and added a note. We should have officers on the scene in four minutes or less..."

"Thanks, Kimberly. I owe you one." I ended the call.

Wanda looked on with obvious anxiety.

"The cavalry is on their way," I said. I picked up Horace's revolver.

Wanda blanched. "Are you taking that with you?"

I went to her side of the bed and placed the revolver on her nightstand.

"No, I want you to have it. We're in the middle of something here, but until I know what it is, I want you to keep this close."

Wanda put on a short satin robe, grabbed the pistol, and followed me through the TV lounge to the vestibule door.

"Could this be another of Florabelle's made-up stories?" she asked.

"It's crossed my mind." I touched the control panel on the door, which slid open with its loud pneumatic sigh. I stepped into the dimly lit vestibule. The air was cold.

Wanda stood staring at me. Tousled hair, bare legs and feet, the loose robe, a revolver in her hand—she looked like the cover of a thriller spy novel.

"Call me as soon as you know anything," she said.

THIRTY-SEVEN

THE OLD FORD, AS IF RECALLING EARLIER DAYS OF GLORY, stepped up and owned the streets of Tucson one more time. Her engine roared, her siren bawled, and her emergency lights lit up whole city blocks. Her fat tires screeched through turns. Cars in our path moved swiftly out of the way. I was Miles Keogh on Comanche, General Sheridan on Winchester, Broderick Crawford on *Highway Patrol*. I didn't take my foot off the accelerator until I bore down on the gate-house at the entrance to the Saguaro Mesa Resort & Spa.

"You're the fifth car through!" called the guard as the gate slid open and I hit the gas.

Three marked patrol cars and a black Ford Explorer were parked in the 100 block of Staghorn Drive. I entered Bunny's courtyard. The front door was wide open. All the lights were on. Inside the tiled entry, a uniformed police officer was conferring with Bunny, who turned and received me with a warm embrace. Her eyes showed panic.

"He seems to be gone, whoever he was," she said. "I'm so sorry."

Outside the living room's sliding door, on the patio, flashlights moved around. Their bright white beams swept the garden and golf course.

"Where are the girls?" I asked.

"In the dining room," said the policeman.

I made my way to the dining room. Two female officers, both standing, turned as I came in. One of them was Kimberly. She wore a perplexed expression. Jane sprang from one of the dining chairs and gave me a big hug.

"Jack, I'm so glad you're here!"

On another chair, Florabelle was curled in a semi-fetal position. Her eyes were glazed, and she exhaled briskly into cupped hands.

Kimberly took a few steps in my direction, the black handle of her Glock protruding from her gun belt, three silver stars glimmering on the collar of her uniform shirt.

"Not sure what transpired, but the child's clearly traumatized," she said in a low voice. She turned to the other officer. "Check the neighborhood. Talk to the gate guard. See if any suspicious cars entered or exited the property. Get me a license plate number if he has one."

The officer left the room.

Florabelle kept puffing into her closed fists. She stared straight ahead.

Kimberly searched my face for an answer.

"She's hyperventilating," I said.

"We should get her a paper bag," Jane said.

Bunny found one in the kitchen pantry.

Kimberly, Bunny, Jane, and I stood around the dining table, watching helplessly while Florabelle breathed into the bag and slowly recovered. Lining the walls of the room were colorful nylon backpacks laden with school supplies.

"Better?" Kimberly took a chair and sat with Florabelle. "Sweetheart, can you tell me what happened?"

"I don't know."

"Someone was trying to break in?"

"A man, I think."

"You think?"

Florabelle blinked at a spot on the floor.

"What can you tell me about this man?" Kimberly asked.

"Very scary."

"What made him scary? What did he look like?"

"I don't know—"

"Was he short, tall, white, black?"

"I can't remember."

"Did he get inside the house?"

"Maybe."

"Did he touch you?"

"No."

"You were in the living room?"

"He was at the door. He ran away when I screamed."

"But you can't tell me what he looked like?"

"He was tall."

"Tall like me? Or tall like Jack?"

"I don't know. Maybe he was short."

Kimberly gave me a look of suppressed annoyance. She turned back to Florabelle. "You aren't giving us much to work with, honey. We have to know who we're looking for."

"I need to use the bathroom."

Kimberly looked away as the color rose in her face. Grinding her teeth, she glanced at Bunny and me and asked Jane to escort her friend to the bathroom.

"While you're there, help her get into some clean clothes," Kimberly said to Jane. "And then we'll try this again."

Jane took Florabelle down the hallway.

Bunny stifled a gasp and turned to Kimberly. "She had an accident?"

"No question about it."

Bunny stole a glance at the dining chair Florabelle had occupied. "Poor thing. Obviously scared to death." She pushed the chair away from the table.

Kimberly bit her lip and fixed her eyes in a different direction. She stayed silent a moment. She turned to Bunny.

"Mrs. Lorillard, what can you tell me about what happened tonight?"

"I don't know, really," Bunny said. "The girls and I were in the kitchen, sprinkling the popcorn with salt and having a fine time, and all of a sudden Florabelle disappeared. Next thing I know she's in the living room, screaming bloody murder."

"And what did you do?"

"I went to see what was wrong, and that's when Florabelle said this person was trying to break in. So I called 911."

"You never saw anyone?"

"No. Only Florabelle did."

"And the sliding door—was it open or closed?"

"Closed. I double-checked to make sure it was locked."

"And Florabelle, she left the kitchen and went into the living room because...?"

Bunny stood there looking blank. "I don't know. I hadn't really given it any thought. She just seemed to wander off."

Heartened by Kimberly's questions, I pushed in. "It's not inconceivable she made the whole thing up."

Kimberly gave me a penetrating look. "Go on."

"Florabelle's a troubled child—trouble at home, trouble at school. She and Jane have been known to concoct crazy stories."

"Keep going, I'm listening."

"Chasing a blackmailer through Disneyland—that was last week's tall tale. I'm thinking maybe she got bored and decided to inject a little excitement into the evening."

Kimberly blew a forceful upward breath. Her hair was pulled back in that same elaborate, rigid braid. Not a wisp moved.

She shook her head. "Let's hope not. It means I pulled three units out of the field for nothing." Her voice had a hardened edge: "I'm here as a cop to help Senator Pepper's daughter, not play social worker to some whack-job kid."

"I know, Kimberly," I said. "If that's the case, I'm sorry."

By the time Jane and Florabelle returned to the dining room, Florabelle was facing a decidedly jaundiced questioner.

"Let's go through this one more time," Kimberly said. "Describe this intruder you saw."

"It was a man. Well, maybe a man—"

"Are you saying it might've been a woman?"

"Don't get mad at me. I don't know what it was!"

Jane interrupted. "You have to tell her, Florabelle."

Kimberly looked quickly at Jane. "Tell me what?"

"What she told me in the bathroom," Jane said. "He was wearing a mask. That's why she doesn't know what he looked like."

Kimberly bit her lip. She turned and glowered at Florabelle as if considering an act of murder.

"You've got to be freaking kidding me," she said. "All this time, and you're just now getting around to telling me he was wearing a mask? I don't believe you for one second."

"I didn't know what to say. I thought you might throw me in juvie."

"Florabelle, why would I throw you in juvie?"

"For lying to my psychiatrist. I told her I never see drippy skeleton faces."

Kimberly lifted her chin and gazed with narrowed eyes at Florabelle.

"This mask you saw tonight," Kimberly said. "Was it a drippy skeleton face?"

"It was a skeleton face. I don't know if it was drippy. My eyes stop seeing when I scream."

Kimberly considered Florabelle with a growing wonderment. "When you say drippy, do you mean, like, leaking water?"

"More like it gets so hot the skin melts away from their faces and they turn into dripping skeletons, you know? I can be walking down the street and some old person walks by and their face melts off and they turn into a drippy skeleton. It happens all the time."

Kimberly's eyes met mine. Her mouth opened slightly, but she made no comment. She turned back to Florabelle.

"This drippy skeleton you saw at the door, can you describe the clothes he was wearing?"

"Something dark on top. A hoodie, maybe."

"What else can you tell me about the mask?"

Florabelle hesitated. She glanced at the doorway and then looked at Kimberly.

"It had a lot of bright colors, but it was still creepy, you know? It was painted with, like, green and yellow hippie flowers, daisies, maybe, coming out of the eye sockets."

In my head I pictured the exact skeleton mask. I'd seen it—or something very similar—the day before at El Whisky. The mask Florabelle described was Santa Muerte, or at least one artist's interpretation of the Mexican folk saint. I took out my phone and Googled *day of the dead images*. A collage of colorful skeleton faces quickly populated the screen. I set the phone on the table in front of Florabelle.

"Anything like these?"

Florabelle tilted her head and peered at my iPhone. Suddenly her eyes grew wide. She screamed, lifted her feet off the floor, and spun away from the table, clutching the chair stiles with both hands, thrashing her Vans on the upholstered seat, trying to climb over the back of the chair. Kimberly took her firmly by the shoulders and urged her to sit.

"Florabelle, stop! Calm down! You're safe."

*   *   *

"The child's obviously got problems," Kimberly said. "On the other hand, it's hard to imagine she didn't see something."

We were standing in the entryway. Jane and Florabelle were down the hall, collecting their things. The police had taken the investigation as far as they could, Kimberly explained, given the circumstances: an unreliable witness, a sketchy description of a masked suspect, no evidence of tampering at any of the doors or windows. The guard on duty at the front gate had reported a typically quiet Sunday night with no suspicious vehicles entering or exiting the property.

"What about neighborhood boys, Mrs. Lorillard?" Kimberly asked. "Could it be some local teenagers trying to play a practical joke on the girls?"

"Oh, that isn't possible," Bunny said. "It's an over-fifty-five community. No one but me knows the girls are here."

"Do you know of anyone who might have reason to commit forcible entry?" Kimberly persisted. "A subcontractor or a service worker who'd know where you keep your valuables, anyone who'd want to see you hurt?"

Bunny shook her head solemnly. "No, nobody I can think of."

I was astonished at seeing how easily she lied.

"Even so," Kimberly said, "you might consider staying somewhere else tonight, if only for your peace of mind."

"Phooey," Bunny said. "I'm not going to let some two-bit prowler scare me out of my own bed."

Resting a hand on her holstered pistol, Kimberly assumed a stance of unrivaled authority, an air of battle-hardened street chops. She looked at Bunny somewhat contentiously.

"This is no time to let down your guard, Mrs. Lorillard. Something may have happened here. I'd hate to have you wake up in the middle of the night and find a drippy skeleton standing over your bed."

Bunny's granite countenance showed a crack. Her eyes flashed with fear.

"Well, when you put it that way," she said, giving me a lighthearted laugh, "maybe I'll check in to the local hotel."

"We've got an empty stateroom on the *Pioneer Mother*," I said. "Why not pack an overnight bag and come with us?"

Kimberly had an encouraging nod for the idea. "Sounds like a solid plan."

"I hate to do that," Bunny said. "I don't want to put anyone out."

"Not putting us out at all," I said. "In fact, I'm sure Mr. Button would be delighted to wake up in the morning and have you as a breakfast guest."

"And maybe you can talk some sense into him," Kimberly said to Bunny. "Encourage him to resign as chief of police, for the sake of the community."

In the end, Bunny relented. She threw a few things into a shoulder bag, locked up her duplex, and joined us for the ride across town to the Union Pacific yard. By the time we boarded the *Pioneer Mother*, Pierre and Wanda had the guest stateroom stocked and ready for its overnight guest.

THIRTY-EIGHT

IT WAS NEARING MIDNIGHT but there was no point in trying to sleep.

I couldn't help but link the Santa Muerte artwork in El Whisky to the mask that had so terrified Florabelle. I ruminated on culinary justice and envy of an award as motives for murder and found both notions unlikely.

Nevertheless, my thoughts kept circling back to the restaurant. There was Truman's claim that El Whisky was a conduit for drugs. Were the restaurant's main players—Carmen and Miguel Ramirez—somehow involved in a conspiracy to commit murder? If so, what did they want with Bunny Lorillard?

With nowhere else to turn, and with Wanda preoccupied in Jane and Florabelle's bedroom, comforting Florabelle, encouraging her to sleep, I settled behind the desk in the alcove under the *Alaska*'s vista dome, powered up Jane's laptop, and inserted Igor's flash drive into the laptop's USB port.

There are prettier ways to die than to overdose on fentanyl. The death-scene photos showed Chef Jean-Claude's lifeless body from every angle. He lay crumpled on the ground, one arm pinned beneath his body in an unnatural position. The facial close-ups were gruesome. His eyes bugged. His lips were blue. A pinkish foam bubbled from his mouth. I knew from the preliminary autopsy report that Jean-Claude had died with a lit cigarette between his fingers, but I didn't know the cigarette burned a hole in his white chef's jacket.

The debris surrounding the body was also exhaustively documented. The endless images of wind-strewn trash rendered me glassy-eyed. I was fast-forwarding through the photographs when a familiar voice sounded over my shoulder.

"What are you looking at?" Jane asked. She was barefoot and wearing her favorite circus-animal-print flannel pajamas.

"Not for public consumption," I said.

"Why? What is it?"

The current picture on the screen was harmless—scraps of paper and a small cardboard box near a foot of one of the dumpsters. I turned to Jane.

"These are pictures of where the chef passed away."

"Can I see?"

"No. You've had enough trauma for one night without seeing a dead body."

"Really? There's a picture of him dead?"

"Too many. But they're for your uncle's eyes only. It's official police business."

"You're not official, and you're looking at them."

"I'm semi-official. I drive his police car."

"That thing's embarrassing."

"Go to bed, Jane."

"Come on, Jack. I'm a mystery writer. I should know what an overdose looks like."

The remark took me by surprise. "Who said it was an overdose?"

"Mrs. Lorillard. Tonight. She said he was a drug addict. It was his hidden flaw."

I closed my eyes.

Expect nothing. See the good. Accept what is.

"How's your story about the evil principal coming?" I asked. "Are you making progress?"

Jane crossed her arms. "Not really. Florabelle can't sit still long enough to write, but she doesn't want me working on it without her. Plus she's making it impossible to sleep. It's making me mad."

"Is Wanda still in there?"

"She's, like, trapped by a schizoid. Every time she tries to leave, Florabelle starts crying and hyperventilating again."

"Well, be patient. She's been through an ordeal."

"Maybe. If you believe her." Jane stepped past me and peered at the image on the screen. "What is this? What came in this little box?"

"Cookies."

"In there?"

"Chocolate, with some kind of mint filling. You can still see part of one, see, in the corner?"

"I've seen this box before," Jane said. "Black with the little window and all those gold pointy things on it."

"Those are called fleurs-de-lis." I looked at Jane curiously. "Where've you seen it before?"

"The coconut macaroon cookies, remember? At Mrs. Lorillard's? They came in that same box."

*   *   *

A soft yellow light emanated from beneath the stateroom door. I knocked softly.

"Mrs. Lorillard? Are you still awake?"

"Jack?"

"I need to ask you something."

"Of course. Give me a minute."

I stood waiting in the *Pioneer Mother*'s narrow corridor. The red velveteen window treatments were infused with the salty leather scent of Horace's cigar smoke. The dining room and observation lounge were dark.

After a moment, Bunny opened the door. She wore a robe. Her hair was down. She held her reading glasses.

"Sorry to bother you," I said.

"That's okay, what's up?"

"That catering company you mentioned the other day—did they send you another gift pack of cookies?"

"Catering company?" Bunny stared back at me blankly.

"When you served us brunch last Thursday, you passed around cookies from a catering company. You said you get unsolicited things all the time. This same caterer—did they by chance send you chocolate mint cookies last week?"

Bunny's eyes suddenly brightened, and she smiled. "Yes, the winter-mint whoopie pies. I remember now."

"And what did you do with them?"

"I gave them to Jean-Claude. He was curious, so he took them to work. Why do you ask?"

*   *   *

Wanda entered the stateroom behind me.

"What in the world are you doing?" she demanded. "Why is every light on?"

"Because I can't see a darn thing in here," I said, standing before the open closet, digging through our hanging things, which were packed tightly together. I shoved the shirts, coats, and slacks apart until I found my blue blazer.

Wanda raised an eyebrow.

"I'm looking for the name of a caterer," I explained.

"Oh, are we throwing a party?"

"Not a party. I have a new theory." In a side pocket of the blazer, I found the printed notecard I was looking for. I had to step back from the closet and angle it toward the light in order to read it.

Enjoy these sweet treats. We're a local company. We provide catering services for corporate and private events. We'd love to consult with you on your catering needs for your next Los Picadores event...

The name of the company was Wild Rosemary. It had a Tucson address.

"All right, Majordomo, I give up," Wanda said. "What's your theory?"

*   *   *

"Jane, come try this and tell me if I'm missing something." I stood and let Jane have the desk chair. "The name of the company is Wild Rosemary. Do a search. See if you can find a website."

I watched over Jane's shoulder as her nimble fingers worked the laptop's keyboard. She tried several combinations of keyword searches. Nothing came back for a Tucson catering company with that name.

"A catering company without a website?" I said, looking at Jane. "In this day and age?"

Jane wrinkled her nose. "Definitely weird. Unless it's run by, like, a really old-fashioned grandmother."

"Now try this. Go to Google Maps and type in this address: 762 South Alessandro Road, Tucson. Tell me what you get."

Jane typed the address and blinked at the screen. She turned to me with a bewildered expression. "The Desert Paws Pet Cemetery?"

*   *   *

"The address comes back to a pet cemetery," I explained, talking on the phone with Igor. "The whole thing's a ruse."

Igor was silent for a time. "Unless it's a start-up caterer who took over the address. Mrs. Lorillard said they were blindly soliciting her business. That's something you'd expect of a start-up."

"But how do you move a pet cemetery? Don't they have plots and headstones like a regular cemetery?"

"Don't know. It'd be easy enough to drive by and have a look. I'm just now leaving the park. South Alessandro's close. What's the street number?"

I gave him the pet cemetery's address.

"Still, it's a bit of a leap to conclude this makes it a case of murder," Igor said, going back to my theory.

"But consider what they did," I said. "They started with maple-glazed donut cookies followed by coconut macaroons. Then they sent wintermint whoopie pies laced with fentanyl. It's wham night for the squirrels all over again, only with humans."

"Ha!" Igor said. "I like your analogy. And your theory is Mrs. Lorillard blew up the plan when she gave the cookies to Chef Jean-Claude?"

"It explains the masked intruder. He was coming back to finish the job."

"You may be getting a bit over your skis here, Jack, but it's kind of an interesting theory. Give me a chance to check out the pet cemetery. I'll call you back."

"You don't mind? It's late."

"Don't mind at all. I've had my fun for the night—delivered four model citizens to their new quarters at the duck pond. You should've seen the glee on their faces when I opened up that trap. That's my reward. I'll call you in about fifteen minutes."

*   *   *

"Okay," Igor said, calling me back at 12:30 a.m. "I'm looking right at the Desert Paws Pet Cemetery and Crematory. It's very much still in business so you're a hundred percent right. The catering company's a sham."

"So what's next?" I asked.

"I'll swing by Papillon and see if that box is still anywhere near the dumpsters. Where were these cookies shipped from, do we know the city?"

"The card said Tucson."

"But do we know that for a fact? Are you looking at the actual shipping labels?"

"Not the shipping labels. My guess is they've long since been thrown out with the trash."

"Well, it's not the end of the world. We can start with the destination address and work backwards. What was the delivery service, did Mrs. Lorillard say? And was it the same for all three packages?"

"It was." I gave Igor the name of the carrier. It was a well-known, international delivery service.

"Good. I have a contact who works graveyard in their Phoenix distribution center. I'll call him right now. I'll ask him to send me a printout showing all the packages delivered to Mrs. Lorillard's address in the time frame we're talking about. That'll give us pickup locations and origin cities. Maybe we'll get lucky and see a pattern."

I gave him Bunny's address.

"She said she got the packages over about a two-week period," I added. "The cookies in question were delivered probably last Wednesday or Thursday."

"All right. We'll go back a month for the report."

"That should cover it."

"Keep in mind, unless they were laced with poison and the intent was to do physical harm, sending cookies isn't a crime. The likely scenario is this guy had stress in his life and turned to drugs as a way of coping. Listen, Jack. You said you and Chief Button had some information about this guy's drug use. I really need to talk to one of your confidential sources as soon as it can be arranged."

"I get what you're saying. I'll bring it up with Mr. Button—"

"I mean, we can chase phantom catering operations all day long, but if this guy simply took a wrong pill, we'll be running around in circles till kingdom come."

My impulse was to blurt out Bunny's name, but I knew that would come back to bite me.

"Tell you what," I said. "Come by the railroad yard in the morning and I'll pour you a cup of coffee. We have an interesting house guest. You might like to meet her."

"Who's there?"

"Mrs. Bunny Lorillard."

"Interesting."

"Get here whenever you can. First pot of coffee's usually on by seven."

THIRTY-NINE

"MUST'VE BEEN QUITE THE FIGHT if she made you spend the night under that table."

The sound of Pierre's voice woke me. I cracked my eyes to daylight and a forest of carved dining-set table and chair legs. I had indeed spent the night beneath the *Pioneer Mother*'s dining table. I rolled over and reached for the .38 snub-nosed revolver.

Pierre held his hands up. "Okay, don't shoot. I'm making the coffee!"

I climbed out from under the table. My joints were stiff and sore, and my eyeballs felt coarse. Pierre was going through the observation lounge, putting up window shades, turning on lamps. The aroma of brewing coffee drifted in from the galley. Pierre always made it suitably strong.

"What time is it?" I asked, setting the revolver on the table.

"A hair past seven." Pierre saw something out the window and turned to me. "Are we expecting a guest?"

I stifled a yawn. "As a matter of fact, I am."

"Looks like he's here."

I joined Pierre at the window. A shiny black-and-white Tucson Police SUV sat parked alongside the tracks, not far behind the old parade car. I studied the police cruiser, but with its tinted windows I couldn't make out who was inside.

"That definitely isn't his car," I said.

Curious, I went out to the back platform and stepped off the *Pioneer Mother* into a clear, cool morning. The trackside ballast crunched under my feet.

As I approached the idling SUV, the driver's window came down. Behind the wheel sat Horace's chief of staff. Her red lipstick was as bright and startling as a Broadway marquee.

"Good morning, sir."

"Lucianna! What brings you here so early?"

"Deputy Chief Earhart, sir. She thought it would be a good idea to minimize Chief Button's inconvenience, in the event he decides to step down today. She asked me to stand by with a pen and a copy of the resignation letter."

"That's very thoughtful."

"Thank you, sir. Anything I can do to help—it's my pleasure. May I ask, is he up yet?"

"I haven't seen him."

Lucianna took the news with a discernible pang.

"Won't you come inside for a cup of coffee?" I asked.

"Thank you, sir, but I hate to be any trouble."

"No trouble at all. The pot's already on. Please, come in. I insist."

"Well, if you insist, I'd love to see what the inside of that thing looks like." She killed the engine and grabbed a brown leather briefcase off the passenger seat.

"I'll take the letter in with me," she added, "so as not to inconvenience the chief."

Inside the *Pioneer Mother* I led Lucianna through the observation lounge and to the bar, where I introduced her to Pierre. Wide-eyed, she surveyed the lavish interior before placing her briefcase on a chair. She turned to me reprovingly.

"Do you know there's a loaded .38 revolver on your dining table?" she asked.

"It belongs to Chief Button," I said. "We have a houseguest who might be a target, and I spent the night standing guard."

"I heard about the attempted forced entry. Thankfully, no one was harmed."

"I attribute that to your department's quick response. Chief Button and I couldn't be more grateful."

"He knows about it?"

"He will as soon as he wakes up."

"How do you take it?" Pierre asked Lucianna. He was filling her coffee cup when there was a knock at the door.

Igor stood on the back platform, peeking in a window, waving to get my attention. His black Crown Vic was parked behind Lucianna's SUV. I quickly opened the door.

"We're making headway, Jack. Wait till you hear this." Igor stepped inside with a big smile. He nodded at Lucianna. "Captain."

"Detective." She used two hands for her coffee—one cradled the saucer, the other held the delicate china cup by its handle loop. Her guarded expression revealed nothing of her feelings about the homicide detective, one way or the other.

Horace came down the corridor and stopped in surprise.

"What is this, a convocation at a precinct station?" he asked, a sparkle in his eye.

"Good morning, sir," Lucianna said, placing her cup on the saucer.

Igor gave Horace a heady grin. "Chief."

"I'm honored by the title," Horace said, "but circumstances have changed, and I've got a plane to catch. Whatever brings you both, take it up with Kimberly." His face was freshly shaved, and he wore his favorite suit for travel, a three-piece brown tweed.

"You need to hear this, Mr. Button," I said. "We've had an eventful night."

"Oh? Tell me."

"Not here, I'm afraid." I glanced up the corridor and looked back at Horace. "It's a fairly sensitive matter. It involves Mrs. Lorillard, who happens to be our overnight guest in the second stateroom."

Horace's face brightened. "Bunny's here?"

"Well, not if our murderer had his way."

Horace's eyes widened.

"I suggest the vista dome lounge—we can bring you up to speed there," I said.

Horace turned to Pierre. "As long as I can get some coffee."

Lucianna lifted her briefcase off the chair. "I'll bring this along," she said, "just in case."

I took the revolver from the table and led the way forward: up the *Pioneer Mother*'s darkened corridor, through the vestibule, and into the *Alaska*'s TV lounge, where we passed Wanda, who was on her way to the galley to start breakfast.

"I hope you got enough sleep for two of us," I said.

"Not even for one of us," she said, shaking her head.

We ascended the steep staircase and settled into the upholstered booth on the port-side of the lounge, Horace and I seated against the bulkhead, Lucianna and Igor across the table from us. Pierre followed with coffee service on a silver tray.

"Now what's this about Bunny?" Horace asked. "She spent the night?"

I told him about the masked intruder and about Florabelle's hysterical reaction to the Santa Muerte images on my phone.

"Carmen," he said.

"My first thought as well."

"You'd never get a warrant on a connection that nebulous," Igor said. "Masks, statues, painted skulls—those Santa Muerte doodads are all over the place. Even the hotel gift shop was full of them, remember?"

"All right," Horace frowned. "What else?"

Next, I told him about the bogus catering company.

"This is where it gets interesting," Igor said, cutting in. "We traced the pickup location for Mrs. Lorillard's Thursday delivery, which we believe consisted of the wintermint whoopie pies." He looked at me directly and eagerly. "This is the big news I came to tell you, Jack. That package and two others in the last couple of weeks all go back to an identical pickup location. Want to guess where?"

"Tell me."

He smiled as if presenting the winning hand in a poker game. "Lake Tahoe Boulevard, South Lake Tahoe."

Horace bristled. He glared at Igor with growing ire as the full significance of the location sank in. Lucianna looked with interest from Horace to Igor. I was shocked. I'd have wagered a month's salary the pickup locations would come back somewhere around Tucson. Carmen and Miguel Ramirez, it seemed, were off the hook. More significantly, the Lake Tahoe location implicated Chef Jean-Claude's estranged wife.

"It can't be," Horace grumbled. "Odette Garin a murderer?" He glared at Igor. "What do you take me for, a monkey?"

"I'm sorry, Chief. Whether or not the cookies were laced, it looks like we start with the wife." For a moment, Igor was reflective. "Was our chef seeing someone else, do we know?"

Horace pressed his lips into a grim line. He turned and gave me a look that said, *God Almighty.*

I did a double take. My mind raced.

"Perhaps," I said to Igor.

He smiled. "I'll take that as a yes." He leaned back in the booth and studied me savvily. "Was he by chance seeing Mrs. Lorillard?"

I looked at Horace. "Um, Mr. Button... you want to take that one?"

Horace lowered his head and ran a hand across the back of his neck. "Lordy."

Igor eyed the two of us sternly. "Guys, it's time we put everything on the table. Either Mrs. Lorillard's boyfriend had a thing for drugs, or she's been targeted for murder. We have to determine which. But you need to stop papering over the truth because that could get her killed. Can we agree no more secrets?"

I looked at Horace. He blinked into his coffee.

"About that. There's another development I need to tell you about," I said, turning to Igor. "Last night, Mrs. Lorillard threw Chef Jean-Claude under the bus. She didn't say it outright, but she left the door open that he may have been using."

"We have a visitor," Lucianna said, her gaze focused at the top of the staircase. Jane, still in pajamas, stood halfway up the stairs, clutching the two mahogany handrails.

"Hi," she said to Lucianna, "is my uncle or Jack up there?"

Horace leaned toward the staircase. "Jane, won't you join us a minute?"

Jane stepped into the vista dome's sunken aisle and faced our booth. She kept glancing at the silver bars on the collar of Lucianna's uniform shirt.

"Meet Captain Gomez and Detective Ivanovich," Horace said. "My niece, Jane."

Lucianna took a minute to converse with Jane, asking how old she was and where she went to school. Igor complimented her on her bravery the night before.

"Thank you," Jane said, "but I didn't really do anything."

I asked Jane if she was alone.

"Florabelle's still asleep. I was about to do some homework."

This was what I'd hoped to hear.

"We were filling your uncle in on last night's excitement," I said, "and you made an interesting comment when you and I were on the computer. Can I ask you a question? Off the record?"

Jane's face flushed. She transferred her weight from one bare foot to the other and regarded me nervously. "Okay."

"When Florabelle says she saw that skeleton mask, should we believe her?"

Jane hesitated. She cast her eyes downward and then looked at me almost angrily. "Most times I wouldn't trust a word she says, but last night I think she really saw something."

"A drippy skeleton face?" Horace asked.

"I don't know, Uncle. But she was really, really scared."

Horace meditated on this.

"Jane," he said, "can you get on that infernal machine of yours and give me a list of all the flights this morning from Tucson to Reno? I want anything that leaves before noon—where it stops, what time it lands."

With an insolent smile, Igor looked at Horace. "Are you suggesting the chef's wife actually traveled to Tucson—"

"I'm not suggesting anything," Horace snapped. "I'm looking for facts that would rule it out. It's critical for the next phase of our investigation."

"Sounds like you're not resigning after all," Lucianna said to Horace, smiling. "Not today, anyway."

Horace crossed his arms. "No, not as long as Bunny's life might be in danger."

Jane's mouth dropped. She took stock of her uncle's steadfast eyes.

"I'll get that list," she said quickly, flittering off like a bird.

Horace watched her go. He turned to Igor.

"I'm sorry, Detective. I should apologize for my hostile reaction to your Lake Tahoe news—"

"I assure you, Chief, no apology necessary."

"Please, let me explain. I've always considered Odette Garin some-what of a friend, and it's my natural instinct to protect a friend. But your point is well-taken. If this is a case of murder, and if our murderer had her way, Bunny would be the one in the morgue right now. The facts are the facts. Your revelation shifts our investigation to a new array of suspects. I'm prepared to follow this thread wherever it takes us, with-out prejudice. If Odette is guilty, you'll have my full cooperation in bringing her to justice."

"Most gracious of you, Chief. If you can facilitate it, I'd like to spend some time with Mrs. Lorillard. We need to clear up this issue of the chef's drug use."

"Were you able to find that box with the leftover cookie?" I asked.

"No, I looked, but the dumpsters had been emptied and the place swept clean."

"So still no hard evidence?"

Igor shook his head. "It's all circumstantial: the Lake Tahoe pickup location, the phony catering company, the jilted spouse—"

"Who has the culinary expertise to bake those cookies in her sleep," I emphasized.

Igor looked at Lucianna. "I'm guessing we might have enough for a search warrant."

She nodded. "I agree."

"How long would it take to get one?" Horace asked.

"A day or two at most," Lucianna said. "It's out of state. We'll have to get in front of a judge for whatever county."

"Do we even know where she lives?" Igor asked, turning to Horace. "California or Nevada?"

"No idea," Horace said. "I can call Dick Peck and ask." He looked away and his eyes lost their focus. Then, as though galvanized by an idea, he suddenly slapped the table. "All right, it's settled. We'll use our wiles to set a trap. Clear your calendars, everyone. We're going to Lake Tahoe."

FORTY

HORACE HAD HIS CASHMERE OVERCOAT and leather gloves draped over the bar. Single-minded in his determination to get to Lake Tahoe as quickly as possible, he'd left the *Alaska*'s vista dome and moved to the *Pioneer Mother*'s observation lounge, where he bossed us around from his chair with the high-handedness of a mannered lord.

"Pierre, put on a fresh pot of coffee and see if any of our guests would like an eye-opener. Jack, get Dick Peck on the phone." He looked up the hallway. "Where's Jane? I need that list of flights."

Igor was seated at the dining table, working on an affidavit for a search warrant. Lucianna had taken her phone out to the open platform. She had the unenviable task of explaining to Kimberly why she wasn't yet the acting chief of police.

Jane came dashing into the observation lounge and stood ramrod straight before Horace, presenting him with a printed sheet as if it were battle orders for a general. "Here it is, Uncle. Every flight this morning to Reno."

Horace took the report and gave it a cursory scan.

"Exactly as I suspected," he said. "Itineraries that read like a roll call for torture: seven hours, thirty minutes; nine hours, thirty minutes; twelve hours—" His basset-hound eyes implored us. "Good god, who'd spend twelve hours flying from Tucson to Reno with layovers in Dallas and Phoenix?" He studied the paper again. "Wait, here's an interesting flight. A 7:39 departure, lands at Reno eight minutes past noon, goes through Salt Lake City." He turned to Igor. "We've missed it, but it could've worked for Odette. It would put her in Reno in time to get up to the lake and cook the Chairman's Dinner."

I offered my phone to Horace.

"Dick Peck on the line," I said.

Horace set Jane's report aside and took the phone, his shrewd gaze focused on my face. "Dick, my friend, I'm afraid I have soul-crushing news. Are you ready?" His voice was somber. He crossed his legs at the knee and looked at Igor, who'd stopped working and was listening intently. "I'm sitting with a homicide detective from our Violent Crimes Section, Central Investigations Division. He's preparing an affidavit to get a search warrant on Odette's house. She's emerged as the prime suspect in Jean-Claude's murder... Yes, horrifying, isn't it? Needless to say, I won't be hitching a ride on your Gulfstream this morning... She poisoned him, that's what we believe... We conjecture he was seeing someone, and she found out about it—you know how these hot-blooded French birds can be. She lost her mind and hatched this diabolical plan to exact revenge on a cheating husband... I know, Dick, me, too. The whole thing makes me ill, nearly sick to my stomach... Listen, Dick, two things. Would you talk to Wayne and have him use his sway at your company to get us Odette's home address? We need it for the search warrant, and I'm sure it's in his records... Great. And the other thing—this is hard to ask—but may I have your permission to search Thunderbird Lodge? We're convinced she packaged the deadly poison as the product of a dummy catering company, and there might be evidence of that up at the Lodge. It's got that wonderful commercial kitchen, you know, and she's there by herself most of the time... Excellent. Thank you, Dick. Bring Wayne up to speed if you would and call me back with that address as soon as humanly possible... You know, that's a good question. Probably tomorrow at the earliest. We have to fly to Reno, rent a car, drive up to the lake, and get in front of a judge before we can do anything, so I'd say tomorrow best case..." With minimal formalities, Horace ended the call. He passed the phone back to me.

"How'd he take the news?" I asked.

"He was suitably shocked," Horace said. "Practically screaming with horror."

Igor sat looking at Horace. "Chief, you know we can get Ms. Garin's address from the records database, right?"

Horace shook his head. "She's a chef, Detective. They're a nomadic breed, often roaming from place to place without notifying the DMV."

"That's very true!" Wanda called from the galley. The peppery smoke of bacon was beginning to drift through the railroad car.

Horace steepled his hands and gave the door to the back platform a long meditative look. Lucianna was out there, still talking on the phone. Horace turned to me.

"I need you to make another call. Get me the reservation desk at the Arizona Inn."

"Are you going to give them a piece of your mind?"

"I need to check on rooms. I don't want Bunny going home just yet— not until we resolve this mystery of the drippy skeleton."

Within a minute, I had the reservation desk on the line. I again handed my phone to Horace.

"Jack," Wanda said, "can I get a little help in the galley?"

Pierre was setting the dining table around Igor and his notes.

"Need me to move?"

"No," Pierre said, "you stay right where you are."

In the galley, Wanda worked with her back to me, loading a big silver platter with bacon and scrambled eggs. She wore her hair up and tied in a black bandana. I stepped behind her, put my arms around her waist, and nuzzled her soft, downy neck.

"Missed you last night," I said. "How're you holding up?"

"I'm worried about Florabelle. I honestly thought she was on the brink of a nervous breakdown."

I drew back. "Did she and Jane have a falling out?"

Wanda shook her head. "Don't know what's happened. They've been at each other's throats since last night." She turned and put the platter in my hands. "Take this out, Romeo. We're doing this family style."

As I laid the platter in the center of the dining table, Lucianna came in from the back platform. Horace stood. "Attention, everyone. You must eat quickly but you must eat. It may be some time before our next meal."

The rest of us regarded Horace flatly and looked at one another, mystified.

"Lucianna, when you finish with your bacon and eggs, I need you to charter a private jet," Horace continued. "The fixed base operator at Tucson Airport is an outfit called Majestic Flight Support—"

"I know Majestic, sir. We've used them before."

"Excellent. Tell them four of us are traveling, and we're going to the Minden-Tahoe Airport. We need to be in the air no later than 10:45." He checked his watch. "That's a little less than three hours from now. Don't take no for an answer. Commandeer the damn thing if you have to."

"Majestic is very good, sir. I'm sure we can make it happen."

"Atta girl, that's the spirit I like to see." Horace turned to me. "Jack, I want you to talk to the rental car company. We need a big car, a four-wheel drive in case we hit snow. Have them spot the car on the tarmac in anticipation of our arrival. We can't afford a minute of delay."

"Done," I said.

Lucianna spoke up. "Sir, for the jet charter, I'll need the names of the four passengers."

"You, me, Jack, and Igor."

"Me, sir?"

"Yes, Lucianna. You."

"Sir, no disrespect, but I'm an administrator. I have little to add to this investigation."

Horace raised an eyebrow. He looked at Lucianna slyly. "On the contrary, Lucianna, it's imperative you make the trip. You'll be playing the lead role in our sting."

"Sting, sir?"

"Don't press me for the details just yet," Horace said. "It's still a little murky in my mind but coming into focus like a Polaroid. Right now, I'd rather we all eat breakfast and concentrate on getting to Lake Tahoe pronto."

FORTY-ONE

"OUR LADY MAGNIFICO HAS ARRIVED!" Enthralled, mesmerized, a gleam in his eye, Horace sat back in his chair at the head of the dining table and stared at Bunny.

Igor and I quickly stood.

"Horace, these old railroad cars are stunning," Bunny said. "I feel like I should be walking out to an orchestra. And I've met Wanda and Pierre, too. They're lovely."

"Please, Bunny, sit with us and eat," Horace said, directing her to the nearest empty chair. "You've had a hideous night."

"Oh, but I had a wonderful sleep. That bed is so comfortable. And everything out here smells so good."

Pierre held the chair for Bunny, who smiled across the table at Jane and Florabelle.

"Good morning, girls."

"Morning," Jane and Florabelle both said. Ever since Florabelle came shuffling in from the *Alaska*, eyes puffy and hair unbrushed, the two girls had been pushing their eggs around sullenly and without the usual horseplay.

"Forgive us," Horace said to Bunny. "We're eating in shifts this morning. You've missed my chief of staff, Captain Gomez. And this is our friend Detective Ivanovich."

"You're a detective?" Bunny smiled at Igor. "With the Tucson Police Department?"

"Yes, Mrs. Lorillard."

"He's agreed to investigate last night's visitor," Horace said. "Perhaps the two of you could set a time to meet when we aren't rushing out the door."

"Oh, that won't be necessary," Bunny said, her gaze going from Igor to me. "It's already forgotten. Please, gentlemen, sit and finish your breakfast."

Horace glanced at Pierre, who stood smiling attentively to the side.

"The kitchen needs a strategic directive," Horace said to Bunny. "How do you like your eggs?"

Bunny thought a moment and recited a breakfast order: one egg sunny-side up with coffee and a single slice of wheat toast on the side.

"And Pierre, make the toast lightly buttered and bring me a spot of orange marmalade, if you have it," she added. She turned to Horace and feigned an expression of utter surprise. "Now wait. I just got here, and you tell me you're leaving?"

"Police business calls. We're taking a trip," Horace said, sitting forward, frowning, planting his elbows on the table, squeezing his hands together. The gesture shortened the sleeves of his suit jacket and exposed his gold BNSF Railway cuff links.

"Oh? Where are you off to?" Bunny asked.

"Out of state, I'm afraid. But it should be a short trip. I'm hoping to return tonight." Horace picked up his cup and took a long sip of coffee.

Bunny glanced at the door to the open platform. She turned and smiled at Jane and Florabelle.

"Maybe I'll stay here with the girls. We'll get our party after all, and we can deliver those backpacks to the school."

Jane's eyes brightened.

"Oh, yes," she said. "Please stay!" She looked at Florabelle. "And we can conduct follow-up interviews for our papers!"

"Hooray," Florabelle said with negligible enthusiasm.

Horace returned his cup to its saucer. He raised his eyes to Bunny.

"I've booked you a room at the Arizona Inn. It's under my name. Stay aboard the *Pioneer Mother* or stay at the Inn, but I want you to lie low. Don't go home or mingle about in the community until I sound the all clear."

Bunny gave a nervous laugh. "That's painting a grim picture. Is this all to do with last night's masked character?"

"Possibly. It's one subplot we're following."

Bunny shook her head. "The *Pioneer Mother* is looking better all the time. What's going on, Horace? Why all this fuss?"

"Don't worry, my dear. I have good reason to believe the window of danger has passed, but better sure than sorry."

Igor gave Bunny his card. "Maybe we can talk in the next day or two?"

Bunny's eyes flashed with anger. She opened her mouth to speak but quickly put the brakes on whatever she was about to say. She turned to Horace. "We're blowing this way out of proportion. It was probably nothing more than some poor wretch strung out on drugs, looking to break into an empty house."

Igor raised an eyebrow. "You've had a lot of experience with drugs, Mrs. Lorillard?"

"Squat," Bunny said. "Champagne brings me all the bad luck I need."

Horace winced. "Speaking of which, Bunny, I do have another favor to ask, if you don't mind?"

"Why should I mind?"

"It's a matter of some delicacy. I'll tell you the story." Horace toyed with a fork and smiled at his own ridiculousness. "This happened yesterday morning. I was cuffing magnums of Bollinger, apparently, going on a toot, when I decided to drop in on Tatiana Wong at Family Bone. Jack tells me I was boiled to the ears..."

"Oh, Horace!"

"By Jack's account it was an exalted performance. I rose in the center of the dining room, looked Tatiana in the eye, and reeled off the climax to my jail-and-bail spiel. Now she thinks she's won Best Chef Tucson and is cooking tonight at the convention center—a party to benefit Los Picadores—"

"Oh, Horace, you naughty boy!"

"Can you call Tatiana and clear up the misunderstanding? I'm happy to put such a dinner on my calendar, but I simply can't do it tonight. Pick any weekend in June..."

"I'll talk to her this morning. I'll tell her you got a little bit ahead of yourself, and we'll come up with a date."

"Good. You can always blame it on my enthusiasm for her cooking and my keenness to see her named Best Chef."

"And a teensy-weensy bit on the champagne."

"That, too." Horace reached for Bunny's hand and gave it a squeeze. "Thank you. Where would we be without each other to clean up our messes?"

I glanced down at my phone to read an incoming text.

"That's Lucianna," I announced. "She found a plane and they're getting it ready."

Wide-eyed, Bunny turned to Horace. "You, on a plane? But you never fly!"

"The gears of justice leave me no choice," Horace said, shaking his big head. "But I wish to God the Wright brothers were never born." He stood, said his goodbyes, and collected his overcoat and gloves.

Leaving the *Pioneer Mother*, Horace stopped on the open platform and turned to Igor.

"I'd like to keep the parade car parked where it is, while we're away, as a deterrent to mischief. May Jack and I ride with you?"

"Of course, Chief."

I took the front passenger seat. Horace settled into the Crown Victoria's back seat. As soon as we pulled the doors shut, a seaweed-like stench overpowered us.

"For the love of god," Horace gasped, "what's that rancid smell!"

FORTY-TWO

OUR CAPTAIN, A LEAN MAN NAMED RICK, met us inside Majestic Flight Support's lobby. He wore a pilot's uniform and conducted himself with a military bearing. He confirmed we were going to the Minden-Tahoe Airport, traveling without luggage, and that the plane was to wait for us on the ground in Minden for the return trip to Tucson. Details corroborated, he led us through the automatic doors and out to the tarmac, where fifty yards away, a Cessna Citation Sovereign stood waiting. The clear morning air was tainted with the sharp kerosene scent of jet fuel. On the way to our plane, I walked almost under the nose of Dick Peck's Gulfstream.

Lucianna was first to board our sparkling white jet. Four stairs extended from a clamshell-style door. She clutched the narrow silver railing with her left hand while bracing her holstered Glock with her right. Her thick black hair blew in the breeze.

Igor followed Lucianna up the stairs. The coattails of his splashy sports jacket billowed up around him, exposing the badge and gun that were clipped to his belt.

Horace was next. He wore a shoulder holster under his suit jacket and carried his overcoat folded over one arm. He raised his eyes to the jet's narrow doorway, gripped the handrail firmly, and mounted the steps like a condemned man climbing the gallows.

I followed Horace up the stairs and into the jet's snug interior, which was permeated with the rich, loamy smell of leather. The deep seats were tan and faced one another in two groupings of four, a layout known as double-club seating. The cabin's interior had accents of glossy brown burl wood. The light fixtures and cup holders were brushed gold. The headroom was limited; both Horace and I had to stoop our shoulders and duckwalk to our seats.

We had no sooner settled into our chairs—Lucianna and Igor were seated in the row behind us—when Rick closed and latched the door. He gave us a brief safety talk, drew our attention to the self-serve refreshment center at the front of the cabin, wished us a good trip, and turned toward the open cockpit.

"I'll tell you a few things about yourself, Captain," Horace said suddenly.

Taken by surprise, Rick turned.

"You attended the Naval Academy at Annapolis," Horace said. "You went to flight training in Pensacola. You flew that old submarine chaser, the P-3 Orion. You play golf, you smoke cigars, and you drink too much. You're unmarried, but you're actively looking for a wife."

Rick gaped open-mouthed at Horace. His copilot, listening from the second seat, traded incredulous stares with him.

"How did you—"

"I've learned to rapidly draw conclusions based on easily observable facts," Horace said. "I'll give you an example. You're wearing a Naval Academy class ring. You're a pilot, so it doesn't take a genius to conclude you were trained to fly in the Navy. All Navy pilots go through Pensacola."

"But the rest of that stuff?"

Horace waved this away. "Your right hand has a good tan, but your left is white as a ghost. That's because you wear a golf glove on your left hand."

"And the not-married-but-looking-for-a-wife part?"

"You have a trim, muscular physique and no wedding ring. Your keeping fit speaks to your pressing desire to attract a pretty wife."

"What about the cigars? The last time I smoked was last week in Nashville."

"Again, two easily observable facts. The underside of your pilot's cap, hanging on that hook behind your seat, has the initials RSR, same as the initials on the cigar case you left on the shelf above the refreshment center. That tells me the cigars belong to you."

Rick glanced at his copilot, quickly pocketed the cigar case, and turned back to Horace.

"And what makes you say I drink too much?"

"Your coffee cup is full of fizzy water. Your mouth is parched because you got hog-drunk last night, not realizing you'd be asked to fly at ten o'clock this morning."

Rick's jaw dropped.

With a twinkle in his eye, the copilot joined in the fun.

"And flying the P-3s?" he asked. "How'd you know about that?"

"That one was easy. I watched closely as the ground crew stocked this plane. Rick here didn't lift a finger to help. A leopard doesn't change his spots. Our good captain graduated flight school, but unlike most Navy pilots, flying jets was contrary to his ambition. He couldn't stand the thought of being assigned to an aircraft carrier, where no drinking is allowed and where there's no golf to be found, at times for thousands of miles in every direction. The P-3 is a prop plane that's based on land. There's always a drink to be had at the officer's club, and you're never far from a first tee."

"Wow," the copilot said.

"Holy cow," Rick said.

Horace nodded, satisfied. "Let's get this hell cart in the air, boys. And pray get us to Tahoe in one piece. To fly is to play a game of chicken with the gods."

As Rick climbed into the left seat, Horace turned and winked at Igor.

"Guess this old boy's still got it, eh, Detective?"

*   *   *

I slept in my comfortable chair, awash in the drone of the jet engines. At a sudden reduction in power and a corresponding drop in the plane's altitude, I awoke with a start. We were descending through the clouds, already on approach to the Minden-Tahoe Airport. We'd been in the air a few minutes short of two hours.

At ten thousand feet we broke through the weather. The Carson Valley below us was a patchwork of black lines and white fields. To the west, dark roiling clouds cut off the tops of the Sierra Nevada Mountains.

We landed with a sharp jolt, braked hard, and taxied to the apron, where a member of the ramp service crew directed our plane to a stop.

As the engines wound down, Rick opened the door and deployed the steps. I emerged from our comfortable cabin to a dark, bone-chilling day in northwestern Nevada. A sharp wind blew from the north.

Our rental, a white Cadillac Escalade, sat a few feet off the Citation's left wing, its engine already running. I stood with Rick at the bottom of the steps as the others emerged from the jet and made their way to the car.

Rick turned to me. "All set?"

"Thanks, Captain." I shook his hand. "You have to tell me. My boss—was he right about any of that stuff?"

"Total character assassination," Rick laughed. "I flew F-14s and F-18s. Had more than a thousand landings on six different carriers. But I do play golf and the cigars are mine—that much he got right!"

FORTY-THREE

I DROVE THE ESCALADE NORTH ON US-395 through a light rain. The flat fields were patchy with snow. A left turn at a traffic light outside Carson City, Nevada, took us onto US-50. A lone billboard for Dick Peck's Golden Mantle Casino trumpeted an upcoming appearance by Art Garfunkel. We began the steep climb up the grade to Lake Tahoe.

Igor, riding shotgun, turned and looked at Horace in the seat behind him.

"Chief, are you sure we shouldn't get that search warrant first?"

"We can't afford the time," Horace said. "Half the Thunderbird's directors are lawyers. I don't want to do this floor show in front of an audience."

Floor show?

Using the rearview mirror, I made a moment's eye contact with Horace. "I hope you're not asking these good people to fudge the limits of the law?"

Horace turned and stared out the window. I refocused my gaze on the road. The curves of the four-lane highway grew sharper as we entered the heavily wooded forest of the Carson Range. The spitting snow activated the Escalade's automatic windshield wipers.

"You need to concern yourself less with the law and more with driving," Horace said finally. "Even the snowplows are passing us."

As he said this a mammoth yellow snowplow from the Nevada Department of Transportation passed on our left, splashing the Escalade with a tidal wave of slush. Chunks of ice exploded against our windows, sounding as though we were being strafed with gunfire.

"Jack drives at a tortoise's pace," Horace said to Lucianna. "I don't know why we bothered chartering a jet. Odette will die of old age before we get a chance to question her."

Lucianna's eyes caught mine in the mirror.

"For the record, Chief Button isn't asking us to fudge anything," Lucianna said. "Actually, it's a decisive juncture in our investigation. If Ms. Garin's already at work, it's unlikely she was in Tucson last night. But if she arrives an hour behind us and can't adequately account for her whereabouts, it means we may be on to our murderer. The Chief's little sting operation is actually a brilliant plan."

I curbed my initial dark thoughts. "And what exactly is our plan?"

"You'd know if you hadn't gone out like a light the minute we got in the air," Horace said.

I turned to Igor and raised an eyebrow.

"The element of surprise," he said. "We're going to overwhelm her with all that we know."

"Chief Button will isolate her and gain her trust while the detective and I search the Lodge," Lucianna said. "If she wants to confess, we'll come in and read her her rights."

"Any chance Dick Peck called and warned her we're coming?" I asked.

"No," Horace said quickly. "Warning her would open him up to charges of hindering prosecution. I'm certain Wayne cautioned him strongly against it."

Igor turned again and faced Horace.

"You said her home address is in California?"

"The city of South Lake Tahoe. She lives on Raccoon Street, just across the state line from Harrah's. And, as it turns out, not far from the pickup location of the express delivery service."

Igor looked at Lucianna. "So for a warrant to search her house we'll need to go before a judge in what county?"

"El Dorado," she said.

"Should we split up and run parallel investigations? I can go for the warrant."

"No, Igor, I need every pair of hands at the Thunderbird Lodge," Horace said. "After that, as far as getting a search warrant is concerned, you two can do whatever you want. By then I'll have resigned as chief."

"Would you like me to plan a going-away banquet, sir?" Lucianna asked.

Horace wasn't one to pass up dinner parties in his honor, but he hesitated.

"Ask me later," he said. "I hate to be a sore loser, but if we don't have our killer in custody by sundown, I'll probably head into the teeth of the storm and start walking to Hillsborough."

Ten minutes later, through the thick pine forest and falling snow, we caught glimpses of the lake. I kept our Escalade tracking in the wet black ruts of the winding, two-lane road that traced the lake's shore. Horace professed to know the turn to Thunderbird Lodge, or at least its approximate whereabouts, but for a stretch of about a mile, he became disoriented. The gatehouse was set back from the road, and the accumulating snow cloaked all landmarks.

"That's it, Jack," Horace said suddenly, leaning forward and patting my shoulder. "That's the entrance!"

I slowed and made a tight left turn, leaving the highway, steering us onto freshly fallen snow, rising to the crest of a small hill.

The gate sat open. The gatehouse was unattended.

The road to the Lodge was a narrow ribbon of white that fell, rose, and fell again, cutting across the steep mountainside, winding around gargantuan granite boulders, curving between the trunks of old-growth Jeffrey pines for perhaps a half mile. We passed another outbuilding, rounded a hairpin turn, and came upon an imposing stone edifice with steep, gabled roofs and a panoramic view of Lake Tahoe.

Igor let out a whistle. "Quite the castle."

Horace pointed past the Main Lodge. "Keep going round the bend, Jack. We'll park down by the elephant house."

Igor turned to face Horace. "You're kidding—an elephant house?"

"Our boy Whittell once ran off with the circus," Horace said. "He packed this place with animals, including an Indian elephant named Mingo and an African lion named Bill. Dick Peck kept the cages in place. You'll see."

We passed a weather-beaten Subaru Outback parked at a stone wall. It was the only car we saw on the property. Horace directed me to drive through the small parking lot to a service road. He had me back the Escalade into a carport beneath an annex to the Lodge, where the full-size SUV would be hidden from view.

The numbing temperature, the robust fragrance of the pine forest, the snowflakes hitting our faces and alighting in our hair—our rapid segue to this lake in the High Sierras came as a shock to my system. I felt sorry for Lucianna. She was dressed for a day of administrative police work in Tucson, and the long sleeves of her shirt were her only protection against the elements, but she rebuffed our offers to take one of our jackets.

"Don't insult me," she said. "I was a Marine deployed to Afghanistan."

We followed Horace, stomping through powdery snow to the Main Lodge. Two imposing rock chimneys framed the high gabled entry, which had an iron door suitable for a castle. The door was unlocked.

"We'll remain silent from here on out," Horace said, then swung open the door and led us inside.

The great living room had the aura of a stage set. The floorboards and walls, all done in knotty pine, were a marvel. Notched rafters criss-crossed the steeply sloped ceiling, which mirrored the lodge's high gabled roof. An enormous wagon-wheel chandelier could have been stage dressing for *Annie Get Your Gun*. The second-story wraparound balcony, with its precipitous wooden staircases and cartoonishly wide knotty pine balusters, might as well have been a painted scenery flat. A stretched zebra skin hung from the balcony's railing.

Horace led us down a long, window-encased breezeway to a contemporary addition to the lodge. The heart of the added wing was an open, airy banquet room with a raked ceiling and tall windows looking out over the lake. In one massive windowless wall, the clean line of a rustic alder wainscoting was interrupted by a single door. Horace pushed open the door.

The black-haired woman working at the kitchen island wore a white chef's jacket. Above the island, a dozen or more gleaming saucepans hung from hooks. Behind her, the commercial gas range was stainless steel.

"Odette."

She was in her forties, somewhat thick around the middle, with a reddened face. Her mouth fell open and she stared at Horace.

"Mr. Button! You're supposed to be in Tucson." Her lively eyes skipped to Lucianna. She gave Lucianna's police uniform the once-over before she turned back to Horace. "Has this to do with Jean-Claude?"

"This is Captain Gomez and Detective Ivanovich. We've come to warn you. You're being stalked by a ruthless killer."

Odette looked acutely from Horace to Lucianna.

"The Chief's right," Lucianna said. "He could be here any minute."

"We must get you out of this kitchen," Horace said. "Take you into hiding—"

Odette glanced down at her bloody hands. She was using butcher's string to tie a tenderloin of beef. She looked up at Horace. "But I've got twenty-seven coming to dinner!"

"Odette, listen to me. The Chairman's Dinner can wait. This is a matter of life and death."

Odette went back to tying her roast. "I'm a simple cook. Who would want me dead?"

"I can't say. Our killer has yet to be unmasked."

"*C'est fou.* I'm not leaving—"

"You have no choice."

Odette's hands stopped working. She straightened up and eyed Horace warily.

"Mr. Button, is this an elaborate joke? Because I'm in no mood for pranks. I'm about to bury my husband, and I need to get my meat into the oven."

"Tell her, Lucianna."

Lucianna regarded Odette earnestly. "This is no joke, Ms. Garin. Your life is in imminent danger."

Odette put her hands on her hips and looked cheerlessly about the kitchen.

"*Mon Dieu*, all this food—"

"Never mind the food." Horace stepped around the kitchen island and offered Odette a clean chef's towel. "Here, wash your hands. We're wasting precious time."

Odette took the towel, threw it over a shoulder, went to the dish-washing station, and ran hot water from the pull-down spray faucet. As she worked her hands with soap and water, her face paled.

"Let me at least put this food away," she said, looking over her shoulder.

"No," Horace said, placing a firm hand on Odette's back, urging her toward the door. "The clock is ticking. Out we go!"

She shut off the water and began drying her hands. "And where do you propose I go?"

"While Captain Gomez and Detective Ivanovich wait for the killer," Horace said, "you and I will lock ourselves in the opium den."

Opium den?

I laughed out loud, but Horace silenced me with a cold-eyed stare.

FORTY-FOUR

I WAS LAST TO LEAVE THE KITCHEN. Horace led the way into the banquet room, with Lucianna and Igor on either side of Odette, boxing her in. Horace suddenly stopped and turned around to face Odette.

"You haven't the slightest idea why we're here, do you?"

Odette stared blankly at Horace. She glanced at each of us in turn, her gaze coming to rest on Igor's garish sports coat.

"Are you the entertainment?" she asked.

Horace touched Odette's shoulder and said to the rest of us, "Look at this guileless Parisian face. Not a clue. I could as well be asking her to scientifically notate Ethiopian basalt gas. It's as I suspected. She isn't our killer." He turned back to Odette. "What time do the caterers arrive?"

"Caterers?"

"The hired hands, the servers. What time are you expecting them?"

"They should be here around two."

Horace checked his watch. "A little more than an hour from now. If my theory's correct, our killer is only minutes away. Do you have an extra chef's coat?"

Odette thought a moment. She shook her head. "Not here at the Lodge, no."

"Then you must strip that one off and give it to Captain Gomez."

"*Vraiment?*" Odette looked with an expression of great affront from Lucianna to Horace. "This pretty one's going to take charge of my Chairman's Dinner?"

"Au contraire," Horace said. "She's going to role-play cheese to our rat, serve as bait to our killer, sit as duck to our huntsman."

"In that case she can have the jacket. I don't enjoy pushing my luck." With practiced fingers, Odette began undoing the black buttons of her coat. Beneath the jacket she wore a thin white T-shirt. Seeing she was braless, both Igor and I averted our gaze.

This made Odette sneer. "American men. Like Boy Scouts. So pathetically modest."

She handed the jacket to Lucianna. Her ponderous breasts sagged.

Horace shrugged off his overcoat and gave it to Odette. "Please. Take this."

Odette smiled. "Mr. Button. Ever the true gentleman." She looked me in the eye, raised her face haughtily, licked her lips, and took her time closing the lapels of the overcoat.

Horace was busy issuing instructions to Lucianna.

"Keep your back to the door at all times. Act as though you're working the stove. Have your service weapon ready. Jack, use that chair to prop this door open so Igor can keep her in view."

Lucianna donned the chef's coat, flipped her black hair over the collar, and stepped into the kitchen. I saw the genius in Horace's masquerade. Standing with her back to us on the other side of the kitchen island, Lucianna was a dead ringer for Odette.

"Igor, I want you over here," Horace said, crossing the big room to the stone fireplace, which protruded from the wall. Twin glass trophy cases, both filled with awards bestowed on the Lodge's legendary 55-foot wooden speedboat *Thunderbird*, framed the fireplace. Horace positioned Igor to the left of the fireplace, where he'd be concealed from anyone entering the room from the breezeway. "Stand here. Give our culprit every opportunity to play out his scheme but nab him when you must. Don't put Lucianna at risk."

Igor took his assigned position with good humor. "And who exactly are we expecting, Chief?"

"I have my theory. We'll know soon enough if I'm wrong. But for God's sake, don't shoot the caterers."

From the grand piano near the fireplace to the popcorn concession cart in the corner, from the foyer of the breezeway to the kitchen door,

Horace paced around the room, making sure Igor's hiding spot kept him hidden from view.

"Keep your phones at hand," he called to Lucianna and Igor. "Jack will be on lookout in the Main Lodge. He'll text you the moment anything happens."

*   *   *

The leaded glass windows opened on side hinges, like windows out of the fairy tale *Hansel and Gretel*. From this snug little den three stories up, with its whitewashed walls, pine-plank flooring, and simple fireplace, reached by climbing a spiral staircase from George Whittell's bedroom on the second floor, I was hidden among the ceiling rafters. I had a bird's-eye view of the great room and the front door.

Eventually, out of boredom, I took my cellphone and snapped a picture of my view—the crisscrossing Scandinavian beams, the wagon-wheel chandelier, the full tiger skin and taxidermied head strung above the front door—and sent it to Wanda.

"Perhaps witnessing His greatest fail ever," I texted. "Been sitting in this crazy place for over an hour, waiting."

A minute later, from Wanda: "Who does he think will come?"

My answer: "Our killer but won't say who. Half dozen potential suspects…"

Wanda's reply: "The butler did it in the library with a candlestick."

I answered: "Pierre! Hadn't occurred to me!"

Suddenly, two sounds raised my hackles: the soft squeak of a door opening and the creak of a loose floorboard. I went to the window.

The great room was empty.

I leaned out for a better look below, but whatever door had opened was beyond my view.

Horace and Odette had disappeared in that same direction.

Are they returning?

In the next instant, a hooded figure crossed the room. The muscular physique and long strides were those of a man. He stopped and turned. Beneath the black hoodie he wore the grisly green-and-yellow mask of a Day of the Dead skeleton. He scanned the room and vanished up the breezeway, in the direction of the kitchen.

Stunned, I grabbed my phone and tried to warn Lucianna and Igor. With quavering fingers I pecked out a one-word text message and hit *Send* as the autocorrect feature reformatted my heads-up *Coming* to *Congratulations.*

At that point my middle-linebacker instincts kicked in. I needed to cut off his escape route in the event of a reverse. Rushing down the spiral staircase, I took the staircase to the great room two steps at a time.

"Police! Drop your weapon!"

Igor's commands resonated from the banquet room.

"Oh, goddammit, don't make me chase you!"

Our villain was in full-speed retreat, coming at me down the breezeway.

I drew a bead on him and assumed form-tackle position: hips lowered, chest and chin up, hands shoulder-high and ready to rip.

He tore off his mask. I saw neither his face nor the gun in his hand, but the muzzle flashes were clearly visible. The quick *pop pop pop* of gunshots echoed through the cavernous room.

I dove over the back of a long sofa, turning it over, hitting the hardwood floor, my feet striking a side table, sending both it and an antique brass lamp crashing to the deck.

Time slowed. Shocked, winded, my ears ringing, I lay defenseless amid a tangle of broken furniture and sofa cushions.

A blurry figure with a gun loomed over me.

I'm a dead man.

"Are you hit?" Igor asked.

"Don't think so." My head cleared. I straightened my arms. I seemed to be intact.

Igor helped me to my feet, looked me up and down, and smiled. "Not much of a marksman, is he?"

Across the room, Lucianna, still wearing Odette's chef's coat, picked up the skeleton mask, gave it a glance, and cast it aside. She had her Glock trained on a wide knotty pine door beneath a staircase.

She motioned for Igor to open the door.

FORTY-FIVE

GUNS DRAWN, WORKING TOGETHER in a wordless ballet, Lucianna and Igor made their way down a creaky wooden staircase and into the servants' quarters, directly beneath the Main Lodge. I followed at a respectful distance. The low ceilings, tight spaces, and austere white walls were in stark contrast to the exotically decorated, open rooms above. A secretary's narrow bedroom, a cold, windowless bathroom, the butler's bedroom with lime green curtains and New England-style twin bed—these first rooms were quickly cleared, and we proceeded clockwise around the quarters, its footprint a perfect rectangle.

With Lucianna providing cover, Igor opened a hallway door, and we entered what felt like a ship's passageway. The colossal mechanical contraption with its pipes, gauges, and valves, I'd later learn, was an early version of an air-conditioning unit.

We made our way to the antique kitchen, a vintage gas stove and refrigerator along one wall, a long trough-style sink on the other. A marble-topped patisserie table served as the kitchen island. As with the air-conditioning room, there was nowhere here for a grown man to hide, and we moved on.

After clearing the laundry room, we all stared at the same closed door.

Using both hands in a combat grip, Lucianna trained her gun on the door and gave Igor a nod. He stood to the side of the doorframe with his back to the wall, twisted the brass handle, and pushed open the door, revealing the entrance to a medieval-looking stone tunnel.

Igor took the lead. We ventured slowly into the tunnel, which was lit by a series of bare lightbulbs hanging from the ceiling. The air was frigid and dry and smelled vaguely of clay. About eight feet tall at the highest point of its gentle arch, the tunnel was wide enough to accommodate an ore cart—we came upon tracks in the slate-covered floor.

It was slow going and terrifying—the flinty passageway turned slowly left and had few places in which to take cover, so there was no alternative to pressing ahead. We were perhaps fifty feet into the tunnel when we came across a shadowy room locked behind a metal lattice door. The room appeared to be a dungeon. Built into the stone walls were several padded seats.

Odette materialized on the other side of the door, giving us all a start. She wore Horace's big cashmere overcoat.

"He passed by maybe two or three minutes ago," Odette said, speaking in a low voice. "A shadow. He was headed towards the boathouse—that way." She motioned farther down the tunnel.

Lucianna and Igor continued their pursuit.

"Is Mr. Button in there?" I asked Odette. On a wall behind her, a firebox glowed red, illuminating the black silhouettes of twin devils reveling on the fireplace screen.

"He left a while ago. I don't know where he went."

"Are you locked in?"

"Not at all. The door latches from the inside."

"Good. Stay put. We'll come for you as soon as it's safe."

As I caught up to them, Lucianna was standing in a doorway, providing cover, while Igor cleared a stark concrete chamber with a deep pit in the ground. Heavy wooden beams and an old ladder lay on the floor of the unfinished indoor swimming pool, which was ankle-deep in water. Natural light streamed in from a glass-block wall. Igor shook his head. No suspect.

"Let's find this boathouse," Lucianna said. I could see her breath as she spoke.

We were approaching a fork in the tunnel when a gunshot rang out. The sound of the shot reverberated through the passageway, making it difficult to pinpoint its origin. It didn't seem to have been directed at us.

Crouching in place, we stared wide-eyed at one another.

"Overhead, do you think?" Igor asked.

"There," I said. A few yards away, in an alcove off the tunnel, was the base of a steel spiral staircase.

Igor looked at Lucianna, who nodded. Pistol up, he went to the alcove, took aim at the top of the staircase, and began to climb.

Lucianna motioned for me to go next.

She followed me up the staircase, continually turning and sweeping the tunnel below us with her gun barrel.

At the top of the staircase, the three of us gathered on a small landing facing a heavy black door. Lucianna pointed her Glock at the center of the door and nodded at Igor. He turned the handle and pulled the door open. With both hands on her weapon, looking fiercely resolute, Lucianna stepped through the doorway.

"Dear God, what is this place?" she said, barely above a whisper. She was standing in the shower stall of a small powder room. Stepping around a mustard-yellow sink and toilet, she moved to the next closed door, put her hand on the knob, and gestured at Igor to take the lead. She pulled open the door.

"Police!" Igor announced in a commanding voice, stepping through the doorway. The stone walls and hewn rafters of the spacious one-room cabin copied those of the Main Lodge. He quickly lowered his gun.

Horace sat alone at a seven-sided poker table before an out-of-use fireplace, his color high, his expression triumphant. His revolver lay on the table's soft green felt. A chair was upended.

Wayne Clark was slumped on the floor, lifeless and foaming at the mouth. He wore a dark hoodie and had a semi-automatic pistol in his gloved hand.

Lucianna's eyes were trained on Wayne's weapon.

"It's unloaded," Horace said. "I made him eject the magazine."

Lucianna looked at Igor. "All the same, let's get that thing out of his hand."

Igor used the side of his shoe to separate the pistol from Wayne's fingers. He gave the gun a shove with his toe, sending it skidding away from the body.

"Check his pockets," Horace said to Igor. "I believe you'll find a suicide note."

FORTY-SIX

"DID YOU SHOOT HIM?" I asked.

Horace luxuriated in his chair at the poker table, his big pink hands clasped and resting on his ample stomach. Across the room, standing beneath the gaze of a stuffed moose head, Lucianna was on the phone with the 911 operator. On the floor before me, Igor had Wayne lying faceup and was doing chest compressions, though it struck me as a half-hearted resuscitation effort on the detective's part. He wasn't counting out loud, and he took no part in rescue breathing.

"He swallowed a pill," Horace said. "He wanted me to shoot him. I wouldn't bite."

"But we heard a shot—"

"Mine. I fired into the rafters to get your attention." Horace nominally smiled. "We were having a nice little chat until his lips started turning blue and he hit the deck, finito."

I held up the suicide note. "How did you know about this?"

"The note and the pill were part of a death kit. He intended to catch Odette alone and give her a choice: sign the letter and take the pill or die of a gunshot wound to the head. Either way, he'd make it look like she'd committed suicide."

"Nice guy." I reread the note. It was printed on a sheet of white paper:

Jean-Claude is the love of my life, and I now join him in eternal sleep. May God forgive me for what I have done. La culpabilité, la culpabilité!

The note was unsigned.

I looked at Horace.

"*La culpabilité?*"

"French for *guilt.* Ironically, the letter's a suitable sayonara for our triggerman. He told me he considered killing the child—I presume he meant Florabelle—and was fully prepared to murder Odette. He'd already taken out Jean-Claude, and he was convinced he'd just shot you dead. He'd probably have bumped me off, too, only I had the drop on him. By the time I convinced him to sit with me at this table and confess to what he'd done, he was weeping like a baby and calling himself a monster. That's when he took the pill, which I presume was the fatal dose of fentanyl meant for Odette."

Horace was so masterfully dispassionate and matter-of-fact that it rubbed off on me. The adrenaline left my body, and suddenly I felt a great sense of calm and relief. It was the same reconciled, at-peace-with-the-world feeling I used to get walking off the football field after a hard-fought game.

"This guy's dead," Igor declared, standing and going through the motions of dusting himself off.

Wayne's eyes bugged hideously. The whitish bubbles from his gaping mouth streamed onto the stone floor.

Igor turned to Lucianna. "Tell the sheriff they'll need the coroner."

Horace tilted his head and peeked around the poker table as if curious about a drip of candle wax pooling on the floor. He studied Wayne's lifeless body a moment.

"The fentanyl was in the mint filling of the chocolate whoopie pies, if you're interested," he said to me. "He bought the drugs for cash from a casino rat in a back alley."

I shook my head. "The man was obviously on a mission."

With two people dead, and with Odette, Florabelle, and me being close calls, I tried to imagine a motive for Wayne's actions.

"Did he say why he did it?"

"I asked him that," Horace said. "His dying words were *Rebecca Flood.*"

"Who's Rebecca Flood?"

"I have no idea. Never heard the name before in my life. For all I know he was talking about Chef Jean-Claude... maybe trying to say,

'He baked the food.' It can be problematic—expressing yourself clearly when you're losing consciousness and gurgling blood."

"There's got to be some connection. An issue with work, maybe?"

"Can't say, but that reminds me. Can you get Dick Peck on the phone? I owe him the breaking news before it's hot off the press."

"Washoe County deputies are en route code three," Lucianna announced, crossing the room to join us, securing her phone in a nylon pouch on her gun belt between her pepper spray and handcuffs.

As I made the call to Dick Peck, Igor and Lucianna spoke with Horace.

"So Chief, how did you know this was your guy?" Igor asked.

"My first clue was his phony narrative about Chef Jean-Claude being a heroin addict. He was trying to throw us off the scent. Then he fed us the line about the Arizona Inn making a mistake in their room reservations. I immediately knew we'd been hornswoggled. The Arizona Inn doesn't make mistakes. I confirmed it in my call this morning to the reservation desk. They weren't overbooked last night and they never asked Dick and Wayne to check out."

"Dick Peck on the line," I said, passing my iPhone to Horace.

Horace took the phone in his hand but turned to Lucianna. "Lucianna, will you fetch Odette in the opium den and escort her back to the Main Lodge? I'm afraid she's freezing down there, and I want her settled and comfortable when I question her about Wayne Clark. You can assure her there will be no Chairman's Dinner tonight." Horace brought the phone to his ear. "Dick, are you there? I'm at the Thunderbird Lodge, calling from the Card House. Rotten news, I'm afraid."

*   *   *

By 2:30 p.m. the Washoe deputies had the Card House secured, and the coroner was on his way up from Reno. Wayne's body still lay on the floor.

"He acted alone. It sounded to me like he came by snowmobile and entered through the boathouse," Horace was saying to the patrol sergeant, who wore a green Tuffy uniform jacket and a fur-graced trapper hat. "I surmise you'll find his truck and trailer parked some-where around Sand Harbor. Now if you'll excuse me, Sergeant, while you and your boys attend to the body, I need to interview the intended victim."

In brisk wind and falling snow, Horace, Igor, and I left the Card House and walked a narrow, icy path back to the Main Lodge. Whitecaps elec-trified the gray waters of Lake Tahoe. Below us, the waves battered the granite rocks.

Igor strode alongside Horace. "Chief, the chartered jet and the drive up here—how did you calculate so precisely when the crime would occur?"

"A naked mole rat could see it coming, Detective. The staged suicide had to happen before two o'clock, when the caterers were scheduled to arrive."

"That's a lot of moving parts. How could you be sure we'd beat him to the punch?"

"I knew they were leaving Tucson at eleven. Dick Peck always flies in and out of Reno. We left first and we flew into Minden-Tahoe Airport, which is closer by about thirteen miles. That gave us the inside track by at least an hour."

"And how did you know today would be the day? I presume it wasn't just a lucky guess—"

"Certainly not. If you remember, I told Dick we'd execute the search warrant tomorrow at the earliest. That put Wayne in a box. The obvious way to short-circuit our investigation was to have Odette confess to the crime and kill herself before we got here. We'd conclude it was a murder-suicide committed by a jilted wife."

"And he'd get away with both murders unscathed."

"I had a hunch that when we arrived, we'd either be investigating a second homicide or preventing one. Thank God it was the latter."

We reached the Main Lodge. Horace opened the front door. In the serene warmth of the great room, we stomped the snow off our shoes. The wrecked furniture was scattered before us.

"And positioning yourself in the Card House," Igor said. "How'd you know to do that?"

"That was luck on my part. I knew that if things went south, he had two getaway routes: take the tunnel all the way to the boathouse, where it ends, or slip out using the Card House's secret staircase. I had a fifty-fifty chance and guessed right."

Igor smiled. "Maybe you should take your good luck over to Dick Peck's casino and put it all on double zero."

"Not on your life. I'm never setting foot in that place again." Horace walked toward the banquet room.

"And my number is four," he added.

*   *   *

"It breaks my heart seeing you cry," Horace said, passing Odette a handkerchief. "I didn't realize you and Wayne were close."

"Not so close," Odette said, wiping her tears. "Two souls in the winter of our lives, both adrift and solitary by choice."

She and Horace had sunk into a brown leather sofa in front of the banquet room's fireplace. Lucianna, Igor, and I had drawn up antique Windsor armchairs.

"Any idea why he might have wanted you dead?" Horace asked.

"You're asking me? You're the ones who seem to know everything. I have no idea. All this death happening at once—it's too much!"

Horace stayed quiet.

Odette's unfocused gaze found the Indian rug in front of the fireplace and remained there. She dabbed the handkerchief to her cheeks.

"Did you ever cook for him?" Horace asked gently.

Odette responded with a faint smile. "At times. If I knew he was working late, I might leave a dinner on his doorstep."

"He lived in Reno? Or up here at Tahoe?"

"Here at Tahoe. South Lake Tahoe. Not far from the office."

"Forgive me, but I must ask you. What was your relationship with Jean-Claude?"

The question roused Odette from her reverie. She stared at Horace. "He was still my husband."

"But you rarely saw him?"

"By accord."

"You knew he was seeing other women?"

"Again, by accord. I have this lodge. And he had a restaurant to run."

"Can you name any of his mistresses?"

"It wasn't my business to know who they were."

"And this didn't bother you?"

"We had an open relationship." Odette looked at Lucianna. "Is this a crime in America?"

"No ma'am, no crime at all," Lucianna said.

Horace disregarded Odette's professed indignation and gazed placidly at her.

"Did you ever make anything for a company called Wild Rosemary Catering?"

Odette looked angrily at Horace.

"Never. I have never even heard of this company."

Horace glanced at Igor. He turned back to Odette.

"Maple-glazed donut cookies, coconut macaroons, chocolate whoopie pies with mint filling—you've not recently made any of these things?"

Odette's face reddened. Her mouth opened a little, and she hesitated. She looked down at the floor and slowly brought her eyes up to Horace.

"You've always been fair to me, Mr. Button. I won't lie to you now."

"Please, go on."

"I made all of those things. Rather recently. I made them at Wayne's request."

"And with what understanding did you make them?"

Odette turned resolutely to Lucianna and Igor. She licked her lips.

"These were small desserts for the executive staff meetings," she said. "Nothing wrong or illegal. Things for Mr. Peck and his colleagues to enjoy—that's all."

For a long moment, Horace studied Odette's face.

"Does the name Rebecca Flood have any meaning to you?" he asked.

Odette considered this. She slowly shook her head.

"No. None whatsoever. Who might she be?"

FORTY-SEVEN

DICK PECK STOOD AT THE OPEN DOOR of the liquor cabinet.

"This is awful. Awful, awful, awful." He set out two highball glasses and reached into the bin of an under-cabinet ice maker. He struggled to pack the glasses with ice—renegade cubes slipped from his trembling hands and went skittering in all directions.

"Mr. Peck, can I take over for you?"

He took a step back and looked at me with gratitude. "Thank you, Jack. Two brandy sodas."

"Of course."

He'd brought the four of us—Horace, Lucianna, Igor, and me—up the stairs to the sales office, which was in the new annex above the gift shop. The large, open room had several desks. As Memorial Day approached, Dick said, the office was certain to become a hive of activity. In summer, the Thunderbird Lodge hosted any number of winemaker's dinners, weddings, family gatherings, and corporate events.

While I finished mixing the drinks, Dick stood there as if in a trance, looking desperately sad.

"I can't believe what's happened," he said.

"We're scratching our heads as to motive," Horace said. "Is there any insight you can give us, even if it's speculation?"

"I honestly have no idea."

I handed Dick the first brandy and soda.

"Thank you, Jack." He gave me a gloomy smile.

I passed the other drink to Horace. He held off taking a sip.

He scrutinized Dick.

"Do you recognize the name Rebecca Flood?"

Dick weighed the name and shook his head. "No, should I?"

"What about Bunny Lorillard? Is that a name you know?"

Dick's gaze sharpened. "Lorillard. I've heard of a Charles Lorillard. He develops hotels."

"Bunny's soon to be his ex-wife, lives in Tucson. Wayne had it in for her. Any idea why?"

Dick looked at Horace censoriously. "This is lunacy, Horace. It makes absolutely no sense."

"He lied to you about the Arizona Inn being overbooked. He had you move to the Saguaro Mesa to get inside the hotel's security perimeter. He bought the skeleton mask from the shop in the lobby."

"Wayne wouldn't have done these crazy things—not a chance!"

"He confessed. These were his dying words."

"He didn't say why?"

"We didn't get that far. The Grim Reaper had other ideas."

Dick shook his head. "My god, it's hardly imaginable."

"I'm guessing it was Wayne's suggestion that the two of you fly to Tucson and claim the body as quickly as possible."

Dick stared wide-eyed at Horace.

Horace's gaze met Dick's. "If I didn't know better, I'd say these were the actions of a hit man."

The insinuation made Dick bristle. "He was like a son to me, Horace. More than a son… a confidant and friend. After the trauma of Maggie's kidnapping, I chose Wayne to set up a personal-protection detail for my family. He managed it magnificently. He rose through the ranks to become my right-hand man. He devoted his life to this company, and I rewarded him in return. Believe me, I paid him too well to be a hit man."

The room fell silent as we all contemplated this. Horace at last took a sip of his brandy and soda. Outside the big windows, the snow appeared to be falling even harder.

"I owe you some living room furniture," Horace said to Dick. "It seems our gridiron star whiffed on his open-field tackle."

*   *   *

"If he wasn't a paid hit man, then his motive had to be personal vengeance," Horace said from the back seat.

"Unless he was Dick Peck's hit man," Igor said, turning to look at Horace. "Curious how everything keeps coming back to the Thunderbird Lodge."

"A slavish devotion to the boss who's given you everything," Lucianna said. "The need for vengeance comes from the top. If that's the case, the question is why."

We were finally free of the Washoe County Sheriff's interviews and paperwork and headed back to the Minden-Tahoe Airport. Darkness had fallen. The snowplows, with their bright lights and clattering tire chains, were busy clearing the highway.

"'She baked the food,'" Igor said. "Maybe that's what he was trying to tell you with his last breath, Chief. Maybe the cook knew too much."

"I could swear he said Rebecca Flood," Horace maintained. "What about this records system you have access to, Detective?"

"I was just thinking that." Igor took out his cellphone. "I'll call my boss and see if he can put a resource on it."

"Forget that," Horace said. "Who's your boss's boss's boss?"

"That would be Captain Zavala."

"I'll call her," Lucianna said. "I'll ask her to do a records check on any Rebecca Flood she can find."

"Tell her to get right on it," Horace said, "if she isn't too busy shrinking heads."

FORTY-EIGHT

AT 18,000 FEET WE BROKE THROUGH THE CLOUDS and into a clear, moonless evening. Our Cessna Citation Sovereign continued to climb at a steep angle, its muscular Pratt & Whitney engines buzzing behind us. In the seat across the aisle, Horace touched the switch to turn on his overhead reading lamp and shook open a copy of the day's *Wall Street Journal.*

"Chief," Igor said, sitting forward and straining against his seat belt. "I meant to ask you. What was that about Dick Peck's daughter being kidnapped?"

Horace put down the newspaper, hesitated, and turned to Igor.

"It's a true story... proof that money can be both a blessing and a curse. All Dick's life, despite his vast fortune, it's like he's had a dark cloud over his head."

Horace went on to tell the story of Maggie's kidnapping—the ruse about the lost dog, the ransom demand, the game of cat and mouse that played out at the then-abandoned Thunderbird Lodge. Having pursued Wayne Clark through these same tunnels, Igor and Lucianna listened with interest. They quickly discerned how the kidnappers were able to collect the money and usher Maggie from place to place without being seen.

"I hate kidnappers," Igor said. "Those animals need to be locked away for good."

The nose of our Citation dropped and the engines quieted to a background purr as we leveled off at 41,000 feet. The cockpit's instrument panels glowed blue and white. Rick and the copilot wore their aviation headsets. They looked straight ahead into the night.

"What ever became of Maggie?" I asked Horace.

"The subsequent years were a struggle, a long, slow climb out of a deep, dark hole. She floundered in school. She had few friends. The trauma of being kidnapped triggered a severe agoraphobia that required constant counseling and stints of psychiatric intervention. It broke Dick's heart. He blamed himself for her troubles—if only he'd been a more attentive father, a man not so devoted to building a fortune…"

"What ultimately became of her?" I asked.

"Well, fortune finally smiled on Maggie's life," Horace continued. "In all those hours alone in her bedroom, standing before a mirror, she developed a talent for twirling a baton. She came under the auspices of a certain Texas Methodist university, where she became a drum majorette. She thrived in that protected setting of raccoon coats, football pennants, and Cadillacs. By all accounts she was as beloved as her father was despised."

I smiled. "So it's a happy ending—"

"Not quite," Horace said. "It seems fate wasn't finished with Maggie Peck. One rainy afternoon—she might've been twenty—she was traveling in a university van with some other students, on their way to a band competition in Waco. The van was struck head-on by a drunk driver. Maggie and one other student didn't survive the accident."

"My gosh," I said. "That's a horrible story."

"One I don't relish telling. But it was a turning point in her father's life—at least that's what he'd have you believe. He says Maggie's death made him a kinder, more compassionate human being, that it was the catalyst for a personal transformation in the manner of the Dickens character Ebenezer Scrooge. He's been ramming it home ever since, showering bequests on children's charities, making apologies to every enemy he's ever wronged."

I scoffed at Horace for his cynical attitude. "You say that like it's a bad thing."

"I don't buy it for a minute. I see it as a shameless desire for public approval."

He again raised his copy of the *Wall Street Journal*. He quickly cast the first section aside and fixed his gaze on the Business & Finance section.

"Bottom line, Jack, he's a phony," Horace said, his nose buried in the newspaper. "You can put perfume on a skunk, but it's still a skunk."

I leaned on the armrest and looked at him across the aisle.

"What happened between the two of you?"

He folded the newspaper and put it aside. "What makes you think something happened?"

"The other day—he was practically prostrating himself to apologize."

"Was he?" Horace picked up a clear plastic cup full of bourbon and swirled it over the fold-down table. Bags of snacks were scattered before him—peanuts and pretzels and multi-grain crackers.

In the row behind us, Lucianna and Igor chatted amiably but in quiet voices. Occasionally, Lucianna's laughter rang through the dark cabin, brightening the mood like a flowering vine in a winter garden.

"That first day we met at Majestic Aviation, remember?"

"All right, I'll tell you. He said some unflattering things about me in the press. This was several years back." Horace put a handful of nuts in his mouth and chewed.

"What did he say?" I asked.

Horace frowned. "The worst kind of slander, I'll leave it at that."

I continued to stare—a useful ploy, I'd learned, when encouraging Horace to come out with a full story.

He gave me a quick look. "He called me Bacchus in morning coat and striped trousers, a Mr. Peanut with a top hat and monocle and a gold pocket watch that tells me it's always yesterday."

I bit my cheek to keep from laughing. "Dick Peck said that about you?"

"In the *San Francisco Chronicle*. Sunday edition."

"You two were enemies."

"It wasn't always that way." Horace lowered his head, brought the cup to his lips, and sipped. He swished the bourbon around in his mouth and swallowed. "Dick and I were once great friends. I considered him a man of discrimination and good taste, and in those days the Button brand was riding high. You may find it hard to believe, Jack, but for a number of years I was a sought-after pitchman. I had an agent. I endorsed several products, including a scotch whisky and a line of upscale men's clothing. Dick said he wanted to talk to me about a project—"

"He was looking for your endorsement—"

"I signed on as front man for his newest hotel-casino, the Golden Mantle at Lake Tahoe. He sold me on a sophisticated, high-end concept with the European panache and savoir faire of a Monte Carlo, which is why I was willing to attach my name to the whole ball of wax. There were permit and construction delays. The hotel finally opened in May of 1975—a grand opening of heroic proportions, by the way."

"So far, so good."

"One might think. The delays meant we opened our doors in the midst of the '75 recession, which hit Californians particularly hard and tanked Lake Tahoe real estate values. The timing couldn't have been worse. Dick was convinced his new hotel was headed for receivership, and he panicked. He hired a couple rip-off artists dressed in the suits and ties of respectable marketing consultants. They talked him into ditching the Monte Carlo sophistication for the barbarism of a family-friendly resort, complete with casual dining, casual attire, a Ferris wheel, and a water park. My contract with the Golden Mantle was summarily canceled. They gave as reasons that I was out of step with the times and conveyed a snob appeal most customers found off-putting. The contract was so lopsided in Dick Peck's favor that I had no legal recourse, other than to go home to Hillsborough and lick my wounds."

"And you hadn't spoken to him since?"

"For a time we battled it out in the press. I ran a series of editorials in *Sunshine Trails* magazine, saying basically that mendacious psychopaths were intent on turning South Lake Tahoe into another Coney Island, on making it a haven for mothers in stretch pants and screaming children with ice cream. That's when Dick came back with that line about Bacchus and Mr. Peanut."

"I can't help but feel sorry for the guy. He's clearly been blindsided by this latest turn of events."

"Don't let him hoodwink you, Jack. Like I say, once a skunk, always a skunk."

* * *

On the ground in Tucson, at half past eight, the desert air was crisp and cold. A new dynasty of private jets had taken center stage at Majestic Flight Support. They preened on the well-lit tarmac. Rick the pilot led us to the double doors of the lobby, where we said our goodbyes and thanked him for the trip.

Inside the lobby, which was otherwise deserted, Captain Zavala stood waiting for us, a flat clasp envelope in her delicate hands. The way her fierce eyes were trained on Horace told us she had a compelling reason for meeting our plane.

FORTY-NINE

HOLDING A TRAY OF PÂTÉ MAISON SPREAD on sourdough toast, Jane greeted us at the door. The lights in the observation lounge were low. The satellite radio played an instrumental version of "Bohemian Rhapsody."

"How was your trip, Uncle?"

"I'd call it a jack-in-the-box kind of trip," Horace said, reaching for an appetizer. "Full of surprises that pounce when you least expect them."

Next in line, Florabelle offered a platter of oysters Rockefeller. Horace stopped for one of these, too. The girls wore their new tea dresses.

Bunny, perched on a barstool, a flute of champagne in hand, slowly got to her feet.

"Did you show the scoundrel what for?"

"A wild-goose chase, I'm afraid. I'm resigning my commission. This police business is for the birds." Horace used a petite silver fork to take the oyster in a single bite. He put the empty shell back on Florabelle's tray.

"Rumor has it you were at Lake Tahoe. What on earth were you doing there?"

Horace turned to Bunny with a gleam in his eye. "Reports of a Bigfoot sighting. Proved to be false."

Pierre looked on skeptically from behind the bar.

"Is that why I'm not allowed to go home?" Bunny asked Horace. "Because Bigfoot's after me?"

"The dragon has been slain. That's all I can tell you for now, but I hope you'll stay for dinner and for the night."

"Of course, are you kidding?" Bunny raised her glass to Horace. "And I'm going to ask a favor, too."

"Oh?"

"I'd like to take the girls up to Tanque Verde Ranch for lunch tomorrow, show them the grounds and the horses. One last hurrah before you all leave town."

"Whatever you'd like, it's fine with me." Horace went to the bar. "Pierre, I'll have a highball of bourbon. All engines full. It's been a particularly vile and ugly day."

Wanda stepped out of the galley. She stared at me. Without saying a word, tears glistening in her eyes, she pulled me into the galley and gave me a firm hug. The smoky, candied aroma permeating the air was a rack of lamb roasting in the oven.

*   *   *

"Girls," Bunny said, "tell your uncle and Jack about your progress on the school reports."

Horace leaned forward and looked from Jane to Florabelle, a fork in one hand, a knife in the other. His tie was tucked firmly inside his shirt, and his broad white dinner napkin covered his midsection. The work of art on the china plate before him—the deep red wedges of lamb ribs with their swooping, upturned bones—typified Wanda's penchant for exploring shapes and heights in her food presentations. "You've made progress?"

"Well," Jane said, gathering her thoughts, sitting a bit taller, "we've got outlines for at least six pages—"

"Maybe even seven or eight," Florabelle declared, looking to her friend for affirmation.

Jane ignored her.

"And how did you do that?" Horace asked.

"They've been working hard all day," Bunny said.

Horace turned to Jane, his eyebrows raised.

Jane leaned toward her uncle. "Bunny—sorry, Mrs. Lorillard—gave us an idea how to organize our papers. We start with the need, and we list everything she does to help make things better."

"Give me an example."

"Undocumented immigrants crossing the desert—"

"They need water," Florabelle said, pushing in.

"So, church volunteers put out water stations," Jane said, "but the volunteers needed transportation. Mrs. Lorillard bought them matching four-wheel-drive pickups, so now they can put out more water and set up more stations."

"And less people will die," Florabelle said.

"Then there's the kids with horrible burns," Jane said.

"She built them a summer camp in the mountains," Florabelle said.

"And a shelter for abused women and children—"

"—she bought a house and donated it to charity."

"And there's all the work Los Picadores does for kids that have problems."

"Seven pages, easy." Florabelle crossed her arms and turned to Jane. "Maybe more."

Horace smiled at Bunny. "I feel as though I'm having dinner with Mother Teresa."

"Stop, all of you," Bunny said, taking up a goblet of red wine. "You're making me blush."

Thirty minutes later, after we had finished the lamb, au gratin potatoes, Parker House rolls, and boiled green beans, Wanda sent out dessert.

"The girls made the vanilla ice cream by hand," Pierre said, bringing bowls of bananas Foster two at a time to the dinner table.

"Wanda sort of helped," Florabelle said. "Like, she did most of the crank turning." She tracked each bowl as it came to the table.

Jane frowned at her friend. "She wasn't even there. God. Why would you say that?"

Florabelle's face reddened and she stared at the floor.

"It looks wickedly sumptuous," Bunny said. "Why should I go home? I may never leave the *Pioneer Mother*." She smiled at Horace.

Horace sat stone-faced. He swirled a snifter of Armagnac and looked on distantly as Pierre served the last of the desserts. Horace drank Armagnac only when he was troubled. He was already on his second glass.

I turned to Jane. "Speaking of leaving, is the Sunset Limited running on schedule?"

Jane had scooped a spoonful of ice cream. "I just checked before dinner. It left Houston on time."

Horace looked over his shoulder toward the corner of the bar. Wanda was standing there, a hand cupped around a glass of red wine. She was without her white cooking apron and had shaken out her hair.

"Accolades to the chef!" Horace said.

We followed his lead in giving Wanda an enthusiastic round of applause. I stood, gave her a quick kiss, and held a chair as she joined us at the table.

"You've outdone yourself again, milady." Horace lifted his snifter of Armagnac. "To the chef!"

Everyone toasted Wanda.

She smiled, shrugged off the compliments, and drank her wine.

Horace continued to extol the lamb.

"*Ummmm…. ummmmm….*" Pursed lips, a hand flapping in front of her face, clearly in a state of panic but unable to speak, Jane drew attention to herself.

"I think she has something in her mouth," Florabelle said, looking at Jane. "She's afraid to swallow."

Wanda turned sharply. "Is that true?"

Jane nodded.

"Can you spit it out?"

"*Ummm…*" Jane glanced at Bunny and Horace.

Wanda held out her napkin. "It's okay, Jane. Spit it out."

Jane leaned forward and opened her mouth. A shifting, fluid mass of vanilla ice cream plopped onto the white linen napkin.

"There's something hard in it," Jane said, poking at the glob with her spoon. "Look."

The tip of the spoon surfaced a piece of white gold jewelry. It was a diamond engagement ring.

"My ring!" Wanda said.

"Oh my gosh!" Florabelle sat up and grasped Jane by the shoulder. "Is there another one? You should check."

"Let me see." Jane dipped the spoon into her dessert bowl and started probing around the caramelized bananas and ice cream.

We all looked on in stunned disbelief.

"Here's another one!" cried Jane, scooping out a similar ring.

"That's my wedding ring!" Wanda said, appearing flabbergasted at her turn of good fortune.

With narrowed eyes, Horace regarded the rings and fixed me with his dubious gaze. He turned to Wanda.

"Your rings—they were missing?"

"Since last Wednesday."

"When we were making ice cream," Florabelle said, her wide eyes going obviously around the room. "They must have fallen into the canister with the recipe mix. And Pierre scooped them out when he put the bananas Foster in the bowls."

Pierre looked on, poker-faced.

"Holy cow," Wanda said. "I feel like the luckiest girl in the world."

"You're quite right about that, my dear." Bunny glanced from me to Horace, seeming a bit disconcerted by this highly improbable series of events.

FIFTY

"ANYTHING ELSE I CAN GET YOU?" Pierre asked as midnight approached.

Horace stayed silent. Perhaps the Armagnac was taking its toll. He finally lifted his gaze.

"No, thank you, Pierre. Go to bed. Jack can look after the bar."

Bunny had been nursing a Bénédictine and Brandy for the better part of an hour. Wanda had gone for a shower. Jane and Florabelle were who knows where—they'd said their goodnights and gone up to the *Alaska*, presumably to sleep. Now, at last, Pierre had been dismissed for the night. The galley was dark. The lights over the dining table had been extinguished. Horace, Bunny, and I sat in the intimate grouping of parlor chairs, alone in our thoughts, holding fast to our drinks. I sipped cognac. Bunny was turned away.

"Wayne Clark committed suicide today," Horace said, breaking the silence.

Aghast, Bunny looked up, her eyes locked on Horace's face.

"He was Florabelle's drippy skeleton, coming to finish you off."

Bunny pressed her eyes tightly shut. She sat so long without moving I thought she'd fallen asleep.

She opened her eyes, suddenly, and stared at Horace. "Should I be worried?"

Horace considered the question. "No, your secret is safe. You're among friends here."

Secret? I looked at him suspiciously.

"Is this the reassurance of my close friend or of the chief of police?" Bunny asked.

"The Washoe County Sheriff will ascribe Wayne's death to a murder-suicide, perhaps the fallout of a lovers' spat, which Odette will deny."

"And what about our Tucson police detective?"

"He won't know what to do with this, either. He's overworked. Every day brings a new haul of bodies, a new surge of mayhem and suspects."

"So I'm simply to go about my business as if nothing happened?"

"You've done more good for the world than any ten people I could name put together. Tonight's sales job at dinner was unnecessary."

Bunny gazed out one of the black picture windows. The railroad yard was still.

"I've spent most of my life atoning for my sins," she said, her eyes not leaving the window. "You're just now figuring that out."

Horace looked at her for a long minute. "The property caretaker, was he one of your sins?"

Bunny brought a hand to her necklace and wrapped her fingers around the diamond pendant. "I knew nothing about that. I try not to think about it. Just as I try not to think about Jean-Claude."

Horace eyed Bunny intently.

"Tomorrow when you go to the Tanque Verde Ranch, I'd like you to take Jack with you."

Bunny weighed this a moment. She gave me a cold smile, then turned back to Horace.

"You don't trust me with the girls?"

"Of course I trust you. You must understand. In the air—all this villainy and savagery—I want Jack there for my own peace of mind."

*   *   *

"Help me better understand," I said. "What were you and Mrs. Lorillard talking about?"

Horace and I were the last ones standing—or, more precisely, sitting back in our parlor chairs, having a final drink before I pulled the shades and snuffed the few remaining lights. I hardly felt the cognac;

I continued riding high on the adrenaline rush of dodging bullets. Horace was smoking a cigar.

"I'll tell you a story," he said. "This involves a young girl. Her name was Rebecca. Her dreams were bigger than the one-hat town in which she was raised—I imagine all those Central Valley apple-knockers called her *Becky*. When she reached the age of twenty-one, Becky moved to Lake Tahoe and landed a job as a cigarette girl at Dick Peck's Golden Mantle Casino. The South Lake Tahoe police got a taste of her ambition and enterprise; she was twice arrested for prostitution but never charged. She was also picked up for questioning in the kidnapping of Maggie Peck."

"Wait, you're not talking about—"

"I am. It's all detailed in Captain Zavala's dossier." Horace paused to dispose of a long cigar ash. "Our girl Becky—Rebecca Anne Flood was her full name—married Charles Lorillard at the First Presbyterian Church of Santa Fe, New Mexico, in the spring of 1985. By that time, of course, she'd dropped the name Becky and was known by the alias *Bunny*."

"Mrs. Bunny Lorillard."

"I kept asking myself two questions: first, why would Bunny forsake Jean-Claude as a common drug addict when it clearly wasn't the case?"

"She knew I'd tell you. She was trying to throw us off the scent, like Wayne."

Horace nodded. "And second, why did Wayne Clark so desperately want her dead—someone he presumably didn't even know?"

"He *did* know her. He and Bunny were Maggie's kidnappers—"

"It was an inside job—the hotshot security pro and the comely cigarette girl, looking to hit the jackpot. The caretaker at the Thunderbird Lodge had to be in on it, too. Soon after the kidnapping he was found dead in the servants' quarters. It was ruled a suicide by hanging. I believe that's one the coroner missed."

"You think Wayne got to him?"

"I have no doubt. Staging a suicide was his countermove whenever things came to a head, to wit Odette this afternoon, alone and cooking at the Lodge." Horace sucked on his cigar and blew smoke. "The Black

Camel was standing in her driveway, and she had not a clue."

I nodded, but there was still the ultimate question. I turned to Horace. "So, what changed? Why did this all bubble up now?"

A cloud of smoke hung in the air, shrouding Horace's face.

"The divorce. Charlie has platoons of lawyers working to protect his interests. The prenup was ironclad. He was leaving Bunny destitute, and she panicked. She turned to Wayne."

"Blackmail," I said.

"I'd call it harvesting an income stream from an old business partner, a partner who built an elite life and gained significant wealth from a man he once wronged."

"In other words, you're whitewashing Bunny's crimes—past and present."

"Am I?" Horace took another puff on his cigar.

"If you condone breaking the law out of loyalty to a friend, you undermine the very fabric of society. You should think carefully about this, Mr. Button. You're still the chief of police. You need to do the right thing."

Horace's expression turned gloomy. "I've begun to miss the magazine. I miss the parties, the easy decisions."

"Then resign."

"I intend to, tomorrow."

"But first go to Igor and tell him everything you know."

The look of anguish and dread on Horace's face transformed, suddenly, into humor. There was a glint in his eye.

"Our good detective and Lucianna are infatuated with each other, did you notice?"

"No."

"It's why he didn't stay for dinner. He was doubling back to her place for margaritas and *pollo en mole negro*. They made plans sotto voce on the plane."

"Hope she likes squirrels."

Horace smiled. "I like to tell myself they'll have a long and happy life together, but I'm admittedly a romantic."

"Will you at least meet with him before you resign?"

"Out of the question, Jack."

"Give me one good reason."

"I'll give you two. First, it would be a waste of the detective's time. He has better things to do. And second, the required course of investigation would needlessly ruffle Tucson's most aristocratic feathers. What's the point in subjecting a woman of Bunny's status to the tribulation of a criminal investigation? It's a fact and everyone in the city of Tucson knows it: lock up Bunny Lorillard and a lot of poor people will suffer."

* * *

I slipped into our darkened stateroom and latched the door. I went to the closet and began to undress.

Wanda stirred. In the air was a trace of her vanilla body lotion.

"Hey."

"Sorry, I was trying not to wake you." I turned in the direction of her voice. The room was pitch-black.

"What time is it?"

"Not sure. Close to one, I imagine."

"I tried to wait up. Guess I fell asleep."

"It's a nuclear bomb, Wanda. Mr. Button solved the crime, and you're not going to believe what's behind this whole mess."

"Yeah? Come tell me in bed."

"Hey, what was that thing tonight with Jane and the rings?"

"She's a good little actress, don't you think?"

"It seemed ridiculously staged—"

"She and Florabelle came up with the plan. Pierre and I figured, what could it hurt? I about freaked, though, when she put that bite of ice cream in her mouth."

"Where'd you find the rings?"

"Jane found them. In Florabelle's suitcase during the sleepover at Mrs. Lorillard's. Something about helping her change clothes…"

"So the little she-devil had them all along."

"She was mad at you after the flap about Disneyland. She came back here looking for something to steal—"

"Jesus." I felt for the edge of the bed.

"She was mortified to think you and Mr. Button and Mrs. Lorillard would know she took the rings. She begged Jane not to tell, but Jane came to me anyway. Believe me, there were a lot of tears on this train today. Finally, to patch things up and make peace, they hatched the plan to find the rings in a dessert. They asked me to make bananas Foster…"

The low rumble of a passing locomotive thrummed through my bones and caused the walls to shudder. I felt for the top sheet and pulled it away.

"So the rings are back with their proper owner?"

"Right here on my finger, Majordomo. See? I'm holding up my hand. They're the only things I've got on."

FIFTY-ONE

TRAIN DAYS ARE SPECIAL. The yen to be on the move again, the satisfaction of a big breakfast, the stowing and securing of breakable things, the preoccupation with stocking the railroad cars and taking on water, and finally, when the train is near, making the switchover to generator power.

The westbound Sunset Limited was scheduled to arrive in Tucson at 6:45 p.m., but there was always a capriciousness to train times. A given train could be twenty minutes early one day and seven hours late the next. The Limited's orders in Tucson this evening included plucking our two private railroad cars from the Union Pacific yard and moving a mile or two up the tracks to take on fuel and passengers at the Amtrak depot downtown.

It was my after-breakfast task to return the old parade car to police headquarters and pick up the Escalade—a signal that Horace's term as chief of police was coming to an end.

I parked the Ford Custom on South Stone Avenue in front of the police building, near the space where we'd first found it. Locking this restored relic for the last time gave me an unexpectedly poignant moment—I'd grown fond of the old jalopy. I crossed the sidewalk, climbed the steps, and took the walkway to the building's entrance.

"Jack Marshall," I said to the angled window of smoked green glass. "I'm supposed to leave these car keys for Sergeant Jimenez." I showed the keys to the window.

"Are you armed?" a disembodied male voice asked through the

speaker.

The question made me laugh. "No!"

"You can come in."

There was a buzzing at the doors. I entered, passed through the metal detector, and went to the reception desk. An older, heavyset uniformed officer—one of several officers working the lobby bullpen—was seated behind the desk. He had his head down, and he was shuffling papers.

"I need to leave these keys for Sergeant Jimenez," I said.

The cop stopped shuffling. He peered at me over his reading glasses and gave me a look that said, *Do I care?*

"He's expecting them," I added.

The cop eyeballed me and the keys as if I were a vagrant offering a bite of my sandwich. He turned back to his papers.

"I'll let him know," he said.

I set the keys in a heap on the counter. I stood there, waiting for the cop to make eye contact again. He finally looked up.

"You need to talk to him?" he asked.

"No, but can you tell me if Detective Ivanovich is in?"

"Detective Ivanovich. I'll check. Name?"

"Jack Marshall."

The officer reached for a phone, put the receiver to his ear, and touched a few buttons.

"Guy here looking for Ivanovich," he said into the receiver, scrutinizing me suspiciously. "Uh-huh... Okay, thanks." He hung up the phone. "Detective Ivanovich hasn't come in yet this morning."

I pictured Igor in a woman's pink robe, having tea with Lucianna in a backyard garden. It made me smile.

"That's a real laugh riot, is it?" the cop said.

"What about Captain Zavala?" I asked. "Is she in?"

*   *   *

The Tanque Verde Ranch, a sprawling hacienda-style guest ranch and spa, is situated in the foothills of the Rincon Mountains, on the perimeter of Saguaro National Park, in the elevated horse country where East Speedway Boulevard narrows to a pair of sand-strewn lanes, makes a hairpin left, and ends in a gravel parking lot.

Bunny had made a 12:15 lunch reservation for us in the cavernous dining room. She was characteristically animated and chipper in Jane's or Florabelle's direct line of sight, but in the course of the long, leisurely meal—the girls kept going back to the buffet to load up on sweets—I caught glimpses of our hostess looking broody.

After lunch, we strolled the tree-lined property. The large, resort-style swimming pool made Jane's and Florabelle's eyes pop. We passed the pickleball courts and the freestanding brick-and-adobe building that was the Dog House Saloon. Eventually we returned to the front of the ranch and its lush lawn, which faced an enormous labyrinth of corrals teeming with saddle horses. Bunny and I settled on a bench in the shade while the girls balanced on a railing and marveled at the sight of all the horses.

"I suppose this trip is going to inspire your next book," Bunny said, her gaze fixed on Jane and Florabelle.

"Depends on the ending."

Bunny turned to me. "I'd like to tell you my side of the story."

"I'd like to hear it."

She was silent a minute, staring at the girls. They held out open hands to the horses.

"In my early twenties I came into some money. I decided to take a few months off. I thought I'd try the Rockies. The Broadmoor in Colorado Springs—do you know it?"

"Of course."

"I checked in for three months, starting in June. Can you fathom that, this silly girl spending a small fortune at a five-star hotel? Every day at the pool, every night in the bars and restaurants. It's where I met Charles. He showed up at the pool one afternoon. I was looking for a knight in shining armor, and he was looking for a party." She glanced at me and smiled wryly. "Guess we both got what we wanted."

"What about Wayne Clark?"

Bunny turned her eyes back to the horses. "I can't say I'm sorry he's gone."

I smiled. "I'm with you there."

"Always on the make—that was Wayne. He ingratiated himself early to Dick Peck, rode his coattails on investments … real estate, venture capital, high-tech IPOs. Wayne convinced me not to put my money in the bank. I left it all with him. He paid me in debit cards—they came in the mail, fifty and a hundred dollars at a time. The concierge at the Broadmoor just shook his head. He'd never seen a guest get so much mail, much less settle her account always with debit cards. Wayne claimed it was a loophole in the Nevada banking laws. If you took debit cards, you didn't have to pay income taxes—"

"That can't be right."

Bunny looked at me askance, her lips slightly parted. "You don't think so?"

"Sounds to me like a scam. Sounds like money laundering."

"That's exactly what Charles thought. When he found out about the cards, he forbade me taking any more, but by that time we were married, and the money didn't really matter. Charles was richer than Midas, even in those days."

"So fast-forward to the divorce…"

"Charles put me on the street without a *sou*. Suddenly I was dirt poor, flat broke. I thought of Wayne and all that money I hadn't touched for more than thirty years. Can you imagine how much he must've been sitting on, money that was rightfully mine?"

"Was he sending you account statements, tax forms, anything?"

"Nothing. He was shocked to hear from me after so many years."

"How much was there?"

"I have no idea. Hundreds of thousands of dollars, maybe more. Enough that he was willing to kill for it. We traded vile words. I threatened him, he threatened me. That morning when you and Horace came to tell me that Jean-Claude had been murdered, I knew it was Wayne sending a message. He'd figured out by then Jean-Claude and I were together."

"You said you threatened him. How did you threaten him?"

"Oh, things anyone might say in the heat of the moment. There's no point getting into that, really. Like I said, I'm not sorry he's gone."

She turned and gazed at the stables.

I stared at her profile. "So how does the story end?"

She hesitated. "I may have to go back to the Broadmoor and sit beside the pool again." She looked over and smiled. "What about Dick Peck? Is he married, do we know?"

*   *   *

Bunny and I walked over to the corral.

"Time to go, girls," I said.

"Jack, look," Jane said, taking a stiff-legged stance on the railing, pointing into the paddock. "We need to come back here. I want to ride that Appaloosa!"

"I'm sure we'll be back someday."

"I'd name him Jacy. He looks like a Jacy." Jane turned from the Appaloosa to a copper-red quarter horse. "Florabelle, what would you name your quarter horse?"

"I don't know."

"Maybe Dakota."

"No, not Dakota!" Florabelle loosened her grip on the railing and hopped down from the fence. Her high-top Vans hit the dirt hard, producing two little mushroom clouds of fine dust. Jane looked down at her friend and back at the quarter horse.

"You're right. He seems more like an Apache or a Cheyenne."

"Who cares about the stupid horse?"

"But Florabelle, if you could have him and name him anything you wanted, what would it be?"

Florabelle's face reddened. She lifted her shoulders and brought her hands over her eyes. "Stop asking me these stupid questions. Just please stop!" She choked back tears.

Jane looked at me and shrugged.

Bunny hurried to Florabelle's side. "My darling, what's the matter?"

With the heels of her hands, Florabelle wiped the tears from her cheeks.

"I'm never gonna get to come back here again. I'll never get to ride a horse, ever!"

Bunny put an arm around the girl's shoulders.

"Oh, my beautiful flower, of course you will!"

"This has been the best trip of my life, and now it's almost over—"

"You come back anytime you want. I'll always be here, okay?" Bunny walked with Florabelle out to the parking lot.

I led the way to the Escalade. The cloudless sky and scorching sun struck me as snake weather. As I walked, I scanned the ground for rattlers.

I had the driver's door open and was about to unlock the doors for the others when a black-and-white Tucson Police SUV rolled up behind us and came to a stop.

"Mrs. Lorillard, may we have a moment of your time?" Captain Zavala asked, climbing out of the driver's seat. Emerging from the passenger side was Igor. They squared off with Bunny. From underneath the cover of Bunny's arm, Florabelle gaped open-mouthed at Captain Zavala, who looked menacing in her uniform and Ray-Ban Aviator sunglasses.

At first Bunny stared indignantly at Igor, and then she turned to Captain Zavala.

"Have we met?"

"Yes, Mrs. Lorillard, at last year's jail-and-bail," Captain Zavala said. "We met in passing."

"Captain Zavala thought we'd do this together," Igor said. "We were hoping to catch up with you."

"Why now, Detective? What exactly do you want from me?"

"A few minutes of your time. We'd like to clear up some details about your intruder the other night."

"You're making a mountain out of a molehill. A harmless prowler is all it was—"

"Nevertheless, we'd like you to come downtown."

The color drained from Bunny's face. She stared at Igor.

Captain Zavala broke the icy standoff.

"I assure you, Mrs. Lorillard, this department has the utmost respect for your time. Your cooperation is purely voluntary."

Bunny looked quickly from the captain to Igor.

"Any other time and I'd be happy to oblige, but Jack and the girls were about to give me a ride home."

"We can do that, Mrs. Lorillard," Igor said. "We'll get you home."

The color rose in Bunny's cheeks. She turned away from the detective, lifted her chin slightly, and affected a brave smile.

"Very well, then. Let me just say goodbye to the girls."

"I'll get your bag," I said.

I retrieved her shoulder bag from the Escalade and gave it to Igor, who set it on the police cruiser's back seat. He held the door open, waiting for Bunny.

The farewell between Bunny and the girls was a tearful affair.

"Please don't cry, girls," Bunny said. "I'll see you again, I promise."

She saved the final hug for me.

"You son of a bitch," she hissed in my ear. "You told them everything."

FIFTY-TWO

"SHE SAID THAT TO YOU?" Wanda reached into the closet and pulled out a white chef's jacket, which was sheathed in a clear plastic dry cleaning bag—her last clean coat for this trip.

"She got it wrong, Wanda. I told Captain Zavala where we were having lunch. That's all."

"So the police suddenly showed up and put her under arrest?" Wanda stripped off the plastic.

"Not under arrest. Took her downtown for questioning. But Igor's a smart guy. He'll figure this out." I was lying on my back on our bed, looking up at the ceiling. It was too late to take a nap. The train was coming early.

"What did you tell the girls?"

"Absolutely nothing. They still think it was about the masked intruder."

Wanda donned the jacket and stepped in front of the mirror. "And you're saying it wasn't?"

I lifted my head and looked at my wife. "It's about blackmail, Wanda. Wayne Clark was being blackmailed by Mrs. Lorillard. She threatened to go to Dick Peck with the truth. It would have destroyed Wayne's life and everything he'd worked for."

Wanda stopped buttoning her coat and stared at me coldly. "This worries me, Jack. You snitched on Mrs. Lorillard?"

"Snitched?"

"You know what I mean. If Mr. Button was determined to protect her, and he finds out you gave her up to the police, he'll have your head. He'll probably throw us both off this train and give us the ax."

"Me, not you."

"Wherever you go, I go. I'm your wife, remember?" Wanda stood sideways and checked her image in the mirror. She turned to me with a start. "Oh, God, what if we lose Jane over this?"

*   *   *

It was a writing posture I knew well, the yellow legal pad balanced on a knee, the rippled brow, as if concentrating on laying an exceptional egg. Horace had spent the afternoon locked in his stateroom, first napping and then drafting in longhand his monthly Letter from the Editor column for *Sunshine Trails* magazine. Now he sat working in his favorite parlor chair in the *Pioneer Mother*'s observation lounge, which, for the moment, we had to ourselves.

"Getting back to your day job?" I asked.

He looked at me. On the side table nearest his chair, beneath an arrangement of fresh flowers, a rocks glass full of bourbon awaited his attention.

"Our adventure in Old Pueblo is about to be one for the ages, Jack. Another twenty minutes of fueling, I'm guessing, and we'll be on our way."

The Sunset Limited, with the *Alaska* and the *Pioneer Mother* bringing up the rear, had arrived at Tucson's Amtrak depot five minutes ahead of schedule, in twilight, at 6:40 p.m. Since then, darkness had fallen, Pierre had set the dining table for four, and Wanda had started dinner. Schubert's Symphony No. 9 played on the satellite radio.

I indicated the parlor chair beside Horace's. "May I?"

"Please."

I sat. Horace had taught me the straightforward approach is always best, particularly when the news is bad. I took my time framing a judicious mea culpa. It felt like my family was on the line.

"The other night, you said dependability and loyalty were the two breasts that feed a friendship. I'm afraid I haven't been very loyal."

Horace shot me a stern look.

"Earlier today," I continued, "at police headquarters, I went looking for Igor. I found Captain Zavala instead. I told her if she was interested, the girls and I were having lunch with Mrs. Lorillard. I told her where she could find us."

Horace lifted his eyebrows but said nothing.

"After lunch," I continued, "as we were leaving the Tanque Verde Ranch, Igor and Captain Zavala showed up. They took Mrs. Lorillard in for questioning. I didn't want you hearing this from anyone but me."

Horace stared.

"Serving as Jane's fiduciary," I went on, "voting the Trust's shares of stock in *Sunshine Trails*, has been my greatest honor. It's because of you I have Wanda and Jane in my life. If you ask for my resignation, I understand completely. But I'd like the chance to explain."

Horace's expression remained impassive.

"See, it's my view," I said, "that no one's above the law—"

"You have a fatal character fault," Horace interrupted.

"Excuse me?"

"You're too principled. It's your Achilles' heel." The amused expression behind his steepled hands, the playful gleam in his eye—he seemed to be poking fun at me. "Your indifference to loyalty, all your harangues about law and order and my duty as chief—quite frankly, you remind me of Jane's mother. She was a tub-thumping moralist nut, too, but then a Nevada cattle rancher probably isn't too different from a varsity man with a West Texas upbringing."

The relief on my face must have been apparent.

"Don't worry, Jack. I might fire *you*," he said, "but I'd never fire my chef. You and Wanda are a package deal. By the way, when I hosted Kimberly and Lucianna for lunch this afternoon, Wanda's coquilles Saint-Jacques was the pink of perfection: a crust of bread crumbs and Gruyère, served in a beurre blanc sauce and accompanied by a lemon-asparagus risotto…" Horace looked off dreamily. He turned and met my gaze. "The lunch was pleasant, but with two uniformed policewomen holding that resignation letter over my head, I felt like Shigemitsu on the battleship *Missouri*, getting pressure from MacArthur to sign the

Instrument of Surrender. I refused to do it until we talked about Bunny."

"You talked about Mrs. Lorillard with Kimberly and Lucianna?"

"I did, Jack. Don't beat yourself up. I wanted to tackle the matter while I was still chief. We all agreed the statute of limitations on kidnapping in the state of Nevada has long since expired. There's nothing for anyone to charge there. As for the conjecture about blackmail, well, Wayne Clark is dead by his own hand, and there's no evidence any secret was exposed or that property changed ownership, cash or otherwise. Kimberly and Lucianna concurred. No prosecutor worth his salt would touch this one."

I started to speak but he held up a hand.

"My duty of loyalty isn't to Bunny alone," he continued. "I have the same duty to Odette and to Dick Peck. They both deserve justice for their loved ones—and to have the full story—which they soon will after I have a long talk with each of them." Horace looked over at the bar. "There's Pierre, back from the stockroom. Get yourself a drink. We'll toast to our enduring partnership and what's certain to be your next book. And when the time comes, we'll adjourn to the dining table for Wanda's roast filet of beef, which is already calling my name from the oven."

*   *   *

Horace and I were enjoying our drinks when Jane, holding a sheet of paper, came bounding into the observation lounge.

"Our train should be leaving any minute now," Horace said, checking his watch, looking at Jane. "Where's Florabelle? You two might like to go out to the back platform."

"I don't know, and I don't care."

"Oh? You've had a squabble?"

"She steals, Uncle. And she copies my homework. I can't be friends with a criminal."

Horace looked at me with wide eyes.

"Anyway, I was hoping you could listen to the start of my paper," Jane said. "Tell me how it sounds."

"Of course."

Jane perched on the edge of a parlor chair. She planted her feet firmly on the floor and wriggled in place until she was comfortable.

"Okay, here goes." She drew a breath and looked down at her paper. "'There are many people in Tucson with completely different needs. Mrs. Bunny Lorillard is a great role model for anyone who wants to help hopeless or very poor people in their community. As the founder of Los Picadores, Mrs. Lorillard always organizes parties and other events to help change the lives of people who cannot change their lives themselves. This reveals she is kind and compassionate and truly cares about other people, especially children. Her good deeds cause poor people to see that they can live happily in society with jobs and houses just like everybody else.'" Jane looked up expectantly.

"That's it?" Horace asked.

"So far."

"Well, as an introduction it's superb. It leaves me wanting to hear more." Horace turned to me.

"Yes," I said. "Definitely."

"Excuse the interruption," Pierre said, "but someone's here to see us off."

Jane glanced out the window behind her.

"Bunny!" She sprang from her chair and went out the door.

"I'll go find Florabelle," Pierre offered.

Carrying our cocktails, Horace and I followed Jane out to the back platform. I doubted Bunny Lorillard wanted to see me again, but I was curious. Her appearance trackside told me Horace was right. She was getting off scot-free.

She stood in the light of the station platform, a few feet back from the rails. We couldn't invite her up; the trapdoor and steps were already stowed and locked for travel.

"Work hard, and I'm sure you'll make it into St. Ignatius," she was saying to Jane. "Take my word—you've got a beautiful life ahead."

"Thank you so much for everything," Jane said.

Bunny shifted her gaze to Horace. "I have to tell you, Horace, when it comes to dealing with the police, you've certainly got the whip hand."

"Oh?" Horace said.

"This afternoon, during my little powwow with the detective, Chief Earhart came by to confirm the Jail-and-Bail for the third weekend in June. She's gung-ho to send out the caravan for Tatiana Wong, and she told me she's reinstating your appointment as honorary police chief for life. You old rascal, what on earth did you say to change that poor woman's mind?"

Horace beamed. "A negotiating tactic I learned from Jane. I took my favorite torch lighter and held it to the resignation letter. I told Kimberly if she didn't meet my demands, I'd incinerate the damn thing."

Without warning, our train began moving.

"You're an extortionist!" Bunny called after us.

Horace raised his glass. "See you in June, my dear!"

Out of breath, Florabelle pushed her way to the open platform's brass railing, but at this point our train had picked up speed and rounded a bend in the Warehouse Arts District. But for the red flashing lights of a crossing signal—and the attendant, earsplitting gongs—the railroad right-of-way was dark. The Tucson Amtrak station and Bunny Lorillard had vanished from sight.

Later that night, as the passing railroad ties flashed in a halo of light behind the *Pioneer Mother*, and the glow of Maricopa, Arizona, faded in the distance, Horace and I were seated in the observation lounge, enjoying an after-dinner cognac. I mentioned my concern for Bunny. I pictured her spending the rest of her life stone broke, and it worried me. She might be a bit larcenous, but destitution didn't become her.

"Trust me, Jack. You needn't worry about Bunny," Horace said. "She's a beacon for wealth and good fortune. She's like a cat that way—guaranteed to land on her feet."

And she did, too. By the time we returned to Tucson in June, Bunny and Charles Lorillard had finalized their divorce, and Bunny had found a new man to marry. Her fiancé was a Mr. Clarence Wetherill II, of Toronto, said to be the seventh richest man in Canada.

Tucson Police Department

This book began with a simple premise: Because Horace Button and his entourage travel by private railroad car, the story had to be set in a city served by Amtrak. I also had the vague idea Horace's efforts to solve a mystery would be complicated by his relationship with the local authorities, but that's as far as I got with my early plotting.

That is, until I came across an auction item on the website Charitybuzz. The item was titled "Spend a Day with the Tucson Police Department," and the experience included lunch with members of the department's top brass, a tour of the Evidence, Property & Identification Center (EPIC), a tour of the department's nationally acclaimed Crime Lab, and a nighttime ride-along with a patrol officer in the department's Westside Patrol Division.

Perfect, I thought. Tucson is a stop for the Sunset Limited, Amtrak's train between Los Angeles and New Orleans, and I can draw on what I learn and see in my day with the police department to add a note of realism—and maybe even a few subplots—to my novel. My winning bid for the day was $500. The proceeds benefited First Tee–Tucson, a nonprofit that introduces kids to the game of golf.

The Tucson Police Department, it's safe to say, never really saw me coming. When Deputy Chief Chad Kasmar, Chief of Staff Michael D. Silva, and Executive Officer Dominic Flores came bounding down the staircase in the high-ceilinged lobby of the police headquarters building, a lobby I describe in the book, they had to ask who I was and why we were going to lunch.

So much for being a successful, well-known author.

Despite their puzzlement, Chad, Michael, and Dominic proved to be good-humored lunch companions, and that delightful meal set the tone for a memorable day.

I want to thank Kristi Ringler, management assistant in the office of the chief of police, for scheduling the day. She had to coordinate across numerous calendars, and she handled my last-minute changes with empathy and good cheer.

At EPIC, Josh Randall in Identification and Bill Brantley in Evidence gave me a behind-the-scenes tour of their astounding facility. And at the Crime Lab, Veronica Kearney, Heather Janssen, and Thomas (TJ) Murphy patiently walked me through the lab's multiple operational units, enlightening me to the science—and art—of catching bad guys. To all my hosts that day, thank you for the generosity of your time.

I owe a special debt of gratitude to Officer Marcos Ramirez, who cordially put up with me as his assigned ride-along, and who proved to be an outstanding ambassador for the Tucson Police Department. In virtually every citizen encounter I witnessed, Officer Ramirez was cool-headed, sympathetic, professional, and courteous. Two months after my ride-along, Officer Ramirez, along with LPO Erika Munoz, responded in the middle of the night to an apartment described as being "fiercely ablaze." For their courageous actions at that scene, both were recognized at the 2018 Heroes Day awards ceremony. Their valor puts my easy days sitting poolside in San Diego, writing fiction, in the proper perspective.

Finally, I want to thank Tucson's chief of police, Chief Chris Magnus, for his commitment to transparency and community oversight. Opening the doors of his department to a casual stranger with a reporter's note-pad shows a great deal of faith in his department and his people.

That faith, in my experience, is well-placed.

Thunderbird Lodge Lake Tahoe

The Thunderbird Lodge is a real place.

It was Tommy Cortopassi, my good friend and go-to resource on everything food and wine, who suggested Horace Button intersect with the Thunderbird Lodge, a historic landmark and prominent food, art, and cultural hot spot on Lake Tahoe's east shore. Tommy facilitated an introduction to Bill Watson, chief executive and curator of the nonprofit Thunderbird Lodge Preservation Society, which operates the historic George Whittell estate. I thank Bill for giving me unfettered access to the Lodge's magnificent grounds, buildings, and tunnels.

I also thank Shireen Piramoon, editor and creative director of *Thunderbird Lake Tahoe Magazine*, who, like Bill, enthusiastically endorsed this book project.

Thunderbird Lake Tahoe is maintained entirely by charitable gifts and contributions from the public at-large. For more information about visiting the Thunderbird Lodge, please go to www.ThunderbirdTahoe.org.

Card House at the Thunderbird Lodge

Tunnel at the Thunderbird Lodge

ACKNOWLEDGMENTS

Writing a contemporary novel involving trains—and Amtrak—is a ticklish business. Get one detail wrong, and you'll hear about it for years. My efforts to get things right have been supported by three friends particularly conversant with the ins and outs of modern railroading:

Doug Spinn, owner of the vintage private sleeper *Pacific Sands*, who has always been quick with answers to my questions;

James D. Porterfield, author of several authoritative books on railroad culture, including the now-classic *Dining by Rail: The History and Recipes of America's Golden Age of Railroad Cuisine*, who corresponds with me on a regular basis. Besides our conversations about trains, Jim has shared with me his considerable wisdom on matters ranging from Nero Wolfe to father-of-the-bride wedding toasts; and

Patrick Henry, CEO of Patrick Henry Creative Promotions, Houston, who one gray morning in San Diego genially answered my knock on the door of his private railroad car *Warren R. Henry*, and who's been a great friend and source for information ever since. Readers might like to know the upper lounge in the *Warren R. Henry* served as inspiration for the vista dome lounge in Horace Button's *Alaska*. You can get a virtual tour of Patrick's two stunning private railroad cars at www.phcp.com/the-train.

None of my train friends were given the opportunity to proof this manuscript. If I've flubbed a fact, the mistake is mine.

I'd like to thank several other friends who've contributed to this novel, a few unwittingly.

Chef at-large John Ogburn talked me through the logistical issues, from a chef's perspective, of transporting and staging a gastronomic tour de force in a ballroom setting.

Sergeant John Jennings, Los Gatos, CA, Police Department (retired), described for me a subset of hit men called "sparrows," and I adopted the term—and modus operandi—for this book.

It was at a San Diego cocktail party that Mike Lawton, talking about his backyard vegetable garden, detailed his strategic plan for dealing with squirrels. I shamelessly pirated Mike's game plan for this story.

Commander Philip A. Winters, U.S. Navy (retired), advised me on the nuts and bolts of shipping gourmet food items ordered online from a theoretical content-aggregation website. I also gleaned from this veteran naval aviator and accomplished golfer—Phil captained the varsity golf team at the U.S. Naval Academy—why a talented Navy pilot might steer clear of flying combat jets in favor of the less-sexy P-3 "Orion," a land-based, long-range maritime patrol aircraft.

The aforementioned Tommy Cortopassi, a stickler for fine-dining protocol, answered my numerous questions about food and wine. (Tommy also insisted Jack serve Château d'Yquem with Wanda's terrine of *foie gras*.) As with my train friends, Tommy was not afforded the opportunity to proofread this manuscript. Any errors with respect to descriptions of food, wine, and American-style food and beverage service are mine alone.

John Cornfield introduced me to two of his favorite places in Tucson, the Arizona Inn and the Tanque Verde Ranch, both of which became settings for scenes in this story. John was also one of my early readers, and I'm grateful for his advice, perceptive edits, and continued encouragement.

Thanks, also, to my other early readers: Debbie Larson, Dr. Edward Brand, G. Bruce Dunn, and John Patrick McGovern.

I thank my cousin Doug Lodato, a director and producer of popular feature films, for taking the time to review our final proofs. Doug catches errors the rest of us miss, and over the years he's been a valued champion of my work.

For the difficult job of converting a bedraggled manuscript into a praiseworthy book, I relied once again on a proven team of talented professionals.

Jennifer Silva Redmond, story editor and line editor, pinpointed for me the beginning of this story, suggested where and how it ought to end, and fine-tuned the tempo of the book. Jennifer's talent for separating the wheat from the chaff remains unrivaled.

Kathy Wise, designer, aced another book cover, provided an additional layer of rectitude and logic to the story, and worked her wizardry on the interior design—including bringing to life the floor plans of the *Pioneer Mother* and the *Alaska*. Thank you, Kathy, for contributing your considerable talents to this project.

Through her sharp-eyed edits and discerning suggestions, copyeditor Laurie Gibson greatly improved this narrative. Thank you, Laurie. Your feedback challenges me to be a better writer.

And my heartfelt thanks to photographer-at-large Cannon Daughtrey, who put her busy life as a Tucson-based archaeologist on pause long enough to make several treks to the Amtrak depot, where she captured a much-needed shot for our cover. (For her time and camerawork, we paid Cannon in El Charro salsa—lots of it!) Cannon provided me with information on Tucson's plant life and history, which helped fill in several gaps within this text.

For me, writing a novel is a slow, tedious undertaking. That I can finish a book-length manuscript is a testament to the organization and management skills of two people who make the business side of my life much easier. Thank you, Shelley Cortopassi and Amanda Flynn.

In 2007, Jill Treadwell Svendsen agreed to help me restart Huckleberry House as a commercially viable, midlist publisher. As our first managing director, Jill was instrumental in mastering the process of getting a book to market. I'm indebted to Jill for her pioneering work with our press—and for her encouragement to this day.

A supportive family has been an essential element in my writing career.

I credit my brother, Chris Peterson, a lover of food-related nonfiction, for introducing me to the bon vivant, food writer, and social critic Lucius Beebe (1902–1966), who is the inspiration for the fictional character

Horace Button. Chris, a retired patrol sergeant for the Placer County, CA, Sheriff's Department, also answered a number of my questions about police procedures.

For advice on matters relating to parochial-school administration and behavioral traits of thirteen-year-old girls, I looked to my daughter Katie Brand. Katie's keen insight, earned from years working as a high school English teacher, continues to inform my fiction.

I thank my mother, Dion Peterson Russell, and my stepfather, George F. Russell, Jr., for their continued encouragement and support for my work. I also thank my father, Gregor G. Peterson, the founder, in 1989, of Huckleberry Press, Lake Tahoe, Nevada. We lost Dad in 2001, but I like to think these modest book projects would make him happy.

I finished this manuscript in a turbulent year, a year that brought challenges—and opportunities—to my immediate family. The details are too private to share, but I can tell you this: when the time came, those around me showed courage, determination, and grit. To Teresa, Katie, Lucas, and Caroline: I love you, and you make me proud.

The thrill of writing and selling books pales in comparison to the joy and meaning you bring to my life.

ABOUT THE AUTHOR

Eric Peterson's debut novel, *Life as a Sandwich*, was a finalist in the San Diego Book Awards. His second novel, *The Dining Car*, won the IBPA Benjamin Franklin Gold Award for Popular Fiction, the San Diego Book Award Gold Medal for Contemporary Fiction, and the Readers' Favorite book Award Silver Medal for Literary Fiction. *Publishers Weekly*'s BookLife named *The Dining Car* a "Book to Watch."

A third-generation Californian, Peterson attended the University of California at San Diego. He completed his Communication degree at Stanford, majoring in journalism. He lives in Southern California with his wife, Teresa.

ericpetersonauthor.com

CPSIA information can be obtained
at www.ICGtesting.com
Printed in the USA
LVHW030938181221
706570LV00010B/159/J

9 780982 486085